SHOOTING FOR JUSTICE

A JOHN POPE WESTERN

G. WAYNE TILMAN

**WOLFPACK
PUBLISHING**
— EST 2013 —

WOLFPACK PUBLISHING
— EST 2013 —

Shooting For Justice

Paperback Edition
Copyright © 2021 G. Wayne Tilman

Wolfpack Publishing
5130 S. Fort Apache Road, 215-380
Las Vegas, NV 89148

wolfpackpublishing.com

Paperback ISBN 978-1-64734-929-5
eBook ISBN 978-1-64734-928-8

SHOOTING FOR JUSTICE

ACKNOWLEDGEMENTS

Appreciation is expressed to Denise Kearns,
Becca Payne, and Susan Stecker
for their contributions as Beta readers.

CHAPTER 1

Wells Fargo Detectives John Pope and Sarah Watson walked out of San Francisco's exclusive Bohemian Club. They were with their boss, the company's famous chief detective, James Hume.

The meeting had been unexpected until the day before. The person who had called it was a surprise. He was the president of their firm.

The case offered them was a bigger surprise. They were to be loaned to the US Department of Justice to investigate a potential attack on the safety and sanctity of their country.

The type of attack and specific target were unknown. Also unknown was whether it was a coup attempt, an assassination attempt on President Chester A. Arthur, or both.

Determining the type of attack and target was their assignment. As was stopping the threat at all costs.

Exactly how was left to the two detectives, one a gunfighter and former San Francisco detective, the other, formerly one of the elite women detectives of the Pinkerton National Detective Agency.

Hume had warned them before they knew anything about the case. He had said it would be the largest and most difficult of their careers.

Though the partners had not yet had the chance to share their feelings on the case, each knew from the other's body language and expressions, it was worrisome. Hume did also. He had misgivings.

"Let's go back to my office and chat a bit," he suggested. He knew they would want to talk with each other at length, but it would have to wait. He had a few unshared details for them first.

They walked back from the club without speaking. Once back behind closed doors, he took a deep breath and began to share what little he knew.

"For my own clarity of thought as well as yours, let me start from the very beginning. I will be more specific than our president, Lloyd Tevis, with whom you just met, is. He's a big picture man. People like us know the devil is in the details.

"Tevis was called to Washington on a ruse about potential business matters. He met with Attorney General Benjamin H. Brewster. Brewster will be one of the two Cabinet members who will be your direct contact. I was not told who the other person will be.

I doubt Tevis was either.

"General Brewster got wind of an imminent threat against the Administration. President Chester Arthur has done some wonderful things. He is accomplishing good way beyond many insiders' expectations. The people seem to love him. His own cabinet, now largely replaced from the late Garfield's, apparently does not. This is in spite of the fact he appointed all except one himself," Hume said.

"Mr. Hume, who was the carryover?" Sarah asked.

"Well, technically the whole cabinet carried over upon the assassination of President Garfield. Over time, Arthur has replaced all except for one. The one, since I suspect he is who you are asking about, is Robert Todd Lincoln. He's the son of the other slain president. He is the secretary of war. I understand he, like his father, has unimpeachable integrity."

"Could he be the other direct contact, Boss?" Pope asked.

"Probably. It's logical. I'm afraid you will have to get there and be told officially by Brewster.

"Now, Tevis expects the world to drop everything and do whatever he says immediately. Like mandating the two of you getting married for the company's propriety.

"Quite frankly, you don't have time to have the wedding you deserve. I do not think the company ordering you two to marry is conscionable. Marry now, marry later, or don't marry at all. Just pretend to be married while you are on the case." The two nodded appreciatively.

"Do you have any idea of what the threats against the country or the president are?" Pope asked.

"Not a clue."

"We will be undercover, I guess. Will the government specify cover stories and identities?" Pope continued.

"I do not know, John. This is very hush hush. I will tell you your salaries here will continue, we will cover transportation to and from. Once you get there, you need to negotiate with Brewster about your housing and expense needs. I gathered from Tevis he's pretty upset and will take good care of you to get this thing to go away."

"When do you want us to leave?" Sarah asked.

"As soon as possible," the chief detective said.

"I wonder about taking my horse," Pope mused.

"I would let the government provide transportation appropriate to the cover they give you."

"Without having to worry about Caesar," Pope looked at Sarah, "we should be able to leave tomorrow." She nodded affirmatively.

"Excellent! I will apprise Tevis and he will telegraph Brewster. 'Detectives John and Sarah Pope'?" Hume asked as he handed them two very sizeable travel drafts.

"Sounds good to me," Sarah responded. Pope just

grinned at her.

"Stay in touch and let me know if you need anything. No need for weekly check ins. This is not criminal activity. It is more like sedition or espionage. I don't know who is going to be watching you. I am pretty confident someone involved on the wrong side will. So, be very careful," Hume said as he rose. Rising and shaking hands was his normal way to dismiss his detectives to depart to begin a case.

"One more thing," Sarah said as they were standing to leave.

Hume raised his eyebrows and waited.

"Pinkerton's was effectively his secret agent operation during the war. Why didn't he reach out to Allan Pinkerton?" she asked.

"I asked Tevis the same thing. He said for two reasons. Brewster and the other cabinet member have read about your exploits for the first thing. With Allan's rapidly declining health, they are unsure of the future capacity of the agency to handle something this big."

"Thank you, sir." They walked out the door.

"Let's go to the cashier and cash these so we can get our tickets. I want to send Grandpa a letter saying we will be back East on business and can be reached via Hume. I'm thinking, depending on our cover, we may need more formal clothes than we own for this case," Pope said.

"I agree. We will have to get them in Washington, DC," Sarah said.

The cashier was able to issue train vouchers not charged against their cash drafts. They went to the train station and found they could leave at nine in the morning. Pope added some cash to the vouchers and got one sleeper car ticket in the name of Mr. and Mrs. John Pope. His partner smiled mischievously as she heard him order it.

"Something worries me, Sarah," Pope admitted.

"Yes?"

"It worries me we have had so much newspaper exposure two members of the president's cabinet have read about us on the other side of the country. Notoriety will harm our ability to go undercover and do our jobs. Not just on this case, but any case."

"I did not know we were famous. You are right. It won't help us doing our jobs. I am more worried about your fame as a fast gun. There are a lot of wannabes like Kid Taos out there who would like to be the one who outdrew you."

"Maybe this case will be all investigative and my so-called fame will die down a bit. I guess it depends on how long it lasts."

"My suspicion, John, is a coup or assassination will not take long to reach its fruition. How in Heaven's name we are going to come in from the cold and solve it first is beyond me," Sarah said.

"We will solve it. We just won't know our investigative plan until we get there and talk with our contacts. I have no idea why the Department of Justice does not have any investigative agents. It makes no sense, does it?"

"My understanding is they borrow Treasury agents for investigative cases," Sarah said. "Lafayette Baker, who found John Wilkes Booth, ran the National Detective Bureau during the war and worked with Allan Pinkerton. Pinkerton's influence on him ran over into the subsequent formation of the Treasury's agent cadre. Baker had listened in on Secretary Stanton's communications and believed Stanton supported the attack against Lincoln. He possessed Booth's diary and said some missing pages contained information about Stanton and Booth. These allegations made him unpopular, and he was subsequently fired. Yet, his influence lived on. Maybe all of this has to do with a distrust in using the treasury agents for a case like this one. Alas, who really knows?" she ended.

"Interesting. Maybe one of the conspirators here is the Treasury Secretary. I don't even know who he is or exactly what he does, other than print money," Pope said.

"I reckon we will find out," Sarah said as they approached their rooms.

The conversation continued after they arrived and took their coats off. Sarah started brewing coffee.

They knew they would take minimal luggage since they did not know whether they would spend their time in downtown Washington at dinners, riding around or travelling.

"Sarah, do you know Detective Ed McEnroe?" Pope asked.

"Vaguely. Isn't he somewhat older? Maybe mid-fifties?"

"Exactly. Between assignments and well before Wyoming, he and I happened to have lunch together. He told me he had been a spy for the Confederacy during the war. It appeared from what he said, the South had a far more sophisticated spy network than the North. I listened closely to see if it was just bias on his part, however, I think he was correct.

"Anyway, he said being a spy was very different from being a detective. We deal with crooks and with snitches. A spy deals with a variety of entities and never knows what side somebody is on at any given time. Is the person a double agent, agreeing to spy for your side? Or a triple agent agreeing to spy for you, when he is actually still loyal to his original agency and feeding you disinformation? Is he a patriot, a disgruntled job seeker, or just someone in it for the money? He said you have to actually live your cover. You cannot just come home and be you until you go back out again. You have to be careful about every word you utter, no matter who you are conversing with.

"I believe, my Sarah, this is what we have gotten ourselves into. It will be different than anything we have ever done, or even imagined.

"McEnroe said you don't put the nippers on your enemy, you slit their throat and leave them in an alley as you walk away. He said you never attract attention by running. Sometimes you join the crowd of onlookers surrounding the person you killed."

"I wonder if we made a mistake taking this case, John?" Sarah asked.

"I don't know. He certainly pulled our patriotic chains on it. There really was no option, the way I see it. And, despite what Tevis said, turning it down would be tantamount to resigning.

"I believe we must meet with the contacts, try to get the lay of the land. If necessary, we have to admit to them and Wells Fargo if it's beyond what we can do. Then, begin to look for a new job," Pope added.

"We always agreed Harry Morse would hire us. But, if we got fired by Wells Fargo, I think it would jeopardize both his friendship with Jim Hume and future business with Wells Fargo. I suspect the company is his largest client," Sarah said.

"Looks like we will be spies for the Justice Department then, oh wife of mine!"

"I kinda like the sound of it," she admitted. "The wife part, I mean," she added.

"Me, too. I would like it better with us choosing

the date, not Tevis."

They put a few things in carpet bags for the four days on the train and the first few days of Washington. They managed to squeeze a short-barreled shotgun and Pope's carbine into the combination gun case and saddle scabbard. Both doubted they would need long guns in the city, however, they did not know where their inquiries would take them.

Pope walked over to the livery and visited with Caesar, his horse. He had arranged for young detective Jake Bell to deliver the horse to his grandfather in Marin County next weekend.

While he was visiting with Caesar, Sarah was out shopping for snacks to take on the train trip. Though their expenses would cover meals en route, it sometimes was just simpler to eat in their sleeper room than go to the dining car.

They left at nine in the morning. They took the Central Pacific eastwards to Ogden, Utah Territory and changed to the Denver & Rio Grande. The next day, they were about twenty miles outside of Pueblo, when a post-lunch conversation was interrupted by the train sliding to an emergency stop.

"Badges and guns!" They already knew the express car was about four cars in front of their sleeper car. They had visited it and conversed with the express messenger, former shotgun messenger Thomas Hyland. Both knew him from a small case they worked in California.

Pope rushed down the aisle and car to car dressed in his suit minus the jacket. Both of his guns showed in their shoulder holsters and his badge was prominent on the left lapel of his vest.

Sarah kept up with him through the train, her guns strapped on and the short ten-gauge shotgun menacingly in hand. She, too, wore her gold badge where everyone could see it.

They slowed their pace as they approached the express car. From the edge of the door glass, Pope peered in.

A man with a bandanna tied over his mouth and nose was raising his gun to shoot Hyland. The guard's shotgun was on the floor.

Pope drew his right gun and shot through the glass panes in the door of the car he was in and the ones in the express car. The glass shattered and with a clearer shot, he fired again. The wounded man was hit solidly this time and began to crumple as a second robber stepped into view facing Pope.

The second robber swiped his revolver across Hyland's forehead, and he hit the floor.

The man aimed at Pope, who stepped aside and let Sarah operate the ten-gauge with its double-aught buckshot. He fell, dead before hitting the aisle floor. Another man popped into view shooting wildly.

Sarah jumped back to avoid the barrage of bullets

aimed at her.

From the left, Pope emptied his right-hand Colt .44 and stepped outside the train door. He jumped five feet to the ground to the surprise of four men holding horses. They swung around and aimed at the detective.

He dropped two with the five cartridges in the cylinder of his left Colt. He was now empty. With a shoulder holster instead of a cartridge belt around his waist, Pope did not have reloads.

He ducked between cars as bullets careened towards him. He could hear the men coming and knew he was in big trouble.

Pope did not even have his Bowie knife, something he doubted he would live to admit to his grandfather, famed mountain man Israel Pope.

He could hear their boots on the sharp gravel beside the rails. They were mere feet away, when above, the door swung open, and Sarah dropped both with horrendous effect from such a short distance.

Pope knew there was no need checking for pulses. The buckshot from four feet had literally destroyed both men.

"Honey? You alright?" came a soft, caring female voice.

"I am now. It was close. Thanks!" he said.

He came out from between the cars, and she tossed him her .44 caliber Russian S&W double-action revolver, retaining the smaller .38 version in its left-hand holster.

Pope saw one man on a horse from thirty feet wheel the horse and start to ride off.

"Where in hell was he?" Pope asked himself aloud as he cocked Sarah's revolver for a more precise shot than the long, double-action trigger pull would allow.

He took the classic target shooter's position, right arm outstretched and left on his hip. He was bladed towards his target.

"You on the horse! Halt!"

The man turned. It was obvious to Pope he had been heard. And, ignored.

Pope pressed the trigger. The short barrel emitted a crack and a foot of flame. The man flinched and rode ten feet before falling off the horse, headfirst against an iron rail.

The engineer and conductor both approached Pope. The three of them checked the five on the ground. All dead. They climbed back onto the train.

Sarah was kneeling beside Hyland, who was regaining consciousness.

"Are you alright, Tom?" she asked.

"Things are still swimming around. I should be able to focus in a minute. I do know one thing thought. The treasure is safe. The vault was not opened before you and John opened up."

"Gentlemen, we need to remove the saddles from

seven horses and bring the saddlebags with us to give to the sheriff in Pueblo. Wouldn't be right to abandon those horses to fend for themselves with saddles and bridles on," Pope said.

The train pulled into Pueblo and Pope, the engineer and the conductor gave a full report to the county sheriff. Sarah sent a telegram to Hume.

An hour later, the trained rolled out of the station and headed to Kansas City.

"I guess I have to carry a little bag of cartridges attached to my shoulder holster," Pope said, once the train was underway and he was ready for a quick nap.

"Yes. I guess a third gun would be a bit much with a business suit on," his partner observed.

"Out of curiosity, what did you tell the boss about our little shoot here?" Pope asked Sarah.

"Not much. I told him seven robbers hit the train. They were getting ready to shoot the express messenger. We intervened. In the ensuing firefight, you killed four and I killed three. No injury to any civilian or WF employee. No loss of treasure. I told him we figured we had gotten enough exposure and made a report to the sheriff and headed to our original assignment."

"Good job, honey. Short and sweet. He won't recall us to investigate. Nobody left to catch. Our assignment takes precedence over any company business. Thanks for bailing me out back there. I'd be dead meat if it weren't for you and your alley cleaner."

"If I hadn't, I'd have to find another husband and partner real fast. I have invested a lot in shaping you the way I want you, so it saved me years of looking and changing some fellow."

"Sarah, I am so happy you are able to look at it so logically. It certainly signifies true love," he said.

"Come here, cowboy. I'll show you some true love."

"Well, if you insist," he said, losing no time departing one bed for the other.

**

During the fourth day of their trip, their third train of the journey pulled into the Baltimore and Potomac Railroad Station at Sixth and B Streets. Ironically, it was the very location where Charles Guiteau shot President James Garfield less than two years earlier causing the succession of Vice President Chester A. Arthur to president.

Without any plans, the two detectives asked a hansom cab driver to take them to a hotel near the President's House. He recommended the Willard. He said President Grant used to enjoy a frequent whiskey in the lobby. He went on to them about people US Grant referred to as "lobbyists" bothering him with their special interests when he was there for a bourbon and cigar.

Mr. & Mrs. John Pope checked in with no problem,

though the room tariff was choking. They decided, since they did not know their cover story yet, they should shoot high.

Once checked into the hotel, the two detectives had to track down the location of the attorney general. Though his office had been created in the 1700's and had become a government department thirteen years ago in 1870, the department was scattered all over the general Pennsylvania Avenue area of Washington.

Sarah subtlety inquired of the concierge at the Willard Hotel about the address of her distant cousin Ben Brewster, who had "some sort of lawyer job in the government".

The concierge knew right away and wrote down the address of the post office at 700 F Street. They walked over and checked the Directory Board in the lobby. The attorney general's office was listed and they walked up the steps.

Entering, they introduced themselves to a male receptionist as being from San Francisco and having a mutual friend with General Brewster. The man said although the attorney general was in a meeting, he should be through shortly. They were directed to a hard wooden bench to wait.

They waited almost forty-five minutes before a clean-shaven man in his late sixties came out and introduced himself as Benjamin Brewster.

"Hello, General Brewster. We are from San Francisco and work for your friend Lloyd Tevis. He said to be sure to look you up when we visited the Capitol."

"Oh, yes. He mentioned you to me. You work with his friend Hume?" Brewster asked.

"We do."

"Are you just arriving?" the attorney general asked.

"We arrived about an hour and a half ago and checked in to the Willard Hotel. We thought it would be convenient until we found a more appropriate accommodation," Sarah said.

"A very good choice, for sure. Listen, I would like to chat with you at great length and have a friend who I am sure would like to join us. Are you doing anything for dinner?"

"We are at your disposal, sir," Pope said.

"Why not get a private dining room for four at the hotel for dinner at seven. I will send a messenger over to the friend and see if he is available. Either way, I will join you."

"We look forward to it, General Brewster. See you at seven o'clock then," Pope said, and they shook hands and departed.

Once they were sure they were clear of unwelcome ears, Pope said quietly to Sarah, "This must be really big, when the attorney general of the United States and another unknown cabinet member drops everything to talk with us."

"Yes, it's kind of scary, actually," she said.

They returned to the hotel and went straight back to the concierge. He secured a small dining room for them for the appointed time.

"Should we dress up?" Pope asked his partner.

"Let's stay like we are and play it by ear. We need their input on who we will pretend to be to best discover the scheme behind disrupting or killing Arthur."

"After sitting on a train for four days, let's loosen up by reconnoitering the area. We can stroll like Grandpa did in San Francisco when he was watching out for the kidnappers," he said, referring to a major case they had solved.

"Except you have me instead of your hound dog, Scout," Sarah said.

"I love you both. But I love you more. He saved me when the Irish gang tried to gun me down in Marin County. I was wounded and he came flying through the air and knocked a man off his horse as he was getting ready to shoot me. However, even Scout's actions were not as gloriously performed as yours several days ago."

"Humph!" was the full response he got.

They walked around the downtown area. Upon passing a gun store, Pope insisted they walk in.

"I have been concerned about wearing my large Western Colts under a suit. I suspect few government types here wear guns in town. I don't worry about my shoulder holster printing in town in Wyoming when wearing a badge. We are supposed to be secret agents here and it would be a bit of a giveaway. I am thinking of picking up a S&W First Model Double-Action in .44 Russian like your larger gun and a deep cover inside the waist holster. One which would not print under a suit, but would still provide a fast draw," he said.

He told the manager what he was looking for and the man produced a blue steel model with black rubber grips. Pope asked about stag replacements and he said he would have to order them, which Pope did. He bought the revolver and a leather holster designed to be worn well behind the right front suspender attachment. Pope was aware of several people who had gotten their guns tangled in their braces during their draw and died because of it.

He bought two boxes of cartridges and they continued their reconnoiter around DC.

Freshened up a bit and Pope armed with his new revolver, they went down to dinner fifteen minutes early. While Sarah checked the small dining room they reserved, Pope sauntered around the larger dining room and looked for anything or anyone seemingly out of place or particularly interested. He observed only well-dressed men and some women engaged in quiet conversations or eating. Nothing aroused his attention.

Pope made a conscious effort to look pleasant and smile a lot. Sarah constantly reminded him he looked like a detective. He knew she was right. In this investigation, a policeman was the last thing he wanted to be taken as. What persona he would adopt may come out tonight. He hoped so. It was important to study and prepare for a cover identity. As a San Francisco detective, he would skip shaving, mess up his hair and put on ragged clothes to portray a bum. He would go home for dinner, get cleaned up and make or buy dinner after as himself. This persona, whatever it might be, would last day and night for the duration of the case. He was anxious to get into it and knew Sarah also was ready.

Pope returned to the small dining room just before the appointed time. Sarah did not find peepholes or explosive traps. She pointed out the server entry door and said it went, as one might surmise, directly to the kitchen.

Water, silver and menus were already on the table, which was set for four.

They heard a tap on the door and two men entered. The first was Brewster. The second, who had to be Lincoln, was a medium height man about forty years old. He was dressed elegantly as befitted one who had become a millionaire as a prominent lawyer. Brewster greeted them with a smile. Lincoln had a pleasant but unsmiling look.

After introductions were over, they sat. Pope pulled out her chair for Sarah.

"Thank you both for coming across the country to meet, and hopefully help us. We will have to talk between trips by the waiter. The Willard is "spy central", according to Robert's Army agents," Brewster began.

"I am sure you have some preliminary questions before we get into the meat of the matter," Lincoln said.

"We do, Mr. Secretary," Pope began.

"Before you ask anything, please refer to us as Ben and Robert in private and in social events. In our offices, you can be more formal. If it is alright with you, we will call you John and Sarah," Brewster said. Both detectives nodded.

"Lastly, everything we discuss is for the ears of the four of us and not to be repeated to anyone at Wells Fargo or anywhere else. Do you agree to this unchangeable requirement?"

Both said, "I do."

"How did you select us? You have military intelligence, treasury agents, and Pinkerton's. We are glad to serve, but just curious," Sarah said.

"I have taken the Western US, indeed almost all, of the country's newspapers since the death of my father. I am friends with Lafayette Baker who ran the National Credit Bureau. He is convinced my father's murder was political and if not engineered by people in the government, was at least supported and helped by them. Neither of us are a fan of the short Scotsman from Chicago."

"I worked for him and don't blame you. He is on his last legs and it is unclear what the future capabilities of the company will be here on out," Sarah said.

"In those newspapers, I read of first Pope's, then both, of your investigative and firearms prowess. You are not insiders here. I doubt your fame has spread to the Washington area. I figured you would be able to go undercover and dig with less scrutiny than Pinkertons, treasury agents or similar. Ben agreed with me," Lincoln said.

"Ben and Robert, does the president know of whatever threat we will mitigate?" Pope asked.

"No, he does not," Brewster said.

"It occurs to us he may be the best person to reveal known potential threats to us."

"I believe you are correct. But we made a pact to keep him on the path of the legislative goals he has and not bother him with other mysterious threats," Lincoln said.

"How did you become aware of the threat?" Pope asked.

"I was on a train, heading to New England," Lincoln said. "I heard an argument in the next parlor of the car. I listened at the wall. I heard, "We have to get rid of Arthur, either kill him or somehow disgrace him sufficiently to cause his impeachment. We do not have time to mess about deciding which to do. We need to quickly execute a plan," one of the men said.

The other agreed. This occurred as we rolled into an intermediate stop. I planned on getting descriptions as we got off the train, but by the time I gathered my things, they were long gone."

"What stop was this?" Sarah asked.

"Scarsdale, New York."

"So, they were the only words you were able to pick up?" Pope asked.

"Yes. Do you know where they got on the train?" Sarah asked.

"I believe in New York City. There was a family in the compartment from Washington to New York."

"How long was the trip from New York to Scarsdale?" Pope asked.

"It is a bit over an hour by train, I believe."

"Did either of the voices sound familiar?"

"No, not at all."

"How about your estimate of ages, accents and the like?"

"They were grown men. Not elderly. No discernable accent. They sounded educated. I truly don't have anything more for you."

"Then," Sarah began, "could the two of you run through a list of what you think might be the reasons for an assassination attempt or coup attempt?"

"Let me lay some groundwork about Chester Arthur," Lincoln said.

"He is a handsome man, those silly sideburns

notwithstanding. He became very wealthy and powerful in New York. He's an attorney and ran the Customs House. He got the job through patronage, something he has tried to do away with since. His actions for merit jobs throughout the federal government have made a number of people angry. People who had their hats set on certain jobs and people who had no qualifications and just wanted to be given a job *gratis*. He is aloof but can be charming when necessary. His greatest two traits are he is very smart, and he supports legislation according to his ethics. Most politicians legislate driven by political reasons. His ideas on immigration and Chinese and everyone else's civil rights would have thrilled my father. He is converting our sad, small, and obsolete Navy to one which will be world class. He is converting from wooden ships to steel-hulled ones. There is a bit of grumbling about steel versus wood even by some admirals. The same type chaps who think single shot rifles are better than repeaters. As good as modernizing the Navy may seem, a number of people are angry over the funding for the Navy instead of their pet interests.

"He was connected very closely with a man named Roscoe Conkling. Conkling is an arch conservative called a Stalwart. He ran patronage in New York and has always been for harsher, more punitive treatment for the South. He has wanted Arthur to put him in the Cabinet, but the man he mentored in politics has refused. Conkling is a dangerous foe."

Both detectives had been writing notes as the secretary of war spoke.

"So, we have a major political boss not only disagreeing with him but feeling betrayed. Related, Southern power brokers in politics and elsewhere may consider Arthur an enemy. We have people whose agendas are negatively impacted by the financial rebuilding of the US Navy. Perhaps, anger resides in the heads of the Army, especially generals. We have anti-civil rights people against him. Particularly, I would think, railroad tycoons who virtually use Chinese immigrants as slave labor. In addition to Conkling, we probably have many job seekers and political bosses who pass out federal jobs as part of their power base, mad about his merit system," Pope summarized.

"It's a good start," Brewster said.

"It strikes me any of those could lead to attempted assassination or coup of some sort," Sarah thought aloud.

"We agree, though this is the first time Robert and I have listed them," Brewster said.

"We have our work cut out for us, gentlemen. Have you given thought to cover positions to allow us to begin?" Pope asked.

"We have one for you but have had difficulty coming

up with a plausible job for Sarah," Brewster admitted.

"John, I would like to make you Provost Marshal for the secretary of war's office," Lincoln said. It is a senior level, non-appointed position. The salary is high enough to help cover your wife's time. Since your emphasis would be base and personnel security and investigations, your job history would tie in. It would give you reason to travel widely as needed. It carries a badge and certain arrest authorities and the ability to be armed anywhere. Of course, both of you would be covered for expenses."

Lincoln handed Pope a badge and told him to raise his right hand. Minutes later, he was a civilian Army Provost Marshal at a colonel level.

"Sarah, Robert and I cannot figure how to position you in this operation. We know you are an experienced and noted investigator," Brewster said.

"How about just as John's wife who is writing a book on President Arthur? Book research would cover me asking lots of questions, going to libraries and the like."

"Excellent! We may even be able to work an interview with the president where you can ask historical questions without giving away the threat," the attorney general said.

"I could absolutely question him without him having the slightest idea I have an ulterior motive," Sarah said confidently.

"General Brewster, would you prepare a letter of introduction for me, explaining I am doing some research for your office? The letter would facilitate getting into some offices and asking for files."

"Of course. I will have it prepared and sent over to your hotel room first thing tomorrow," the attorney general said.

"The president and his sister, who is social director since his wife died, are having a cocktail party three days from now. I will make sure you get an invitation. Be advised the party will be formal wear. It will be in the President's House."

"We will be there!" Pope said.

"Gentlemen, we have two separate sets of issues here. Assassination and having him removed from office under false pretenses. What precautions have been taken relative to the first?" Pope asked.

"There is a guard at the President's House during public hours," Brewster said.

"We have had two presidents assassinated in the past sixteen years. Why not detail five military guards there on three shifts each day? Your new provost marshal can train and supervise them," Pope said.

"I have the authority to do it. Getting the president to accept it could be an issue. Since Garfield was shot about two years ago, it should be something I can sell," Lincoln said. "Arthur has spoken candidly with me about Garfield and my father. I don't think he is frightened, but I know he is aware. I will tell him Ben and I have been discussing tightening security at the President's House as a matter of course. I should be able to introduce you both to him Friday night at the party. Assuming I've had good luck, I will mention you will be overseeing the strengthened security as well as a number of other things," Lincoln said.

"John, come to my office in the War Department Building. It faces Pennsylvania Avenue and is just northwest of the President's House. Look for 17th Street. Make it about ten in the morning, and I will introduce you around and assign an office for you," Lincoln said.

The two cabinet members rose, and Pope signed the bill to their room. All shook hands and departed.

Back at the room, Sarah asked, "What is your overall view of what we just heard and the men from whom we heard it?"

"A number of things, darling. One, it amazes me we do not have armed guards at the President's House. Two presidents have been assassinated in the past sixteen years. We guard military bases, but not the home of the president? It is beyond belief.

"Second, I cannot believe a president's son, who was a military officer on Grant's staff and is a member of the cabinet did not figure a way to see the two men whose conversation started all of this.

"Third, I adamantly disagree with not telling the

president about this matter. You will have your work cut out for you drawing who he should be worried about from him without his knowledge.

"Fourth, we have made inroads today into possible reasons someone may want him killed or removed. However, we are approaching it logically. The reason may not be logical. It may be a splinter group of crazies whose reasons we could never guess," Pope finished.

"Do you think we can trust them? Brewster and Lincoln?"

"Not yet. What better way to test the security of your plan than to hire two detectives to ferret it out then kill them?"

"Yes, it crossed my mind, too. We really don't have much choice though," Sarah said.

"No, we do not. We will go with them until we think we no longer can. Who we will turn to then is a complete unknown. Perhaps we will find a trustworthy confederate in our socializing."

"You mentioned confederate with a small 'c'. What's the possibility of powerful Southern senators and congressmen seeking to disrupt the government for retribution reasons?" Sarah asked.

"I fear it's as good a probability as anything else we have. My gut reaction lies with Conkling, the political boss in New York. I don't believe he is still a senator. The probable reason he wants a cabinet appointment. We will check on his job and whereabouts as a first step. I think a quick trip to a library is in order," Sarah said.

She found there was a dearth of libraries in DC and Sarah ended up at the Library of Congress. Its location was in congress itself. She located and hand copied a list of members of congress and the cabinet.

At the same time, Pope reported for duty as the Provost Marshal for Security and Investigations for the War Department. He was assigned a private office. It was small, but on the prestigious fourth floor down the hall from the secretary's office. He quickly found the department maintained its own small library and familiarized himself with it.

Lincoln summoned Pope around lunch and said he was to accompany the secretary to the Washington Arsenal by carriage. At the Arsenal, site of the hanging of the Lincoln conspirators, they met with a Colonel Willoughby. He assigned a half platoon of eighteen infantrymen to the President's House. Instead of the lieutenant which headed a full platoon, he put a senior sergeant in charge. The sergeant, George Wilders, was to report to Pope onsite. The secretary set up the guard staff preemptively, not having spoken to the president.

"I'd rather risk him telling me to dismantle it than to give him a chance to say not to do it," Lincoln said, showing genetic resolve and management from the paternal side of his family tree.

While Lincoln met with a general and several colonels, Pope sat with Sgt. Wilders. He outlined his ideas for the duties. They would work out patrols and emergency actions once they got to the President's House and studied the building and its weak points. They then went to the supply warehouse and selected items they would need for the President's House mission.

"I do not know if the President's House has a telegraph. If it does not, it certainly ought to. Let's meet there tomorrow morning. Meet me at the front door at nine. Bring three of your top troopers with you and the gun safe and other items."

On the way back, Lincoln advised Pope the President's House not only had a telegraph room, but a telephone was installed in 1877. They would be able to add a set to whatever guard room they were assigned and call either the Washington Police or the Washington Arsenal for reinforcement in an attack situation.

Lincoln and Pope returned to the War Department and walked over to the President's House. They called on the chief of staff and the secretary asked for a room as near as possible to the telegraph room. A very small room was sufficiently close, so a second telephone set was not required. Pope requested several keys to the telegraph room and two desks and a file cabinet.

Back at the War Department, Pope obtained a

draft voucher and went shopping. The single shot .45-70 trap door Springfield models of 1873 were overly powerful for what he wanted and too slow to reload. He purchased ten 1873 Winchester carbines, five double-barrel shotguns, and ten Colt revolvers. He also purchased twenty boxes of .44-40 cartridges, ten boxes of twelve-gauge buckshot, and five cleaning kits. The Army's handguns, Colts and Smith & Wesson .45's would have caused confusion with the rifles and revolvers shooting similar looking but non-interchangeable cartridges. With the standardization of .44-40's, the soldiers would have a familiar handgun, except with a different cartridge of the same power class. They would fit in the issue holsters as well. His last purchase was a holdover from his San Francisco Police days. He bought twenty-five loud brass police whistles on lanyards.

Pope had his purchases scheduled for delivery after noon on Friday. He wanted to give Sgt. Wilders and his troopers time to offload the equipment they were bringing and put it in the President's House security room.

******

Friday morning the two detectives parted early. Pope walked to the President's House, and Sarah headed down Pennsylvania Avenue towards the Capitol. She was armed with her letter from the attorney general. The letter was worded much like a federal subpoena and signed by the deputy attorney general. It was much more powerful than what she had imagined. The most interesting aspect of the letter to her was it was done by a Remington typewriter of the Sholes and Glidden design. It appeared to have been printed just for her on engraved stationary.

At the Capitol building, she was directed to the records room. It was managed by a gnome-like older man. He was quite taken by the beautiful detective and her letter. She spent three hours going through records and copying items of interest to her investigation. Much of her time was spent with Washington newspaper articles on the president's more controversial agendas, such as the Navy, the Chinese situation, immigration in general, his proposed merit system, and arguments with increasingly powerful Southern Democrat senators and congressmen.

Sgt. Wilders met Pope at the front of the President's House. His three men, one corporal and two privates, took their wagon to the rear loading door. Pope and Wilders walked followed and watched the offloading of a gun safe and miscellaneous items the two had selected from Army supplies. The current President's House guard was a Washington policeman. Pope located him and recruited him into the mix. He was glad to have backup and said the officers on other shifts would also be pleased. He was invited to sit in on the briefing and discussion once the items were moved to the room.

"Men, this is Officer Tyron from the Washington Police Department. He has been a roving guard here for a year. He will be an integral part of our security operation. I would like to spend the next hour or so with him walking us through his rounds and sharing events of note with us. We have pencils and some notepads, so feel free to take one and make whatever notes you wish. We will come back here, and I will answer your questions and we will put together standing orders and the report format for this mission. Officer Tyron? Would you begin your tour? If you have a set tour beginning at one point each time, let's start there. My gut reaction would be to have predetermined stations on the tour but begin it at a different station each time. Following the same route day after day leads to predictability. We want to avoid predictability," Pope said as they began their walk through the building and grounds.

As they toured the intricate building and the grounds with so many unprotected entry points, Pope realized they would need a diagram of the building posted on the wall of the security room.

He told the group he felt any persons held for questioning should be detained by the police officer on duty, though the soldiers could assist. He explained *posse comitatus*, which prevented the military from interfering in law enforcement matters unless martial law has been invoked by the president. Tyron, at fifty years old and a twenty-five-year police veteran, told the men about living through martial law during the war. He said with the two opposing capitols, Washington and Richmond, being only a hundred miles apart and having many police officers in the army, President Lincoln had to resort to extraordinary actions to protect DC. Declaring martial law was one of those actions.

The group stopped at several blind entry points and discussed remedies. Upon return, they discussed items for the duty roster, standing orders and checking weapons in and out. Pope asked Sgt. Wilders to set up a range day with the whole cadre, including the Washington Policemen.

They returned to the security room. Pope asked Tyron what types of events he and other officers had dealt with over the past year. The officer explained the incidents involved drunks, job seekers, and crazies for the most part. When asked whether he had been able to deal with each alone, he responded "yes" about drunks and job seekers. However, multiple persons of any type or people with apparent mental disorders were difficult for one man. All agreed a two-person patrol with whistles to alert the desk guard to call DC police would be much preferable.

Once the policeman was released to resume his tour, and the four soldiers returned to the Washington Arsenal, Pope began to develop the types of post orders they had discussed.

He cut it close with regard to finding a suitable tuxedo for the President's House party but lucked out at an exclusive men's haberdashery. Pope specified the tuxedo jacket to be one size larger to accommodate his revolver without printing notice of its presence. He bought some black shoes and socks, a tuxedo shirt, cummerbund, tie and stud set and rushed back to the Willard.

Pope found Sarah bathing and noticed a new ball gown in deep royal blue hanging on the door of the wardrobe. He quickly disrobed and got into the tub with her. Gallons of water sloshed on the floor, but they mopped it up with towels afterwards.

"Nothing on the President's House invitation mentioned food beyond hors d'oeuvres," Sarah observed, "so I hope they are really good and really filling."

"Me, too. I skipped lunch. Probably a mistake," Pope said.

They dressed. Sarah got Pope to turn and could not see his .44 print under his tuxedo jacket. She did not have to do the same. Her smaller gun, a .38, fit nicely in her purse.

At seven o'clock, they left the Willard for the short walk to the President's House, invitations in hand and fashionably late.

The president and his sister were announced fifteen minutes later. Sarah walked around with a glass of red wine. Pope carried and sipped a glass of water with a lime squeezed and dropped in it. Crowds were good for assassinations and he wanted his reflexes to be at their best.

Around eight, Lincoln caught Pope's eye and motioned both over to where he was speaking with Chester A. Arthur, the twenty-first President of the United States.

"Mr. President, allow me to introduce the Popes. John is the new provost marshal for my office. He's the one I was telling you about heading up strengthening security at the President's House."

Pope shook hands and was glad to feel a firm, confident grasp. Sarah extended her hand and the president kissed it. He was clearly taken with her.

Most people she was not shooting were taken with her beauty and smile, Pope thought to himself. She was exceptionally beautiful tonight. The dress, raven hair and the perfect curves all showed her at her best.

"You are young to be a provost marshal, Pope. What did you do before this? Army officer?"

"No, Mr. President. I was a major case detective for Wells Fargo."

The president's eyebrows rose almost imperceptibly.

"Are you the fellow I have read brings 'em in dead or alive, but always gets his man?"

"Oh, I doubt anything much has been written about me, sir."

"My husband is too modest, Mr. President. I suspect it is exactly him you have read about," Sarah said.

"I believe he was alleged to have a beautiful female detective partner."

"He certainly had a partner at Wells Fargo. The beautiful part was probably a misprint," she said.

"Mrs. Pope was also a detective with the Pinkerton's, sir," Lincoln added.

"So, I see the journalist did not overstate his point. Well, welcome to the People's little house. I appreciate you making it, and me, safer."

Several senators walked up, and Lincoln ushered the two detectives off.

"As you can tell, the sales job about increased security went well. He even admitted he lamented there was no agency or person responsible for it. He was playing you both. He knew exactly who you are and some of your more notable accomplishments. I am not sure what his game is, so watch him. I believe in what he is doing, but I suspect you have figured out, I am not a great personal friend. He can be a pompous ass, funny sideburns and all," Lincoln said in a place and voice where it was impossible for anyone else to hear him.

"I almost hit him up for an interview, but felt a bit uneasy," Sarah said.

"Yes, it's not like you can knee him in the groin if he got too forward," Pope said.

"You think his title would deter me a whit? Think again, cowboy!" she responded with vehemence.

Lincoln smiled. He liked these two and felt comfortable with them. His father would have too. Abe had more enemies in his cabinet than Chester A. Arthur did. However, he put his trust in Pinkerton instead of more properly placing it with his friend and self-appointed bodyguard US Marshal Ward Lamon and General Lafayette Baker. If he had had these two teamed with Lamon and Baker, he might be alive even today, his son thought. Brewster found them in the crowd and introduced Frederick Frelinghuysen, the secretary of state and his wife, Matilda.

During the several hours, the attorney general and the secretary of war introduced them to the full cabinet and many senators and congressmen. Pope was not sure what to expect with the leadership of the country. He kept his thoughts to himself until he and Sarah were alone in their room at the Willard.

"What did you think?" she asked.

"I had figured these would be real impressive powerful people. I came away thinking they were just regular people, some with money, some without. They all put their pants on one leg at a time."

"How about the president?" she asked.

"I did not care for him. Lincoln as much as told us he was a good, honest president. But a man who was neither warm or likeable. His smile is put-on. I thought the only genuine thing he said was about liking us making it safer. The reason was because it made *him* safer, not the institution."

"As I admitted to Lincoln, I did not feel comfortable around him. Realistically, you are right. If he got out of line, I probably would hesitate to squash his *huevos*."

Pope grinned. "You are picking up some Spanish, I see."

"From hanging around you, my darling unofficial husband."

"Perhaps we should not mention your book or article, whichever cover story you use. Interviewing him can go in the case's rubbish can."

CHAPTER 2

The next day, Pope went back to the President's House and continued to write procedural orders for the security staff. He finished midday, spoke with the Saturday guard from the Washington Police and the three Washington Arsenal soldiers who reported for the first duty rotation. Sgt. Wilders came by at one o'clock and checked on his men. Each had properly signed out a revolver, whistle and pair of handcuffs.

Pope and Wilders went to the police department and met with the duty sergeant to explain changes in security at the President's House and how it was a team effort between the police and the military. He realized it was a meeting which should have occurred earlier and with the chief's office. With the potential imminence of a death threat to be handled, he was going too fast and had to focus.

Sarah left on the first train for New York City. She

used her cover as a writer and supported by the letter from the assistant attorney general to research the files of several newspapers. She used the clipping files for Arthur and Roscoe Conkling. The information she found was inflammatory and she could not wait to share it with Pope. She felt she had solidified Conkling as probably being the man behind the threats.

Sarah found a news article about Conkling and Arthur and a third man, George Chadwick, forming a consortium to sell cotton during the war. The reporter claimed the three each made over a million dollars in the endeavor, then had all records of their dealings expunged from records of the customs office in New York and their partnership was dissolved by lawyers Conkling and Arthur.

She resolved to find and interview the reporter who had since left the paper a decade ago. Using every skill she learned at Pinkerton's, she traced him to a tenement in New York City. There was no response to her knock. She walked to a better part of town, glad for the .38 concealed on her person.

Sarah knew she would not make it back to DC tonight. This was a prime lead.

She found a hotel she deemed respectably safe and checked in. She had brought a large handbag with overnight toiletries and a briefcase with her leather notebook and a couple relevant clippings she had purloined from the New York Sun's clippings file on the president.

Sarah ate a light dinner and walked back to the area where the former reporter lived.

She knocked on the door and a sallow, thin man answered.

"Are you Matthew Ricard who used to write for the Sun?" she asked.

"Maybe. Who wants to know?"

"I am Mrs. Pope. I'm doing an article on the good and bad aspects of Chester A. Arthur. I gathered from your excellent article on the cotton deal during the war you were expert on one of the bad aspects."

"I have suffered enough because of the damn article, lady. I was fired with no notice, beaten severely in a so-called mugging, and told after being beaten to never be a reporter or talk about Conkling or Arthur or Chadwick again."

"Who did this?"

"The important part is who had it done. Any thug can beat somebody up for a fiver and deliver a message. Of the three, who is a known gangster?"

"This is all new to me, Mr. Ricard. Conkling?" she asked for verification.

"I am not saying his name aloud. Ever again. He was and maybe still is the most important man in New York. Actually any of the three could be behind ruining me. Maybe all three."

"How did they expunge the records of the cotton

consortium they ran?" she asked.

"What's it worth to you?"

"Twenty dollars, maybe."

He stood there until she withdrew the money and handed it to him.

"They are big time lawyers and the famous two have been involved with the customs house for years. The deals ran through there," Ricard said.

"I might have some papers with evidence on them…" he suggested.

"If I was to see them and think they were helpful for my article, another twenty might be available."

"Twenty is not worth dying for," he said.

"Let me see them and I will make my decision."

"Come in. I'll dig them out."

She entered and sat on a threadbare sofa while he rummaged around a box of files. It appeared to her his filing organization was no better than his housekeeping.

Finally, he pulled out a sheaf of papers and handed her five pages.

She looked at them. They were bills of lading from the consortium. No duty had been levied. They were transferred to Canada tax free.

"They were like finding pure gold," she thought, keeping her face expressionless.

"These might help. Another twenty is all I can go."

"Make it thirty and you walk out with them in

your hand," Ricard said.

"All right then. You win. Here's the thirty dollars." She handed him the bills and placed the papers in her briefcase.

"Anything else you can tell me, Mr. Ricard?"

"Yeah. Watch your back, asking questions about Conkling and the guy he mentored, and then who left him high and dry. They are both snakes as far as I am concerned."

"Thanks for your help," she said as she went out his door and began a very dark walk back to her hotel.

About four blocks from his building, Sarah felt the hairs rise on the back of her neck.

They came at her fast. Three of them. They were burly and she could smell them before they closed on her.

Sarah was able to draw the dagger Pope had given her. She slashed one attacker and he recoiled in pain. The second one grabbed her arm as the third pulled at her handbag.

She thrust the dagger's seven-inch blade into his throat and twisted the handle.

Sarah was only splattered by a little of the gush of blood, but the man holding her got a face full and let go. She drew the .38 Smith & Wesson and smacked the first man across the face with it. He went down. The one whose throat she had opened up still stood, dying on his feet.

The man who had grabbed her arm was trying to wipe his friend's blood out of his eyes with a dirty sleeve.

Sarah pressed the revolver against his torso and fired it. Being pressed in and between two bodies, the sound was muffled. The man went down for the count.

The sound must have carried further than she thought. Sarah heard a police whistle in the distance. She walked across the street and hid behind a tree as two of the city's finest ran up to the scene.

"What happened here?" the first policeman asked.

"A woman went crazy and shot Tony and stabbed Sean."

"Yeah right! You are saying one woman killed two and severely wounded you?"

"I need a doctor!"

"And I need a hot cup of coffee. We are both gonna have to wait," the officer said.

The man whined more about hurting.

The second officer said, "I know you. You guys rough people up for a living. I think you grabbed the wrong man or two and bit off more than you could chew. Woman? Ha! I'd like to meet the woman who could do this to you pukes! You still want to stick with your story?"

The man nodded.

"Then describe this woman who kicked the hell

out of you and offed your two friends."

"She was big. And mean."

"What race?"

"White, I think."

"Hair?"

"Dark."

"Eyes?"

"I dunno. It was dark here. Still is."

"What did she say?"

"Nothing."

"What was she wearing?"

"A dress, I guess."

"You guess. So, this was a possibly white woman with dark hair, unknown eyes, who may have been wearing a dress, and said nothing as she shot one of you and stabbed two? Am I pretty much right?"

"Yep."

"Your description is beyond worthless, you piece of dung. I am going to write 'Got in fight with unknown person or persons and lost', in my report. The bulls in the suits won't touch this as a case. They will mark it like your two friends. Dead on arrival. Now, let's go down to the lockup. Maybe somebody will patch you up there."

Sarah began slowly walking away from the direction she was originally headed. She knew to walk slowly and not appear to be running from a scene of crime.

She stayed in the dark and under trees wherever possible. Seven blocks away, she stood under a gas lamp long enough to check herself for blood. She had a little on her dress. She used water in a ditch to swab as much as possible off with her handkerchief, then threw it in the bushes and walked on. She brushed her clothes and was fairly presentable when she made it back to near the hotel two hours later. She had made a wide circle. Before going in, she found a number of trash cans in an alley behind a restaurant and deposited the .38 in one and the bloody dagger in another. She walked back and entered the hotel. Knowing in reality she had gone west, she commented to the desk clerk over her shoulder she had gotten terribly lost walking east of the hotel. She could not hear his response as she walked on and began to climb the steps. Her hotel was not tall enough or well-funded enough to have one of the steam powered Otis elevators. She was happy it did not. This way, she avoided the scrutiny of an operator.

In her room, she removed her dress and examined it. She was sure in the dark and from the questions her survivor was answering for the police, she could not be identified. She took a washcloth and soap in the bathroom and stood naked scrubbing the faint remaining bloodstains on both herself and her dress. She then washed out the washcloths until they were clean.

Sarah put out her travel clothes for the return to Washington by train in the morning.

Once back at the train station the next day, she checked schedules. She would be able to take a train up to Scarsdale and look around. The people Lincoln had heard got off there.

She realized there was nothing specific to look for, but it was an "i" one of the detectives had to dot.

A southbound train to New York City was due an hour and a half later.

In Scarsdale, she got off and walked around. Nothing. She had a snack for lunch and sat at the station waiting for the southbound.

Sarah took advantage of this time to watch people surreptitiously and listen to conversations. Again, her efforts were to no avail, but illustrative of detective work.

The southbound came and she boarded for the trip, stopping in New York City and onward to Washington, DC.

While this travel day was non-productive, the trip overall had been very productive. She organized her notes as she rode. By arrival, she had her report ready to share with Pope.

******

Sarah arrived back in Washington and went straight to the Willard. She fired the gas water heater associated with the cast iron enameled tub. Filling the tub with now-hot water, she soaked and later blotted off the last vestiges of last night's fight while drying.

Convinced the New York police would not pursue the killing of two thugs and wounding of another, she dismissed the thought from her mind. Her sense of reason was much like Pope's. Bad men decided to attack her and died by her self-defensive action. So be it.

She waited until Pope returned to the hotel instead of trying to find him at the President's House. Her wait was not long.

Pope returned for lunch, primarily to assure himself his partner had safely returned.

In the privacy of the room, she told him about the attack and of being convinced there would be no repercussions. He agreed whole heartedly with her.

"Is there any way the attackers could have been watching your snitch's house? Maybe Conkling's men?" Pope asked.

"I really don't think they would be watching him after this long. And I was careful about someone following me there. I truly doubt they did. I believe I was a victim of opportunity," she said.

"Ha! You were the wrong 'victim' darling!"

Sarah had the records spread on a table in the

room. She gave him the background on the cotton deal, and they discussed Conkling in detail.

"I think this is enough to have a meeting with one or both of our contacts. I will leave a letter for Lincoln and let him decide who, when and where," Pope said.

She accompanied him and they dropped the letter on the way to lunch.

Pope, since his vague letter said he would be in the security office of the President's House, returned there to await a response.

A message was left for the provost marshal by telephone to the telegraph room next door.

"Provost Marshal Pope. Please meet with me and a guest in my office at three o'clock. Bring your partner." It was marked "from the Secretary of War" by the telegrapher.

Pope looked at his pocket watch. It was almost two. He returned to the Willard and he and Sarah quickly choreographed their presentation. Armed with the notes and five pages of records which had been redacted from the Customs House, they walked over to the nearby War Building.

Lincoln's secretary walked them down the hall to a very private conference room. Lincoln was there. Brewster sat at the head of the conference table with an open pad in front of him. Both men rose as they entered. All sat down once brief greetings were exchanged.

"What do you have for us, Mr. & Mrs. Pope?" the secretary of war asked.

"Two things. Let me do the briefest one first. We have established an eighteen-man cadre from Washington Arsenal to protect the President's House. The office is adjacent to the telegraph room, to give us quick access to a telephone and telegraph. I have coordinated with the Washington Police Department. One officer and one trooper will be on 24/7 patrols with a soldier remaining at the desk for communications purposes. They have been provided specific weapons and have both standing orders and orders of the day. Sgt. Wilders from the Arsenal detachment will conduct daily inspections. I will split most of my time between there and my desk here."

"Excellent. I trust your planning. Ben, any questions?"

"Not really. I am glad Washington Police remain engaged for arrest purposes from a constitutional standpoint."

"I addressed the issue of *posse comitatus* in my briefing to the men," Pope said.

Sarah stood.

"I will commence the second phase of our reports to you today. Please ask questions at any juncture.

"Our investigations have turned up some things we did not know about someone on our unofficial suspects list. Perhaps you know these things but have no proof. We have proof.

"The suspect is former Senator Roscoe Conkling. As I am sure you both know, he and the president were cronies in New York, but seem to have fallen out due to the president's reluctance to appoint Conkling and the president's lack of support and, indeed, opposition to a number of legislative things Conkling feels strongly about.

"It seems Conkling, Arthur and a man named George Chadwick formed a cotton consortium during the war. They made millions of dollars. On the surface it was good business. But, if it was honest, why were all records about it expunged?

"We have in front of you five pages of records from the Customs House in New York. They are allegedly the only ones left from the cotton consortium records destroyed.

"The pages show five instances of where large cotton sales to merchants in Canada were made without report or any sort of duty, tariff or tax being paid. Each should have specified who was responsible for paying—the sender, the Canadian recipient, or a third party. None is stated. It appears nobody paid anything.

"Now, we doubt Conkling would use this against the president without implicating himself, though as a sharp attorney he might find a loophole.

"However, this is proof alleged misdoings did occur and we think the three principals are culpable."

The two secretaries were quiet for a moment.

The attorney general took possession of the five sheets and studied them.

"Where did you get these?" he asked, immediately putting the two detectives on the defensive.

"From the man who found or stole them. I bought them for a token amount."

"Who was this?"

"A source whose identity I promised to protect, sir."

Brewster thought about her reply for a while.

"Alright. I will accept your position. We cannot prosecute or even publicize this without putting the president in an untenable position. If, at some juncture, he goes off the reservation and an impeachment is underway with which we agree as a point of fact, these will surface. We will revisit their use. If Conkling is impacted negatively, so much the better. He is a very dangerous man and, to me, of dubious character.

"I agree, the cotton deal is something one as canny as Conkling could use to influence Arthur. Don't you agree, Robert?"

"I do, Ben. I believe this solidifies the case for Conkling being a prime suspect."

"Sarah went to Scarsdale and looked around. We have not determined a link there with Conkling but will continue to seek one. At this time, we are not putting all of our eggs in Conkling's basket. We just feel we have validated him as a threat. We will continue pursuing the others and whatever new ones pop up. And will, of course, continue to advise you both right away," Pope said.

"I am intrigued our detectives located evidence which eluded the ones in New York," Lincoln said.

"Robert, Conkling runs New York. He is a man who exercises daily, is a boxer himself, and is intimidating even without his henchmen. Nonetheless, Popes, this is good work on the hardening the President's House and investigation standpoints. Keep it up," Brewster said.

Pope and Sarah went to a gun shop and replaced the .38 with a matching one. A hardware store had a six-inch blade Bowie and she bought it to replace the dagger discarded in New York City. Pope bought both weapons. He attracted less attention with the purchases than Sarah would have.

"Where to now on the investigation?" Sarah asked.

"Let's move to enemies of Arthur's pro-Chinese and pro-immigration reform efforts. We assume railroads are against the efforts. This may or may not be true. Let's figure out a way to validate our suspicion or mark it off our list."

"I think I will go back and visit my friend who is at the Congressional Library, if you could call the crammed together room a library," Sarah said.

"I'll look for discussions on the floor of both houses

of Congress about immigration and see who is loudest against it. Then, I will try to tie those Senators and Representatives back to the railroads and any other more covert financial supporters they have."

"Sounds like a fine plan to me! Safer than your last trip, too."

"I don't know. The gnome-like little man seems to have taken a fancy to me."

"Probably heard about your plan to turn the president into a gelding…"

"There is a remote possibility of it happening. It's made more remote by your increased security."

"Lincoln told me some interesting history the other day and this is the first time I have had a chance to share it with you," Pope began.

"It seems a house painter was mad with Andrew Jackson about fifty years ago and shot at him point blank on the Capitol steps. His gun misfired. The old president began beating the living hell out of him with his cane. The man pulled another pistol and it misfired too. Fully enraged, Jackson was beating him senseless until some congressmen pulled him off."

"My kind of president!" Sarah said.

"There's another story more germane to our situation. It seems a number of people suspected Conkling was behind the assassination of Garfield at the train station where we arrived in Washington."

"I thought Charles Guiteau was a deranged job

seeker acting alone," Sarah said.

"The job seeker version was the official story. Apparently either Conkling got the version with him in it stifled, there was not sufficient evidence for a grand jury, or all of the above. Lincoln told me the story whispering as if he was afraid to say the words."

"I don't think he is the rough and ready fighter his father was," Sarah said, adding, "or as crazy as his mother was. Or is."

"She is dead. Almost a year ago to the day. I gather she may have had an unpopular personality but was beside Abe Lincoln until the night he died. There is some question about the truth of her being crazy. Our friend Robert had his mother committed to an insane asylum. She was released several months later and deemed sane. A number of people do not respect him because of how he treated his mother. Maybe he was trying to save his political career from embarrassment and, in turn, embarrassed himself more? I do not know.

"I do know this is an odd lot we have fallen into," Pope said.

"You have amassed a lot of information. Have you been doing research?" Sarah asked, thinking she had the research abilities of the pair.

"A small bit, mainly by listening and asking vague but carefully pointed questions," he said.

"Let's go back to the Chinese and overall immigration matter as a possible cause for the threats. I will ask both of our contact secretaries for as much as they will, or can, share on the subject and try to get a feel for how the railroad tycoons may play in this," Pope said.

They retired early and were awakened by a tapping on the hotel room door at two in the morning. Both had guns in their hands before the covers were down.

"Yes?" Pope called from beside the closed door.

"Bellman with a message we got at the front desk telephone, Mr. Pope."

Pope eased the door open and found it was, indeed, a bellman. He took the message and closed the door. Sarah raised the gaslight's brightness and they read it. It was from the desk soldier at the President's House security room. They had a suspect in custody and asked him to come over and interview him.

Pope dressed quickly and trotted over to the President's House. He saw the policeman and soldier on their rounds. He found from them the man had been apprehended only fifteen minutes ago. The subject was trying to get in the front door of the President's House.

The two said they approached him with their revolvers drawn, so the man was unable to put his own into action before being disarmed. Pope thanked them and proceeded to the security room.

An unshaven man was sitting handcuffed at the

worktable. The duty soldier was watching him carefully.

"I understand this man was apprehended trying to get in the front door. He was armed and the patrol took his weapon away. Has he made any statements?" Pope asked the man, Corporal Smythe.

"He started babbling and I told him to shut up until the provost marshal got here. He did."

"Good work by all three of you, Corporal. Let's see what we can learn from this gentleman," Pope said.

He picked up a notebook and pencil and sat across from the man.

"Who are you?" the man asked.

"I am the Provost Marshal for the secretary of war's office. You will not be allowed any more questions until I tell you. What is your full name?"

The man's response was as profane as could be imagined. Pope's response was to backhand the man across the jaw and send him toppling onto the floor. Before he could get up, Pope was around the table and grabbed him at the collar and lifted him back onto his chair.

"You will answer me in a civil and truthful manner, or I will see you tried by a court-martial for coming here to shoot the president. You will be hung at the Washington Arsenal just like the Lincoln conspirators were. Do you understand me?" Pope asked with a growl.

"Go to hell!"

Pope got up and walked around the table, fists balled up ready to knock the man unconscious. For the first time, Pope saw actual fear in the man's eyes.

He grabbed the man by the collar once again and leaned in, inches from his face.

"You aren't helping yourself. I can and will get a lot rougher. You will be in a world of pain before I have you taken to the brig at the Arsenal. You will be hidden away there for a long time before anyone remembers to try your butt in court and hang you."

"Oren Baker," the man said.

Pope walked back around the table and sat down across from Baker.

"Where do you live?"

"Why do you care?"

Pope got up again and began to walk around the table when Baker told him his address.

"Where do you work?"

"I don't have a job."

"Why were you beating on the President's House door at two in the morning with a gun in your pocket?"

"Because it's his damn fault!"

"Whose fault?" Pope asked. He already knew what the man would say.

"The president. He's letting those Chinese stay and others steal our jobs. It's why Americans like me can't work. Somebody read it to me from the paper."

"Did they read you the Chinese and some other immigrants are working under slave labor conditions in hard jobs nobody else will take? Did they read the jobs are thousands of miles from here in the mountains and deserts?"

"Not the facts I heard!"

"Well, you heard wrong then. How many railroad tracks are being laid anywhere near Washington? I will bet your life if even a siding was being laid nearby, it is being done by white workers like you. So, Mr. Baker, you could have gotten killed for bad information. As it is, you will go to jail for bad information," Pope said in a low voice.

"Mr. Baker, who sent you to shoot the president?" Pope asked.

"Nobody!"

"Do not lie to me!" Pope snarled menacingly.

"I ain't lying!"

"If nobody sent you, who gave you the idea?"

"Nobody! We was talking about him loving the Chinese when I was in the bar."

"What bar?" Pope demanded.

"Smileys over to 14th Street," he said. Pope looked at the corporal who nodded.

"Corporal, what kind of gun was Mr. Baker carrying?"

"Something called a New American. It is .22 caliber," he said as he handed the gun to Pope along with three cartridges.

"You hoped to assassinate someone with this?" Pope asked Baker incredulously.

"I doubt this will penetrate his suit, vest and shirt. Besides, he's in bed asleep. You couldn't have gotten anywhere near him. Bad idea, Mr. Baker. Stupid idea.

"Corporal, have the telegrapher call Washington's finest to send a couple officers over to escort Mr. Baker to jail. Have him charged with attempted breaking and entering with a somewhat loaded weapon."

"Should I say 'somewhat loaded'?"

"No. Just B&E with a firearm to shoot the president ought to work."

"Yes, sir."

Pope waited until the police responded and took Baker to jail.

"Sir?"

"Yes, Corporal."

"He's an idiot, isn't he?"

"Sure, seems like one. The problem is the three people who have tried to shoot or have shot presidents so far have had mental issues. So, we have to treat them as real threats. I am going back to bed. I hope the rest of your tour is less exciting."

"Yes, sir."

Pope climbed back in bed. Sarah mumbled, asking if everything was alright. He told her it was, and he would share it with her at breakfast.

The next day, Pope went to his war office first. He wanted to make sure both cabinet members knew about the attempt last night, feeble though it was.

After he shared the situation with Lincoln, the secretary commented it probably was not worth worrying about. He did say he would tell the attorney general who may want to monitor the case.

"Sir, I would not take it too lightly. Even the dumbest pig makes good bacon. It just takes one badly aimed bullet to kill the president. I feel we need to take all attempts seriously and investigate to see if they may have been put up to it by someone else.

We have about four possible areas of interest in these threats. Sarah and I have developed a couple more we have not discussed with you. They need to be substantiated before we waste your time. The ones really worrying me though are the ones *not* on the list. Ones so far afield we have not even considered them yet."

"Your points are well taken. Are you going to investigate this man Baker any further?" Lincoln asked.

"I thought I would dirty up a bit and have some beers at Smiley's Bar on 14th Street. It's in the district marked as off-limits to the soldiers during martial law in the war. The so-called 'red light' district. Maybe I can pick up something on what angry workers are saying," Pope said.

"Let me know if you learn anything, John."

"Always, sir."

Pope left Lincoln's office and asked around the War Building. He got the directions he needed and walked eight blocks to a second-hand store. He located a pair of overalls and two shirts which he thought would fit. A pair of scuffed up boots followed and a beat-up newsboy-type hat. It was too hot during the Washington summer to wear a jacket and cover his gun. He put the Bowie knife in his left boot and tied the sheath to his upper ankle. With the baggy work pants pulled over the hilt, it was virtually invisible.

He was certainly better armed than Baker had been with his dollar and fifty cent gun from Sears Roebuck.

Pope went out the back stairs of the Willard into an alley. He looked and nobody was around, so he rolled around. He wanted to get dirty but not with the urine or garbage he smelled. A bit of dust and dirt from a railing leading into the back of the hotel took care of his face and hands. He tousled his hair and mustache and put the cap on. Pope was, by every appearance, an itinerant who had worked at a basic labor job and was likely sleeping rough.

He walked to the bar and ordered a draft beer. It was warm and weak. The weak part was fine since he would have to spend some time at the bar listening.

After an hour, several men came in and sat at the bar near him. They were clearly day workers who showed up at a location for basic work and employers would come by and hire them for the day to unload wagons or train cars or dig ditches.

After a few beers, the three next to him got louder and friendlier. They felt they could afford to be friendly to someone who was both in their element and appeared to be one of their own.

"Ain't seen you here, fella," the man next to him said as the three and Pope ordered their fourth and his second beer.

"Naw. Just got into town. Found a job for today digging a garden for an old man," Pope said. He did not want to offer too much. He preferred they ask him, and he would consider the best answer.

"Where ya from?" the man asked, his friends listening.

"I came in from Colorado on the very damn rails I used to make a good living laying."

"Ticket musta been expensive," the man probed.

"Nope. I rode in boxcars all the way and avoided railroad detectives. Didn't cost me a cent!" Pope lied.

"You said you laid rails?" another of the men asked.

"I did. Good money, too. Then, the president started molly-coddling them foreigners and a good American like me was put out of work. Just not right, you know?"

"Doesn't seem right. We heard he was giving special rights to foreigners. Chinese and all. We was talking about it two or three days ago in here. Some fella got all worked up over it. He agreed with us and stomped off. We talked after. My pa was born in Dublin. Hans, where are your folks from?"

"Outside of Solingen," the man two barstools down said.

"The same place where they make them knives? In Germany or somewhere?" Pope asked in character.

"Yeah," he said, with it sounding more like "yah".

"So, you see what I mean? None of us been here for a long time. We are all kinda foreigners. I don't see the harm in giving a man a chance. We agreed on it. But the fella the other night got himself worked up into a real lather."

"What happened to him?" Pope asked, knowing the man was talking about Baker who he had questioned in the security office.

"Don't rightly know. Ain't seen him since. Probably moved along, looking for work."

"I might do the same," Pope said. "Go back out West. I like it better there. Too many people here. You boys hang in there. Maybe I'll see you down the road somewhere," Pope said and stood. He downed the beer. The men nodded at him and he put his cap on and walked out.

He thought about the men and Baker on the way back. He believed they did not know where Baker was or what he had tried to do. Baker was still in jail. There was no way they knew his predicament.

Pope did not consider this a dead end. He considered it one more item checked off his to-do list. He walked back to the rear entrance of the Willard and climbed the stairs to his and Sarah's room. She did not know about him being disguised today, so he knew to be careful.

He tapped on the door and said, "It's me, but I am in disguise."

She cracked the door, and he knew there was a .44 in her hand, just out of sight.

"Hello there? Come right in. My husband won't be back for an hour or two," she said in a believably seductive voice.

"Thank you, Ma'am. I think an hour or two will be plenty of time," he said, and she grinned broadly.

"Good disguise. If you weren't dirty and smelly, I might take you up on a little fun," Sarah said.

He grinned at her and asked if she would draw a hot bath while he got rid of the work garments. While he was in the bath, she put them, boots included, in a sack to take to a cleaner. He might need a disguise again before all this was over.

Pope had gotten used to being able to walk to a Chinese laundry in San Francisco. He would have to look around for a laundry in Washington. It would be bad tradecraft to have the soiled workman clothes washed by the Willard staff. Too many questions could arise.

Clean and redressed in clothes appropriate for an informal dinner, he briefed Sarah on his trip to Baker's bar the day before.

"While the men at the bar are unlikely to be involved in a plot against the president, I don't think it was a futile effort. We eliminated one specific concern and need to continue investigating. What was your experience today?"

"I came up with something worth further investigation. I just hit on it reading local newspapers in the Congressional Library. You and I discussed some senators and representatives were agitating to expand the boundaries of the country. We also were concerned about the growth in disruption by newly powerful Southern members.

"Well, I found three senators and two congressmen have some sort of group pressuring other members to vote for expansion into Mexico. Maybe even Canada, though Canada is lower on the list. Here is the list."

She handed him a list of three senators and two congressmen and had their states in parentheses beside their names.

"There was also mention of funding possibly available from a finance firm in Dallas. It operates like a private bank and is very secretive. It's called GC Financial. A man named Joe Selby Jr. is the president. The bank and he popped up in an article once and was never mentioned again. I thought it was pretty odd.

Like somebody called the reporters off," Sarah said.

"I will see if either secretary knows anything about it. It sounds significant enough to make a quick train trip to Dallas. Sure, wish I had Caesar with me."

"Your horse is in high cotton. Or, maybe high grass, with your grandfather. You may have to arm wrestle the old mountain man to get your massive horse back from him!"

"I might. He'd probably win too," Pope said. She grinned, having seen him lift an outlaw who smarted off at her. He grabbed the man by the collar, lifted him up with his feet off the ground, and threw him several feet. Pope did this with one arm. Sarah would put her money on Pope in a match off with about anyone.

Pope stopped by the President's House security office and reviewed the reports from last night. All was well. He then headed for his office at the war building.

Upon arriving, he requested a meeting when possible with Secretary Lincoln. He took notes during the hour wait before he was summoned.

"Hello, John. What is happening?" Lincoln asked.

"First off, I used a disguise and a lot of dirt and visited the President's House attacker, Baker's, bar on 14th Street. I spoke with the men he met with before coming to try to shoot Arthur. I believe he took what he wanted to hear and remembered only it. These men are all second-generation Americans and have no issues with immigration. If anything, I think they would support opportunities for people like their parents.

The anger over immigration is probably there, but I believe it resides in railroad executives who are patrons of various congressmen."

"Makes sense, John. Second off?"

"Sarah did a lot of research. It seems there are some senators and representatives who are pressing for more domain for the United States. Here are their names and states. A funding source was mentioned, then dropped from the press like a hot potato.

"It's GC Financial in Dallas. The chairman of the board is a former senator, but she included him on the list I just handed you," Pope said.

"Old enemies of my father," Lincoln said after a while, clearly disturbing memories were emerging in his mind.

"John, Senator Shelby was a Confederate officer. Perhaps more importantly, he was one of the founders of the Knights of the Golden Circle. The 'GC' in GC Financial stands for Golden Circle.

"The founders had one initial goal. It was to expand the land area of the United States by annexing northern Mexico and parts of southern Canada. Cuba was a possible target, too. The primary interest was on Mexico to avoid issues with England over Canada. The founders were not all southerners. They were power barons from a number of states.

"During the war, it became a southern thing and helped finance the Confederacy.

"It is rumored the Knights of the Golden Circle removed the gold and silver from the Confederate treasury in Richmond prior to burning and evacuating Richmond.

"How much and where it was put remain secrets. They are a powerful and secret organization. And a dangerous enemy. Dangerous both physically and legislatively.

"They absolutely would have the wherewithal to kill a president or change a government.

"We need to talk with Ben together before you go any further. My initial impulse is for you to go to Dallas, maybe with the attorney general and tell them why you are there and ask them straight out if they are involved. I can, however, be swayed by your and Brewster's thoughts on the approach."

Lincoln went to the office's telephone and called the Attorney General's office. They waited several minutes until Ben Brewster answered.

"Ben. Robert and John here. Do you have a few minutes for us? Yes, it could be very important. Alright. Thank you. See you in five or ten minutes. Bye."

"He has a meeting scheduled but will cancel it. Let's go over now," Lincoln said.

They walked the short distance, then went up the stairs to the Attorney General's office and presented themselves. His secretary ushered them in immediately.

"John, you must have found something important," Brewster began.

"I believe it's more counsel on what to do about what Sarah found," Pope said.

"John and Sarah's research has suggested the Knights of the Golden Circle as a possible group behind the threat against Arthur. Especially since the chairman of their funding source is none other than our old enemy, General Shelby," Lincoln said.

"The Golden Circle was an expansionist movement. One which may have millions if not more in gold secreted around the South and West, right?" Brewster asked.

"Yes. And a number of powerful industrialists and senators and congressmen have been associated with it, by fact or suggestion. Their money may be the Confederate stock of bullion and coins. However, the leadership has never been totally Southern.

My initial thought is you and John go to Dallas and confront them with it. What do you think?" Lincoln said.

"Well, let's think through it. If we go as attorney general and investigator, it will add an official aspect to the questioning. However, we will spill the proverbial beans on the table about the threat against the president. What if we couched it in terms of an 'operation' in the Virginia-Washington area? We could refuse to comment on the nature, leaving a criminal enterprise open as a possibility perhaps," Brewster suggested.

"And refuse to give details? Perhaps suggest we have heard GC was behind funding it?" Pope asked.

"Yes. My fear is by me being there, it ratchets up the curiosity factor."

"Ben, what about a subpoena from a federal court to see their records?" Lincoln asked.

"They have been a secret organization for twenty or thirty years. We have no idea who they are, what they want or how much money they have. They have not maintained such a level of security and anonymity by being stupid or without good counsel. They could tie the subpoena up in courts for years without our willingness to admit why we want the information. Years!" Brewster said.

"Perhaps I should just go down alone and push them hard. Could you get me a treasury agent badge? Or some non-military credentials?" Pope asked.

"I agree with John, Ben. He needs to go in without a military angle," Lincoln said.

"If I tried to 'borrow' a treasury badge, it would raise too many questions at the treasury. I am still not sure I trust them to not be part of this mess.

John, I can swear you in as a deputy US marshal. Or, have business cards prepared naming you a member of the Assistant Attorney General for Criminal Prosecution's office," Brewster said.

"How about both, sir? I could give the card as my

introduction but have the badge in case I need it."

"Your idea seems reasonable," Brewster said.

"Be sure to keep your badges straight. A provost marshal with a deputy US marshal badge would raise a lot of questions," Lincoln said.

"I will, sir. Not a problem. Even if caught on it, I could say I was on loan to the Attorney General's office from the War office. I can finesse it alright."

"Go ahead and get a ticket to and from Dallas. How can you keep us apprised?" Brewster asked.

"Wells Fargo uses a coded telegram system. I can send telegrams to Sarah. She can decode and deliver to you."

Pope left and, since he was returning to the West, picked up his boots, Stetson and Colt .44. He swung by the train depot and picked up roundtrip tickets for Dallas.

He and Sarah walked down to the Old Ebbitt's Grill near the hotel and the President's House. They recognized several diners from the cocktail party, but names and titles eluded them. They had originally thought social mixing was going to be the way the investigation would run, but quickly found it not to be the case. Both admitted they were glad of it.

Sarah had pork chops and Pope had a steak. They still chatted at dinner like new lovers instead of old marrieds. The dinner was a delight and they walked back to the Willard anxious to arrive at the privacy of their room.

CHAPTER 3

Pope left for the train depot at dawn and boarded the train south, then connecting west.

He arrived in Dallas the next morning. This train trip had been brutal with storms buffeting the train and rocking the cars like a boat in rough water. He was beat as he climbed down from the train. His return ticket was open, so he found a hotel. Pope took a nap and cleaned up before going to the GC Financial offices.

Looking like the native Westerner he was, he arrived at the offices at ten o'clock.

There was a man at a desk. Nothing identified him as to name or title.

Pope asked to see Mr. Joe Shelby, Jr.

"What is your business with Mr. Shelby?"

Pope presented the new engraved Attorney General's Office business card.

The man read the card, taking an inordinately long time to do so.

"Let me repeat myself. What is your business with Mr. Shelby?"

"I am here on behalf of the US Attorney General. My business with Mr. Shelby is not your affair unless you happen to be him."

The man glared at him.

"Are you, in fact, Mr. Shelby?"

The man continued to glare. Then, he threw his coat back and reached for a gun in a shoulder holster.

Before the gun cleared leather, he felt a Colt Frontier Model pressed against his mustache, just below his nose. Looking cross-eyed up the barrel, he could see the Colt was cocked and ready to fire.

"This could have been so easy. But you had to be stupid. Now, before I decorate this office with your brains, where in hell is Mr. Shelby?" Pope asked.

"I am Joe Shelby. Is this a robbery?" a portly man in his forties said from a doorway behind where the covered man sat.

"Of course not. I work for the attorney general. I asked to see you and this man tried to draw on me. He's the first one who did and lived to tell about it."

"You are with the Texas Attorney General? I may have to have a talk with him," Shelby said.

"I am with the Attorney General of the United States. You are most welcome to have a talk with him.

In fact, it's beginning to look like he will be wanting to have a talk with you."

"Perhaps we should come into my office."

Pope removed the gun from the man's mustache and slipped the gun out of the shoulder holster and stuck it in his own waist.

He nodded for the man to precede him into his boss' office. The man hesitated but was sped up by a hard barrel prod in the middle of his back.

"Does my secretary need to sit in with us?" Shelby asked.

"It was not my plan. But I will not have him bushwhack me while we are talking, or run and get some accomplices," Pope said.

"Talbot, sit at your desk and do not move. Do not take any action or go anywhere. This gentleman and I need to speak in private."

"I want my gun back."

"You may get it when I leave. Or you may not. You came real close to dying just now. Why don't you sit at your desk and contemplate on it?" Pope suggested.

Shelby sat at his desk. Pope moved the chair around to the side so he could control the door and sat.

"Do you have any identification?"

"I gave the man who drew on me my card. Here is another," Pope said, handing it to Shelby.

"Assistant US Attorney for Criminal Prosecutions. Ominous sounding for a visitor," Shelby noted.

"Maybe, maybe not. I am here to ask your cooperation and maybe help on a major criminal investigation."

"What type and how can GC Financial assist? Also, should I have my attorney present?"

"I don't think you need him, but you are most welcome to have him present if you wish," Pope said.

"Ask me a few questions and I'll decide."

"Fair enough. I am out of Washington. I am heading up an investigation for the Assistant Attorney General. I cannot tell you about the crime we are investigating because it has not happened yet.

"We have a fair number of facts about an event which will occur in Washington. We have received information from a good source saying your institution will be involved in the funding of the operation. I was sent here in good faith to ask you about it. It's entirely possible someone is soliciting your financial support under false pretenses. If such is the case, it would certainly behoove you if we work together to nip this in the bud."

"How should I address you?"

"Provost Marshal Pope."

"Isn't provost marshal a military position?" Shelby asked.

"Yes. I am a head investigator for the War Office. I am on loan to the Attorney General and deputized as a marshal during my deployment."

"What is the nature of this crime?"

"It is an operation against the government of the United States of America, Mr. Shelby. I am not at liberty to say more. I need to ask you some questions to take back to the attorney general. He will decide what further information we can give you based on your responses. We are attempting to do this informally without taking you to Washington, deposing you and making it an interrogation. I will tell you the crime is a serious one, probably with capital punishment."

Pope saw Shelby fidgeting and beginning to perspire. Instead of waiting for permission, he pushed ahead.

"What sort of institution is this? A bank? A trust?"

"It's a private bank and trust. Our assets are related to a blind trust. Most recently, we have evolved into a philanthropy organization."

"You mean you give money to deserving charities?" Pope asked.

"Precisely. Orphanages, church missions and the like."

"Most admirable, Mr. Shelby. Was charity always your mission?"

"No. We were an expansionist movement originally. The expansionist movement ended during the war. Our assets were devoted to the Confederacy's efforts. I am afraid it did not work out well for us or the effort. So, we evolved into a charitable organization," Shelby said.

"Mr. Shelby, what did you say was the source of your assets?"

"I didn't actually. The source is a blind trust. It and its trustees are protected under very tight trust law from being identified. The trustor wrote it into the trust document."

"So, if the attorney general subpoenaed you for the information, he could not get it?" Pope asked.

"It would be tied up in court for years. Well past his term as attorney general. I suspect it would go to the Supreme Court in four or five years. We could tie it up until then."

"The secrecy sounds like illegality, Mr. Shelby."

"I am sorry you think so, Marshal. Nothing we do does anything except help people who need help. I am required as a trustee to exercise due diligence to protect the tenets of the trust document. Hence my reluctance to speak further."

"Would you be willing to tell me under oath your organization is not involved in any operation against the United States?"

"I can tell you with all honesty I am unaware of any operation against the United States. I have been here for six months. Before then, I was a Dallas bank president. I cannot swear to anything my predecessor may have concocted before he left."

"How might I contact him?" Pope asked.

"Very conveniently. He is near you. He has a small

estate east of Charlottesville, Virginia. It's called Topping. His name is Michael Kane. You might be careful approaching him."

"Why should I be careful?" Pope asked.

"He is quick to shoot."

"A banker?" Pope was confused.

"He ran the organization from more of an operational standpoint. I run it as a financial professional."

"Is your father still chairman of the board of trustees?"

"I am not at liberty to say under the constraints of the trust," Shelby said.

"Thank you, Mr. Shelby. If we have more questions, someone from the office will be in touch. May I give you a bit of advice?"

Shelby said "yes" with great hesitation.

"The man out front could get you and him killed. He's not very good with a gun."

"Kane met him on a rare visit after resigning and laughed. I guess I should have taken my predecessor's reaction seriously."

Pope unloaded the man's gun, a Smith & Wesson Schofield, and laid it and the six cartridges on his desk. He said, "Only a fool has a loaded round under the hammer in this type of gun," and left.

The man stood menacingly as Pope walked out. Pope walked past him aware, but not showing his disgust with the man's incompetence.

On the street, he turned and walked back to his hotel. He believed Shelby. He also thought Shelby had told him much more than either his father or this Kane person would. Regardless, Pope knew Kane would be his next visit once he got back to Washington. He avoided the Wells Fargo office and opted for the Western Union Telegraph. He sent a coded telegram to Sarah for the two secretaries. It outlined his findings and plans to call on Michael Kane at Topping in Charlottesville when he arrived back in Washington.

The weather and ride were smoother on the return trip. He sat thinking the whole time. The talk with Shelby had been an interesting conversation. Depending on the board of trustees, the Knights of the Golden Circle probably did have the power and money to pull off a coup against the government. Certainly, an assassination.

No matter where the case took them, Pope knew he would not dismiss the group readily. They would be on the suspect list until the very end of the case.

He got off the train in Richmond and found a westbound train to Charlottesville.

The conductor was walking through forty minutes outside of the former capital of the Confederacy. He stopped and looked at his pocket watch and announced to the passenger in the car, "We will be having a big bump in the tracks soon. Nothing to worry about."

A few minutes later, there was a bump and the whole train rattled as each car went over it.

"We used to stop at a watering station there. Newer equipment makes it all the way to Charlottesville without a coal or water stop. The pronunciation of the place is 'bumpas'. It was a bit of humor by the railroad. The official name of the station and little community is Bumpass. You can see why!"

Pope grinned. He had seen some pretty crazy place names traveling around the country for Wells Fargo. So far, Bumpass was on the top of his list.

He got off at Charlottesville and went to the post office, again avoiding Wells Fargo during this secret investigation.

"I am looking for a nearby estate. It's called Topping," he said to the postmaster.

"Actually, it's Topping Castle. Take Richmond Road east for five miles. You will see a sign for it on the left. It's owned by the Kane family. Has been for over a hundred years. The old man is dead, but his son lives there now. Rumor has it he's married to a beautiful actress."

"Thank you. One last question. Where can I get a horse to ride out there?" Pope asked.

"Two blocks to the left of the post office and one block over to the right. There's a good livery stable. Tell the man Honus sent you. He'll take care of you."

Pope stopped at a café along the route and got a

ham sandwich and cup of coffee.

The livery owner set him up with a handsome Morgan gelding. Unfortunately, the saddle was the British style popular in the east.

No damn place to wrap a lariat or hang a canteen and no latigos to lash on a rifle scabbard or saddlebags, he thought to himself.

He swung up on the horse with the ease and grace of a cowboy, his first job.

Following the postmaster's directions, he found Richmond Road and headed away from Charlottesville.

Knowing his day on the horse was not going to accrue much mileage, he rode at a fast trot and saw the sign for Topping Castle quickly.

He turned into a long, one lane entry. It was lined with trees on both sides.

If I was going to live back East, this would be it, he thought. *And was rich,* he added.

He was totally convinced when he rounded a curve in the lane and saw the house. It was brick with white columns. As he got closer, he could see well performed repairs almost hiding bullet pock marks and at least one cannon hit. As a Californian, he had never given much thought about the war. Only the fact it had eliminated slavery. At least black slavery. Certainly not helped the way Indians were treated. Or immigrant workers.

It hit him hard to imagine what it might be like to have an invading army attack you at home where your wife and children and animals were. To bombard your house and stables. And, for this to happen when you were not around to help protect them or fight the fires or bury the dead. He decided it was the most horrible war imaginable.

As he approached the house, several fine-looking hounds, tri-color fox hounds, probably, came out and set up a ruckus. It made him think of Scout.

A tall man appeared on the front porch. He stood near a column he could duck behind if shooting started. Pope would have done the same thing.

He was darkly handsome and probably forty years old. His hands were loose at his sides. Pope would have bet a year's salary a revolver and maybe a Bowie knife were in his waistband in back.

"Buck, Tar! It's okay boys. I have it now. Sit!" he called, and the dogs returned to his side and sat protectively one either side of where he stood.

"Are you Mr. Kane?" Pope asked.

"Who's asking?"

"My name is John Pope. I am an army provost marshal on loan to the attorney general."

"Mr. Pope, do you have a way to prove it?"

"I do. I have a written warrant naming me provost marshal for the secretary of war and a deputy US marshal badge from the attorney general, who swore me in himself."

"Why don't you get down and show me these things, then we can commence talking about whatever brought you to Topping Castle?"

"Fair enough."

Pope had already determined the Morgan horse would stand with his reins dropped, so he walked slowly towards the man and the dogs.

"I don't know about you, Mr. Kane. But I detest the English saddles. How do you all stay on them foxhunting?"

Kane smiled.

"Despite the dogs, I don't foxhunt. I irritate my neighbors by not allowing them to foxhunt on my land. And there is not one of those silly saddles anywhere in my stables, Mr. Pope. Or should I call you Deputy Pope? Maybe Provost Pope?" he asked.

"Most people just call me Pope."

"There is a gunfighting Wells Fargo detective named Pope. Has a beautiful ex-Pinkerton lady detective partner. I read she's almost as deadly as him."

"Actually, Mr. Kane, she's a lot more dangerous. A helluva lot," Pope said confirming his identity.

"What brings you here? I take it you are not Wells Fargo anymore."

"I was asked to come to Washington and investigate for the government. My case is sensitive. It involves an attack on certain government assets in

Washington. I cannot divulge much more. But, in a recent conversation in Dallas I was referred to you."

"How much did Joe, Jr. say to you, Pope?" Kane asked suggesting Kane's knowledge of his talk with Shelby was more than just speculation.

"He was very careful and would not answer any questions about the Knights of the Golden Circle, its leadership or funding. He promised me he was not aware of anything involving them or GC Financial which involved an attack on government resources. He said for anything before his six months on the job, I would have to ask you."

"I am not aware of anything which would imperil the government or any person in it, either," Kane said.

"How about trustees using your funding in a manner where you would be unaware of the actual use?"

"The procedures I set up years ago should prevent such a thing. There are…influencers associated with the group who might undertake getting rid of someone they thought was a problem for some reason.

"To get money to finance an operation, it would have to be applied for in writing and vetted by the entire board of trustees. These men do not act as a rubber stamp, Mr. Pope. They keep each other in line."

A very lovely woman appeared in the doorway behind Kane.

"Michael, do we have a guest?" she asked.

"We do, my dear. And, I suspect hospitality and

prudence should have told me to have our conversation inside and over a beverage and perhaps lunch."

"Let me look to lunch. I will leave you to the liquid refreshments." She moved away. Pope got a sense of her floating away. She was beautiful, but not as much so as his Sarah.

"Pope, please come in."

Pope followed the man inside, through an entry hall, a parlor and to a small dining room. He was sure there was a larger dining room for entertaining. This was probably where Kane and his wife ate. A sunroom, it also had comfortable chairs and bookshelves.

"Perhaps we can finish the official part of our chat before my wife returns with lunch?" Kane said firmly, though posed as a question.

"I'm sure we can," Pope replied.

"I am interested someone who the news rags claim has solved many of Wells Fargo's thorniest mysteries and killed its most dangerous outlaws was called to Washington. The threat must be very major. An assassination at the highest level, an overthrow of a government agency. A defamation with enough evidence to fuel an impeachment," Kane said.

"As you are not at liberty to violate the trust agreement the Golden Circle lives by, I am also not at liberty to say the specific threat," Pope said.

"You are very close to the threat identification, Mr. Kane. I will add the suspect list is larger than one might expect. I am in the process of reducing the suspect list by elimination now."

"I am glad you do not consider the Knights or their funding a major suspect."

"My suspicions are diminishing," Pope admitted.

"President Arthur is an odd duck," Kane began.

"He did not set out to be president and I don't get the impression he wants to be one now. When Garfield was wounded and died of infection, people said 'Chet Arthur is President? How odd!' Yet, he has done remarkably well. Many of his major endeavors have pleased the people and made special interests very mad. Some of those special interests are very powerful. I can see you have your work cut out for you. Is your partner helping?" Kane asked.

"She is, though under her housewife cover, is doing more research than investigations. Nobody but the president has identified us as quickly as you did. Most of the people in Washington are so absorbed with what is best for them they have no time to worry about anyone else. I think it makes them very vulnerable."

"I agree wholeheartedly, Pope. Not to move suspicion away from my former employer, but have you considered how cheap it would be to eliminate a head of government? Or, so simple to amass evidence against him to impeach him?" Kane asked.

"You are right. Just get a crazy and spend enough to arm and liquor him up. Which is why we have subtly hardened the President's House and the movements of the president himself," Pope said.

"My guys stopped a man with a gun beating on the President's House door at two in the morning recently. He claimed under questioning he was going to shoot the president because Chinese were taking "good American" jobs," Pope added.

"You know the scariest thing about our republic?" Kane asked. He proceeded to answer before Pope could respond.

"Uninformed idiots like him vote."

"Yes. Terrifying," Pope responded, "but, perhaps the cost of freedom."

"Afraid so. Changing the subject…" He was interrupted by Rita Kane bringing in a silver tray of sandwiches, followed by a pitcher of lemonade.

"Please join us, darling," Kane asked. She sat down next to him.

"Mrs. Kane, I did not expect lunch, but I will appreciatively enjoy it."

"May I ask, Mrs. Kane, you seem familiar. I know we have not met. Have I seen you in the papers?" Pope asked.

"Perhaps. I was an actress before getting married."

"I'm sure recognizing you is it, then," Pope said without probing further. "The sandwiches are wonderful. I really like the salty ham's flavor," he continued.

"It's Smithfield ham from east of Richmond. Virginia ham is always salty. This seems to Michael and me to be the saltiest and most flavorful. This particular one was from the Joyner's farm."

"With me being from California and my wife from Illinois, we are just beginning to sample Southern cooking in Washington. So far, we love it."

"What does your wife do, Mr. Pope?" Rita Booth Kane asked. Kane watched, enjoying himself. He knew his wife would get more out of Pope than he could.

"Officially, she just puts up with me as a husband now. Previously, she was one of the small cadre of female Pinkerton detectives. Then, I recruited her to Wells Fargo. She is a wonderful detective."

"I love seeing women succeed in manly jobs. And you, Mr. Pope, what is your background?"

"I grew up in Kansas. At ten, I saw an Indian raiding party kill my mother, father and little sister. My grandfather, Israel Pope, was one of the last of the real mountain men. He took me and raised me."

"I have heard of him," Kane said. "I am surprised he did not go after the party."

"We did. He knew the tribe from the arrows and who was raiding in the area. We watched them and identified a raiding party of young braves ride out. We saw there were no more left and reckoned they were the ones who killed his and my only kin.

"We trailed them and picked our place. With lever action rifles, we mowed them down. I hesitate to continue during lunch. The story gets pretty violent," Pope said.

"My Rita is pretty tough, Pope. Please continue," Kane said.

"We killed them all and scalped them. The scalps were presented to the old chief. Immediately, my grandfather and I had developed the ability to read each other without words. I saw my little sister's scalp hanging on display. Grandpa knew what I wanted to do. I saw a flicker in his eyes. Given permission, I shot the chief where he stood. We rode off hoping my family could rest in peace."

"You did this at ten years old?" Kane asked.

"I did. I could not have had a better person to raise me than Israel Pope. He set out to teach me everything he knew about hunting, tracking, fighting, even smelling horses and men at a distance. He turned me into an Indian."

"Do you hate the Indians for what they did to your family?" Rita asked.

"No, Ma'am. Not at all. I more hate what we have done to the Indians. The raiding party did what they did. I often have to kill outlaws, but I don't hate them."

"An interesting, but logical approach. One I have taken myself," Kane said.

"I have taken up far more of your time than I intended. Thank you for your hospitality and delicious lunch," Pope said, rising.

"You are most welcome anytime, Mr. Pope. Next time bring your wife. I would love to meet a lady detective," Rita said.

"I'll show you out," Kane said.

They walked out to where the livery horse still stood.

"This is a good horse. I miss my own, Caesar."

"What type horse is he, Pope?"

"Just a massive walking horse. He is not handsome with his Roman nose. But he can face into a blizzard and trot until I cannot ride anymore."

"I feel the same about my black, Hadrian. He is a stallion," Kane said.

"Mr. Kane, you had a point which the arrival of lunch interrupted. What was it?"

"This country has been through too much disruption since 1861 to survive another coup twenty-two years later, or another presidential assassination, only a year after the most recent one. I will poke around with some sources and see what I can find out for you. I am confident nothing will be related to the organization I used to run. I'd know if it was.

"Shelby Jr. is a good banker. He is not a great leader, so I am often consulted about the impact of requests for large donations on our mission. Nothing even hinting of what you and I have discussed has come up," Kane said.

"One of my areas of inquiry is the impact of the Chinese legislation Arthur has pushed. It reduces free or cheap labor for the railroads. The railroad bosses are a powerful and rich group. If you have contacts there, it may be an interesting inquiry to make."

Kane gave a wry smile and said, "I'll see what I can do. How do I get in touch with you?"

Pope handed him a card.

He also noticed Kane had always faced him. Kane donned a jacket when walking out the door, despite the warm day. As he turned, Pope saw the faint print of a gun butt under the back flap. And something else. Pope went with his first guess. The handle of a Bowie not unlike the one he also wore.

When Pope had met Wyatt Earp, it had been like two lions circling and appraising one another. Two deadly beasts wondering who would win in a fight. Pope decided he would. Earp was without fear. Pope knew he could outdraw and outshoot the sometime lawman. Beyond the shadow of a doubt. He also knew Earp would walk into death without a qualm.

He did not know what kind of gun Kane wore. But he knew to the depths of his heart, if he and Kane drew on each other, Kane would prevail.

Pope had a finely tuned gunfighter instinct. Kane would kill him before he could get a shot off. He had never had such a thought before. It was profoundly unsettling to Pope.

******

He returned the horse and found an eastbound to Richmond and connected for the several hour trip to Washington.

Pope arrived around dinner time and found Sarah at the hotel. Her research at the Congressional Library had yielded a few names of railroad executives complaining about how Arthur's Chinese worker legislation would slow the expansion of rail service countrywide. What Sarah interpreted to mean was it would hamper profits.

Pope told her about his meeting with Shelby in Dallas and with Kane near Charlottesville.

"See what you can find on Rita Kane. She is an actress and must be famous. The only actress I can name off the top of my head is Lillie Langtry," Pope asked.

He related the conversations and what a handsome and interesting couple the Kane's were.

"John, there is a part of this story you are not telling me. What is it?"

He hesitated a full minute before replying.

"I have never met anyone who I knew was better than me. Someone who could kill me in a fair draw down. I did today. Kane made no effort to show his capabilities, but I felt them. He has killed. And, killed fast people. I feel it. He could kill me without a doubt."

"Hmm...I don't believe it's true. I don't know

what to say, darling John. If you feel it so strongly, it must be so. I never thought there could be anyone faster than you."

"Kane is. I know it. The good thing is I think he's on our side. He kept the privacy of the Knights group he used to run. But he spoke candidly, man-to-man with me. Almost like old friends would speak. I don't believe he pulled any wool over my eyes. I think I have a good horse manure detector."

"I would love to meet this couple. It sounds like they are like us in a few years. Just richer."

"I believe Rita is your age. Kane looks to be about forty or so."

"Well, if nothing else, we are working our way through the suspect list. While the Golden Circle people may not be directly involved, we still could have powerful expansionists or railroad interests behind the threat," Sarah said.

"I'd still put my money on Conkling at this point, Sarah," Pope said.

"Could he be tied in with either of the ones I just named?"

"I doubt expansionists or railroads. He seems to be a New York political, if not criminal, boss. Have you found anything tying him to activities outside of New York? Maybe as a national politician?" Pope asked.

"Nary a thing. He seems to have come to Washington to support things benefiting his constituents.

Probably himself in so doing," she said.

"Have you picked up any sense of a new secession-ary movement by the Southern Democrats?"

"Not really. They are growing in number and in-fluence, but only appear to have the interests of their individual state agricultural and industrial growth on their agendas."

"What are we missing, Sarah?" Pope asked.

"If we are wrong about Conkling, I don't know. Like you said the other day, what we don't know is what we don't know. It will be something out of the blue neither us nor the two secretaries never dreamed about."

"What are you seeing as being the most discussed and contentious things in Congress right now?" Pope asked.

"There are always arguments and speeches leading to more arguments about the expansion of the Navy."

"Is it always the same argument?"

"No, not at all. A lot of people in both houses oppose it because the money takes funds away from their states or their pet interests. Those interests tak-en alone are not much. Taken together, they represent a lot of Congressional power.

"Do we need a bigger Navy? So much at one time? Changing from wooden ships to steel ones? Which Navy shipyards should get which slices of the ship-building pie? What ships should come first?"

"Sarah, let's go back to your next-to-last. About the shipyards. Are you saying commercial shipyards don't build Navy ships?"

"I am. The Navy has its own shipyards. Which in itself is a bone of contention. It seems it costs more to build a warship in a Navy shipyard than in one which builds commercial ships. Since the shipyards employ civilian builders, they have to hire crews of specialty workers for each ship approved for them. So, the interests of cities and states come back on the scene because a ship provides more jobs for some period of time."

"Despite Arthur trying to do away with the spoils system for government jobs, spoils still describes almost everything else the government does, right?" Pope asked.

"Right! Spoils in the way of jobs, budgets, building projects. Virtually everything."

"It's clear any special interest group could be behind the threat Lincoln heard. We are looking for a needle in a haystack, aren't we?" he asked.

"I am afraid so. There will always be people against a president. Crazy and legitimate people both. Your moves to protect the President's House and guard the president when he is out and about may be all we can do. Even if we miss the conspirators on the train, but save him from another one, we will have accomplished a lot, John."

The following morning, Pope had the same conversation with the secretary of war.

"You are not giving up are you, John?" Lincoln asked.

"Not in the least, sir. This is not a conversation full of excuses. It's a statement of how very many reasons groups, even obscure ones, could have a gripe against the president. Sarah and I think protecting him from both organized conspiracies and single crazies is the first order of business. While he is being protected as reasonably possible, we will continue to chase down potential threat sources."

"I admit, John, neither Ben nor I had previously given much thought to the presidency or the perils which come with it. I realize, particularly as the son of Abraham Lincoln, it's pretty naïve of me. Try to keep him safe. I have a lead on a townhouse about five blocks from here.

"Please consider moving into it for the duration. It's a few blocks more walking from the President's House but gives the two of you a more established Washingtonian look. It actually will not cost as much as the Willard, is fully furnished and will allow you both to have a more normal life. I can have it billed directly here. Would you like to see it?"

"No, sir. If you think it would be best, we will move right away."

"Oh! And it comes with a live-in housekeeper. Her

presence will allow us to install a telephone so you can be reached or called out in an emergency."

"Sounds good, sir. Perhaps I could take Sarah over today. Would you send the housekeeper a message introducing us?" Pope asked.

"It will be on the way before you make it back to the Willard." Lincoln wrote down the address and handed the slip of paper to Pope as he was leaving.

He walked back to the Willard, happy with the turn of events. As nice as it was, it was still a hotel room with no way to cook. It did not have the space to stretch out. It was a room, not a home.

The two of them walked back to F Street NW and found the address. It was a well-kept brick townhouse with dark green shutters. They met May, the middle-aged housekeeper at the door. She showed them the parlor, dining room, master and second bedrooms and pointed up some narrow, steep steps. "I live at the top of the steps," May said.

"I clean and cook. I can do *hors oeuvres* if you do a party or reception."

"This is beautiful, May. I am sure we will be at home here!" Sarah told her.

"We may be installing a telephone, so there are times you may have to take messages," Pope told her.

"A telephone! How exciting. I have a good handwriting. I never even saw a telephone. Who might call us?" she asked.

"The President's House, attorney general, or secretary of war primarily."

"The president?" she asked excitedly.

"No, the security office there. I head it up," Pope told her. "If they call, especially in the middle of the night, there is a real problem. We will try to keep you aware of where both of us are during the day, in case either gets a call you can advise people."

"There's a backyard and two-horse stable through the kitchen door as well as a privy. The bathroom is just beyond. It's brick to prevent fires from the wood heater for the tub. If you want a bath, just let me know ahead and I'll fire up the water heater. It takes maybe half an hour for real hot water in the tub."

"Thanks, May. We will move in late today. We only have clothes here. I am new to my job with the war office," Pope said.

They went back and packed. The concierge summoned a hansom cab, and they were moved in within an hour. The following day, Pope contacted Sgt. Wilders at the Arsenal and asked for a small key lock gun safe for the house. He would return it when the case was over.

Nothing of note had occurred at the President's House.

Pope gave some thought of buying a horse to keep in the stable behind the house and decided against it for now. They did not know, day to day, how long they would be in Washington.

Sarah met with May and found out how the household worked, grocery shopping, and cleaning. She accompanied May on an initial trip to the grocery and butcher and they bought a week's worth of groceries. Once a representative budget was established, she would create a cash jar for May to draw upon.

The house, though small, was lovely, as were the furnishings and wall hangings. She found it belonged to a senior Army officer stationed overseas at an embassy and had been rented far longer than occupied by the owner.

The house and its furnishings were what a poor Illinois girl had dreamed about. It gave her ideas about what she and Pope should own once they finally settled down.

Pope checked in at the war office and had no messages. Lincoln was on a trip. Pope walked over to the President's House security room. Sgt. Wilders had assigned a corporal for each shift there, a man with more experience than the troopers on patrol. Pope was pleased with the decision.

Pope checked out one of the police whistles to carry on patrol. He spoke with the new corporal on duty then caught up with the Army and Washington Police patrol and walked with them.

Pope decided he would try to join at least one patrol a day on days he was in Washington.

With the warm weather, more crowds were out and the home at 1600 Pennsylvania Ave NW was busier than ever.

He worried about the case reaching a point where nothing arose regarding the listed suspects and no new ones surfaced. He felt like his boss James Hume at Wells Fargo and his friend, private detective Harry Morse felt about Black Bart. They had chased the elusive stage robber for almost a decade and were no closer to arresting him now than in the mid-1870's.

Pope was continually nagged by the possibility the threat against either the president's life or his presidency would come from some unknown and impossible to identify person or group. One whose inclusion in his and Sarah's investigation would only happen when they struck.

1883 Washington was hot and humid in July. The city and its Potomac River smelled due to insufficient sewage handling. It had outgrown itself and many government officials left for the mountains, or just for home.

Later in an uneventful week, Sarah did come up with some interesting material. It had nothing to do with the case.

She found Rita Kane was really Ogarita Booth Kane. She was the only daughter of Lincoln assassin John Wilkes Booth. Information was available about her because she had some renown as an actress.

"So, even without her tell-tale name, her photos in the newspapers are how you recognized her," she told Pope.

"Yes, she could certainly be an actress. She is pretty enough. Yet, in person, she is down to earth and interested in things other than herself. It's odd for an actor or actress to care about others, I would think.

"The other question is more interesting. How did Kane meet and marry Booth's daughter? Something related to the Knights of the Golden Circle?"

"I am convinced, John, we will never know. If the Circle is as secretive as you say, I believe how he met her will never be divulged."

"Probably so," he acknowledged.

******

Lincoln and Brewster met with Pope the following week.

"There is little Ben and I can do to help you and Sarah eliminate suspects. The only area we have been able to identify is the military. We talked about this and have a plan regarding any threats coming from the Navy. We decided to come right out and ask them. Tomorrow, John, the three of us will meet with the secretary of the Navy and whatever senior staff he wishes to bring to a meeting down the street at the Navy office."

The three walked to the building next to Lincoln's the next morning.

Secretary of the Navy William Chandler was there along with several admirals and captains.

"Secretary Lincoln, I thought you and your associate might be here to campaign to wheedle us out of some of the funds President Arthur has designated to grow the Navy. But I fear the presence of the attorney general adds a more somber note," Chandler said.

"No, funding is not our interest today. We are here to talk about the protection of America and her government. You know Attorney General Brewster. The other man with me is Provost Marshal John Pope. He has been tasked with protecting the president and his dwelling. His background, which is quite illustrious, is investigations.

"Allow us to jump right into the topic at hand," Lincoln said. "Ben?"

"Have any of you heard whisperings from any corner about harming or toppling the president? If you have, I believe it is imperative for us to talk," the attorney general said.

There was silence in the room for a moment. Secretary Chandler was the first to regain his composure.

"Who is behind this, Ben?"

"We do not know. Provost Marshal Pope is investigating it. We have also had him harden the President's House and implement stronger protection for the president when he is outside of it. A very senior member of government overheard a conversation between at least two intelligent, well-spoken men on a train northbound out of New York City. By the time he heard words setting off an alarm to him, the train was stopping at Scarsdale and the men slipped off before he could identify them. The nature of their conversation and ensuing argument, which is what got his attention, was about either killing or causing President Arthur's presidency to fall. Arthur is unaware of anything beyond the additional security. He condones those efforts.

"I might add, gentlemen, this whole meeting is conducted at the most secret level. This cannot be discussed with anyone outside this room. If you choose to discuss it among yourselves, it should be in a place and manner where you will not be overheard."

"Without offense to the provost marshal, isn't this a job for a treasury agent?" an admiral asked. The attorney general responded.

"Admiral Belton, you would normally be correct. However, the secretary of war and I felt, since we did not know whether this threat extended within the government, it would be prudent to use a proven investigator from outside. I invite you to research John Pope of Wells Fargo in the newspapers. Especially the Western state ones. I am sure you will agree he is an excellent choice.

"Pope has identified a number of people or organizations with cause to not like Arthur. Midway down the list is the people whose funding will be diminished by the shift of monies to the Navy budget."

"Are Navy officers suspects?" the secretary of the Navy asked.

"No, sir. Except to the extent naval officers may control shipyards which might lose out due to shifting to steel hulled vessels. Quite frankly, knowing little about shipbuilding, I would think it is not Navy personnel on fixed salaries who we should worry about, but specialists, people who supply civilian workers and suppliers. Do you agree?" Pope asked.

"I believe it is safe to speak for everyone and say we agree with you, Provost Marshal Pope," Secretary Chandler said.

"Do you have a man who is knowledgeable in the ship building process to assign to work with Pope on this phase of the investigation?" Lincoln asked.

Chandler turned to a captain.

"Captain Foster, I'd like you to coordinate with Pope," he said. Foster nodded.

"Thank you. Now, has anyone one of you heard anything, no matter how obscure, which might aid Pope's investigation? Hints, rumors, anything against the president?" Pope asked.

One of the admirals spoke. Pope later found he was in charge of naval shipbuilding.

"Sailors gripe. It's their nature, especially during long periods at sea. I suspect soldiers do also.

"There have been universal gripes over going to steel vessels ever since the president announced it. I might add, he did so with the full concurrence of the men in this room.

"The nature of their talk has mainly been 'wood floats, steel sinks'. While the phrase is true, it's irrelevant because of the design of a modern ship with its sealed off bulkheads and inherent flotation. They worry since wood flexes more than steel, a steel ship will break apart in rough seas. Flex can be built into any design. These men largely do maintenance; they are not nautical architects. Lastly, most people are resistant to change. Wooden ships to steel ships is about as large a change as we could make. I daresay they will change their minds once another ship's fire bounces off the new hulls instead of penetrating like it would with a wooden hull.

"The men who complain about this, the cooking, the style of their uniforms don't have the capability to pull off a coup or an organized assassination attempt," he said.

Pope looked around the room and read concurrence on the faces of all the naval officers.

"Thank you, Mr. Secretary and officers. You have satisfied this part of the investigation, at least until Captain Foster and Pope conclude whatever probes they make. We will leave you to running the Navy," the attorney general said. All rose and Foster waited for Pope to approach.

"I have some ideas of actions for us," he told Pope. Pope nodded and held up a finger signifying to wait.

"Secretary Lincoln and General Brewster, I would like to stay and meet with Captain Foster. There's no need for you to wait."

They left and the room was cleared except for Pope, Foster and the admiral who spoke at length.

"Provost Pope, this is my boss, Admiral Hemingway. He is in charge of the construction and maintenance of every aspect of the fleet," Foster said.

"Foster has a major project coming up. How long do you think you might need him?" the admiral asked.

"I doubt more than a few days. We can start right away."

"Excellent. This is important. Very important. But I have a full agenda planned for him." The admiral left the two.

"Let's go to my office and meet behind closed doors," Foster suggested.

They walked down the hall and Foster beckoned him into an office. They sat and Pope took out his notebook and a pencil.

"If we took a day trip to New York, we might be able to kill all our birds with one trip," Foster said.

"Please go on."

"I suggest we take a train to New York or hitch a ride on a naval vessel out of Baltimore or even here if one's available. We can visit the Brooklyn Navy Yard, where we can see the impact of the wood to steel changeover, get a list of types and number of civilians, who is affected, and who the suppliers are, both old and new. If you want, I can send a telegram today and we can begin tomorrow."

"It's a good comprehensive approach, Captain. Let's do it. They are installing a telephone in my house today. If you will give me a number for the Navy building, I will call you later and give you my number to confirm time of departure and where exactly," Pope said.

******

"Do we have a telephone?" Pope asked as soon as he arrived at home.

"We have one and both May and I have been instructed with the use. I have gotten a small notebook and attached a pencil to put numbers in. It will take me less than three minutes to teach you how to use it, John," Sarah said.

"Good. I have to call the Navy building and secure some information about a trip to New York tomorrow. I am not sure if it will be by train or ship."

"Ship? Isn't a train cheaper and faster?" she asked.

"No doubt. But it will be a Navy ship, so it will be fun and free."

She instructed Pope in the operation of the telephone. Several hours later, he made his first call. It was to the Navy building. He asked for Captain Foster.

"May I ask who is calling?" the man at the other end asked.

"Provost Marshal Pope."

"Captain Foster is in a meeting with several admirals, sir. He left me a message for you. You will travel to New York on a Navy ship. It will depart from Washington Navy Yard at noon tomorrow. Look for the USS Miantonomoh BM-5. It is a 263-foot ocean-going monitor attack ship." He spelled out the hard to pronounce name slowly.

Pope wrote this in the notebook and tore the page off. He was excited. He knew this would be a fast ship and interesting ride to Brooklyn Navy Yard.

"Do you know how long it takes to get from the Navy building where you are to the Washington Navy Yard by cab?" he asked.

"Stand by for a minute, sir. I will ask." The man returned momentarily and advised to allow for thirty minutes to get to the Navy Yard and find the ship. It was one of only three docked at the yard, so would not be difficult to find.

"I wish I could go!" Sarah said, looking over his shoulder as he wrote.

"I wish you could, also," Pope said, "but it would be too hard to explain. These people don't know you are also a detective. We probably ought to keep them in the dark."

He left in plenty of time at ten o'clock the next morning. Just in case, he carried a small satchel with toiletries, a clean shirt and the Bowie knife.

Pope walked around the dock area and found the ship. Compared to wooden sailing ships, it looked modern and fast. He asked for Captain Foster. Foster appeared moments later and welcomed him aboard. He introduced Pope to the ship's captain.

"This monitor is a fast, ocean going attack and escort ship. It has a top speed of over ten knots. It's two hundred sixty-three feet long and draws fourteen and a half feet. The ship has a single steam engine turning two screws. It is the newest ship in the Navy at this time.

"Once underway, it will take us twenty-four hours Navy Yard to Navy Yard. We have small officer quarter staterooms reserved for you and Captain Foster. Meals, which are quite good, will be called by bells. I am sure Captain Foster will tap on your hatch at the appropriate time to eat."

"Thank you, Captain. My only other experience has been on a ferry across San Francisco Bay. I look forward to this and am honored to ride on the newest and fastest ship in the Navy," Pope said.

Pope and Foster watched as the last of the coal was run down the chute into the ship's coal bunker. As coal was consumed to build steam power during a trip, it had to be moved closer to the boiler in case a burst of power to catch or evade another ship or render aid to a vessel in distress was required.

"Does the ship have small arms in addition to the eight big guns I see?" Pope asked Foster.

"Yes, there is a small arms locker below with rifles, revolvers, cutlasses and knives. The ship was built in 1876, but just commissioned last year. It will do coastal patrol initially. The patrol will include boarding other ships at sea. It would move in and launch the small steam launch you see on the port, or left deck. An officer and enlisted boarding team, fully armed, will board a vessel to inspect and maybe make arrests."

"I must admit, I find all of this fascinating," Pope said.

The coal shuttle was moved away from the ship. Pope could feel the engine build steam power. Finally, the order to cast off lines came.

The captain sounded the whistle one blast and Pope felt the four-thousand-ton vessel begin to back away from the berth.

The starboard propeller was reversed, and the port propeller simultaneously moved. The result, one pulling and one pushing, caused the big vessel to spin almost in its own length.

The captain straightened her out, and she began to idle out of the Navy Yard at slightly above clutch speed. They maintained the speed of a brisk walk out of the Anacostia River into the Potomac and headed south.

South of Alexandria, Foster pointed Washington's Mount Vernon out to Pope. As the Potomac widened, they sped up to about seven knots.

The ship entered the Chesapeake Bay for several hours. At Cape Charles, they entered the Atlantic Ocean and turned north.

The captain set a course ranging five to twenty miles off the coastline as he made his way past the oceanside of the Eastern Shore.

Foster looked at his watch and said, "We should return to our rooms and prepare for four bells. They will signify our dinner seating as officers at six o'clock. Duty officers and one third of the crew will eat at the next two half hour increments. I will put on a dressier uniform. You will be perfectly fine in your business suit," Foster said.

"I take it from what you said we will reach the Brooklyn Navy Yard around noon tomorrow?" Pope asked and got an affirmative response.

Dinner was as good as virtually any restaurant Pope had eaten in outside of the Bohemian Club in San Francisco and the Cheyenne Club on his last case in Wyoming.

The officers adjourned to a small lounge and had cigars and either brandy, wine, or whiskey. Pope followed Foster back to their rooms through a maze of passageways with doors which could be readily sealed like vaults and several ladder wells.

"I hope the damned thing doesn't run into anything. I would never find my way back to the deck in time to jump overboard," he noted to Foster, who thought the remark to be hilarious. Pope, to the contrary, was dead serious.

Pope was lucky with the seas being calm and slept well. Foster tapped on his door and said, "Breakfast in about thirty minutes." Pope met him in the passageway twenty minutes later and they headed to the mess for breakfast.

They had skirted Long Island and idled up the East River to the Navy Yard on Wallabout Bay and docked by one o'clock.

Pope and Foster thanked the captain and headed for the office of the commander who headed the facility.

Commander Daniel McKellar welcomed them at the dock, and they took a brief tour of the yard before going to the mess hall for lunch. He reserved a small dining room, and they held their meeting in it.

"Dan, John Pope and I are here to assess the impact on the Navy of switching over from wooden to steel hulled vessels. If you would, tell us how marine surveyors, specialty craftsmen like carpenters, suppliers of wood and steel will be affected. And we cannot leave out the unions. What are they saying?"

"Would it be more complete for you gentlemen if I give you an overview, then provide a list of contacts among the unions and company owners who supply our naval yards?" McKellar asked.

"It would be very helpful," Pope said.

"Let's get the ones not affected out of the way first, though I will list them on the sheet in a separate column.

"Any company or union involved in steam fitting, engine design and gear, such as gearboxes, shafts, and propellers should not be adversely affected. They should remain the same regardless of hull material.

"Wood producers, carpenters, wood-related unions would be negatively affected. Quite frankly, it would cost them millions and they would go out of business, unless the majority of their contracts are for commercial vessels. They must realize, as goes the Navy in hull materials, so goes the fishing, transport and passenger industry. However, there are several firms which work on contract to the naval yards exclusively. Those will either have to switch over to steel or become insolvent."

"Please asterisk those companies," Foster said.

"I will. The most popular wood for sailing ships is live oak. The primary source is live oak preserves owned by the government on the north coast of the

Gulf of Mexico. They are primarily in the Florida panhandle and Mississippi," McKellar added.

"How are they impacted if they are owned by the government?" Pope asked.

"They are impacted because the trees are grown, managed, cut down, and properly boarded and prepared for use by contract firms. Those firms will be badly hit by the switchover. Several of them also own the transportation companies which move the prepared boards from the deep South to naval yards such as this one.

"The delivery fees are a large part of their income. It is about twelve hundred fifty miles, for example, from the Biloxi preserve to here by land. It's much farther, around the horn of Florida at Key West, by sea. The Navy has set a miles per pound standard, and it's enormously high for a big enough load to build a two hundred seventy-five- or three-hundred-foot ship."

"What shipyards can you give us information about?" Pope asked.

"The ones you want. As of now, it appears this yard, East Boston, and Philadelphia will be the initial builders of the new steel hull Naval vessels. Perhaps more will follow suit later. I daresay it will be at least five years or so before others are engaged. The funding is not there for it so far."

"How long will it take you to compose this?"

Foster asked.

"Until at least tomorrow."

"Pope, here is what I propose. You put up in the bachelor officer's quarters, or BOQ, here for several days. I will telegraph back to the admiral who runs naval operations and have him prepare a letter of introduction for you to carry to each listed entity. I have to get back by train later today, so you are on your own. Sans a senior naval officer's uniform, you will need some sort of introduction," Foster said.

"Do you think a telegram from the admiral would suffice?" Pope asked.

"No, I do not. Dan, would you prepare a letter for Pope for the ones in Philadelphia and non-Navy contacts here in New York. They will keep him busy until the letter arrives. Then, he can go to Boston, other builders and unions and to the Gulf Coast regarding lumber and transportation."

"I will. Pope, drop by later this afternoon. Ensign Murray?" McKellar called to a young officer outside the door.

"Would you escort Mr. Pope over to the BOQ and get him checked in for an indefinite number of days? On the way, secure transport for Captain Foster to the train station."

"Aye-aye, Commander McKellar. Will do."

They shook with the officer and left with the young junior officer.

"Gentlemen, I will secure a room for Mr. Pope and then pick you up at the entrance to the yard," the ensign said.

The two men walked to the entrance as the ensign left them.

"Captain Foster, thanks for your help. And, for the ride on the ship. It was a once in a lifetime thrill for me," Pope said.

"I wanted to hitch a ride on it myself. It will already be steaming up the coast. Rumor has it hanging a starboard turn and going to Greenland, then to Europe for a while."

"I am not sure I would like to take a long ocean voyage in a steel ship, most of which is well beneath the surface of the ocean," Pope said.

Foster looked around to see whether anyone was within hearing and mouthed, "Nor would I!"

A naval passenger wagon pulled up in ten minutes with the ensign driving. It was not unlike a buckboard pulled up. Foster and Pope shook, and the wagon left.

Pope walked over to the BOQ and checked in.

He walked over to the manager's office after giving McKellar sufficient time to prepare his list. Foster waved him in and had him sit for a few minutes until he completed it. He looked at his list closely, then pushed several sheets across to Pope.

"What do you go by, Provost?" McKellar asked.

"Either John or just Pope."

"I'm Dan, John. No need for a lot of formality inside. Outside, protocol is the Navy's middle name."

Pope grinned at him.

"Seems to be in Washington, too. Few uniforms, but everybody is concerned by the next man's title and how much power it suggests. Pretty silly to watch. I can understand it from a discipline standpoint in the Army or Navy, though."

"Yes. Me, too. You get used to it when you are in uniform. Which I will probably wear until they put me in a box, nail it shut and fire a few rifles up in the air."

"Probably not a bad life. Especially if you don't care about the rose covered cottage for the long term. Just one big, organized adventure."

"True, John. Sometimes you get an assignment which is or gets boring, but even then, you can transfer before too many years pass."

"I have prepared a letter of introduction for you for the local and Philadelphia yards. You will be on your own for Philadelphia and for the live oak preserves in the South."

Following dinner, Pope went to his room and prepared a working list of questions he wanted to ask. The ones for contractors included: "How are you impacted? What will it cost you? Can you make a turnaround and switch to steel hulls? Cost? Retraining time? Cost to retrain. What do your employees or members think? What are you hearing?"

Pope was not seeking the answers to these questions. He was seeking how the questions were answered. Did the questions engender anger? How were the responses couched? In business logic or threats?

In Brooklyn and Philadelphia, he got angry answers from companies who supplied wood shipbuilders and their unions. Most others saw the steel hull handwriting on the wall and were adjusting to change over. The cost to manage the change in their marketplace was simply a cost of business most said. They would build as much of it as possible into the lucrative government contracts. The unions would attempt to cover the cost of retraining into contract negotiations with the builders. Nobody seemed to be taking on the Navy.

He made reservations on a train to Atlanta and onward to live oak preserves in Florida and Mississippi.

Pope planned a one-day break in the trip to report to Lincoln and see Sarah.

******

"So, nobody so far seems to be horribly mad at the Navy, or the congress, or the president?" Lincoln asked at the end of Pope's update.

"They are irritated to have to change. I think resistance to change is a human frailty. But I have not seen the type of anger leading an assassination or a coup."

"This is comforting, John. Keep nibbling away at this thing. Eventually, there will be nobody left but the threat."

"Occam's Razor, sir. Shave away the possible and you will be left with the answer."

"Hmm. Thought I heard such logic somewhere. Perhaps in law school."

"Perhaps, sir," Pope said. "I will let you know which way the wind blows down South in the live oaks."

Pope went home and surprised Sarah. They adjourned to the parlor and he brought her up to date and told her he was on the way to Florida and Mississippi, if not more Gulf states.

"I wish I could go. I'm starting to get cabin fever. There's not much more research I can do at the Congressional Library."

"Why don't you go then? We certainly can afford your train fare and meals. It will be a break for you."

"Are you sure?"

"I am, honey. You just cannot actively be a detective. It's out of the character we are playing. But you can be the loving wife. Very loving would be nice," he said.

"I am beginning to see why you want me to go…"

"Truly, I have missed my partner on the trail. Tell May and pack a few things. Including your armaments."

"Shotgun, too?" she asked. "It will fit in my valise. I checked."

"Then by all means, bring it along. You never know when a nice load of double-aught will soothe a savage beast," Pope said.

She sought May and requested a train picnic to carry for the trip down. Pope had never seen the valise she was packing. It was longer and less deep and wide than most. He was pretty sure his partner had her sawed-off shotgun in mind when she selected it. The perfect wife for him, he thought.

They headed south through Richmond and on to Atlanta, and then to Jacksonville where they changed for a westbound train for the Florida panhandle. They got off the train in Pensacola and checked into a hotel.

Pope got a horse from the livery nearest the hotel and rode to a live oak preserve. He presented the letter from the admiral who was in charge of naval operations.

His reception was cool at first, then heated as the civilian manager cursed the Congress and the Navy. He sounded like the man Pope had arrested at the President's House, ranting about "ruining jobs for hardworking Americans". The difference in his rants was the substitution of changing from wooden to steel hulls instead of immigration.

"Where is the company located which hires the men who tend the live oak trees, cut them, mill them, deliver them to port and load them?" Pope asked.

"ACME Marine Lumber is in Biloxi. At least until they go out of business."

Pope bit his tongue and let the man continue.

He asked about shipbuilding unions in Pensacola. He was told there were no shipbuilding unions in Florida. He suspected the same for Mississippi.

At the end of the harangue, he thanked the man and left. Pope wished he could have decked the man for subjecting him to his temper tantrum but knew it would not have accomplished anything. Except, perhaps, satisfaction.

He went back to the hotel. Sarah left a note saying she was out walking around town. Since the town was not large, he went out looking for her. He was successful.

"There's a seagoing port here. Or rather a Gulf-going," she told him. "Do you think it would be worthwhile to go over to the port area and listen for a while?" she asked.

"I should start keeping a change of work clothes for a disguise with me," Pope admitted.

"Find another second-hand store. Nobody there is going to speak with a man in a navy-blue suit," she said.

"Good thought. I will do some shopping and come back to change. See you soon."

Pope found a second-hand store. It had a rack of clothes and boots and he found some which would work. They had been nicely washed, something he could remedy quickly.

He bought an outfit and went back to the hotel and changed. As before, without a covering coat or pockets, he could not take a gun. He used the same solution. His Bowie in a boot and the sheath bound to his calf.

He worried a bit about lack of stubble but had no remedy. As before, he slipped out the back of the hotel and began the walk to the port area. Arriving by horseback or a hansom cab would be out of character.

Pope walked around the port and watched. He found a saloon. Dive would have been a more appropriate description.

It was fairly full. Seamen and dockworkers drinking lunch and complaining.

Pope sidled up to the bar and ordered a draft. It was weak and tepid.

After a few minutes, the man next to him asked if he was new to town.

"Yeah. A fella in Mississippi told me there were jobs here. Lying bastard!"

"What do you do?" Pope had to think fast. As a gunfighter, he worked diligently to protect his hands. They were a giveaway he was not a laborer.

"I string wire. Sometimes, I do some varnishing. I got a problem with my hands. Born with it. No real strength to do a man's work."

His neighbor seemed to buy the lie.

"Yeah. Not much here. With the Navy Live Oak Preserve near, we used to ship out a lot of lumber to the Navy Yards. With them doing away with wood hulls, it's already died out. Won't come back until some of them steel ships break in half or sink. Men's gonna die with the stupid idea. Mark my words. Everybody here thinks it!"

"Is there anything can be done about it?" Pope asked.

"Shoot them fellas in Washington who came up with this silliness."

"Shooting them would work, I guess. But which ones would you shoot? There's a lot of them up there," Pope said, hoping to keep the man talking.

"Me, I'd start with the president, then the secretary of the Navy and whatever odd admiral walked past my gun."

"Think you or anybody will actually do it?"

"Nope. It would be like suicide. Them guys got guards who are shooters for a living. They'd take me out in a second. A job is worth complaining about, but not worth dying for. They's other jobs out there. The port will figure out something other to ship. Life goes on."

"I guess," Pope began, "but they sure are messing things up for us who work on ships, building ships, loading ships and more," he said.

"Always government against the little man," the

man said.

Pope did not really have a retort, so said nothing. The man quaffed his beer and walked off a bit unsteadily.

If he is a good indicator, it does not sound like the entry level men will be anything other than cannon fodder in somebody bigger's plan, Pope thought.

Pope hit five more bars and one café during the afternoon. He picked up the same sentiments and the same lack of probability of action on the part of marine industry workers.

He was interested in what tomorrow would bring in Biloxi. He would get a slightly different perspective talking with the owners of a marine lumber servicing company. Pope still could not see any tie-in with Scarsdale, New York however. Everything seemed to him to come back to New York. And New York brought him back to thinking about Conkling.

He returned to the hotel and cleaned up.

He picked up a horse and rode to the live oak reservation at Gulf Breeze. The manager hired by the Navy to run it hoped to be able to buy it because of the Navy's decision to cease making wooden hulls.

"There's lots of commercial hulls which will always be wood. I have people trying to buy from me all the time, but I can only sell to the Navy. I make a salary from the Navy. If I owned it, I'd make a lot more," the manager said.

No rancor there, Pope thought.

They had an eight a.m. train in the morning. Sarah suggested eating in the hotel's small dining room, packing and going to bed early. This time, Pope decided to keep his disguise outfit. If he could find a theatrical store somewhere, he even considered obtaining a bushy beard to add to the outfit. Assuming he could find one realistic enough to stand up to close scrutiny by someone on the next bar stool.

Pope and Sarah took a connector train over to the Mississippi River, then a commuter which took primarily businessmen down to New Orleans.

They got off at Biloxi. Pope rode out to the live oak reservation first and spoke with the Navy's civilian manager.

"I may or may not lose my job. I'm not too worried either way. The Navy says they will keep it open along with the one over in Florida. They will still make small boats with wood hulls. They don't really pay so well, so it's no never mind to me if they close her down. I can find something else. Maybe something paying better," he told Pope.

Pope returned to the hotel and got in his same disguise. He hit the bars and a couple of eateries catering to dockworkers. The complaints were similar to those in Pensacola. None were worrisome from a case standpoint.

The next day, he and Sarah reversed their rail trips

and headed back to Washington.

"You know, John?" she began. "Walking around new places is only mildly interesting to me. Traveling with you without investigating as your partner is not a lot of fun."

"What if I needed you to back me up?" he asked.

"I'd probably be shopping or in a hotel room, reading a book."

"You know in this case with the cover we have, you accompanying me and asking questions would cause a lot of questions."

"I know. Just saying, honey," she said as the train rumbled through North Georgia.

The first day back, Pope wrote a ten-page report addressed to both secretaries. He had a clerk at the War office use one of the new typing machines to make it a formal record. Records of everything seemed to be the government way.

CHAPTER 4

Several days later, he received a letter from Michael Kane. The former Knights of the Golden Circle executive told him he had information to impart in person. He went on to say he and Rita would be in Washington for shopping the following Tuesday at the Willard Hotel and wondered if they could meet then.

Pope wrote back and suggested they come to the Pope's house and join them for dinner on Tuesday night. Sarah was pleased, especially during the doldrums of a hot summer in Washington.

He wanted to walk with the guard pair at the President's House on Friday night and stayed later at the War office.

The guard tour was uneventful.

Walking back home from the President's House in the dark, Pope felt the hairs rise on the back of his neck. They had not given false warning yet, so he opened his coat and loosened the .44 double-action he wore in town in its holster.

He stopped and turned, squatting as if to tie his shoe. As he bent his knees and his head lowered, a shot rang out and knocked the hat off his head. It was the derby he wore in town.

Pope drew quickly but could not identify a target. He heard footsteps but could not see anyone. Squatting, he scanned the area from where the shot had come. The muzzle of the revolver followed his eyes. Pope could not identify a target. No additional shots followed.

He took off in foot pursuit, gun in hand.

The man must have ducked down an alley and hid motionless, because Pope was unable to see anyone. He quietly stepped between some buildings and walked on a parallel street. It was Pennsylvania Avenue Northwest. He would walk, turn and listen. When he turned, it was always at a place where he had a barrier to stand behind, such as the corner of a building. He sprinted a block and stepped behind another building but could not hear anyone coming for him. By then, he was a block from his house. He passed the house, not wanting to give away the address. Four houses up, he went between houses and walked back by way of the alley used for accessing the stables many houses on the street had.

He took out his key and unlocked the rear door,

carefully identifying it was he who was entering. May greeted him from the kitchen and told him she had kept a plate from dinner warm for him in the oven.

Sarah came down and the three of them chatted as he ate. Once they went upstairs to the bedroom, Pope told Sarah about the shot from an unidentified person. She reckoned it was the first time somebody ever shot at John Pope and survived. It worried her a great deal. Things were different back East. She liked the Midwest plains and the diverse West better.

The next day, he told the attorney general and secretary of war about the attempt on his life.

"I'd say you are getting close enough somebody is pretty worried," Brewster said.

"I thought so, too. My last week has been about the matter of switching from wood to steel hulls. I did not pick up on anybody being shooting mad. Certainly not down South at the live oak reservations. But somebody had to have telegraphed ahead to a shooter in Washington. Luckily, he was not very good. He was pretty good at disappearing though," Pope said.

"Should we put protection on you?" Lincoln asked.

"No thank you, sir. I am a protector, not a protectee. If he tries again, I may be able to capture or kill him."

"Or he might be successful."

"Much of my life has been as a target. Against what I think are deadlier men than this one. I'll chance it, Robert.

"On another matter, the former head of the Knights of the Golden Circle wrote and mysteriously says he has something to tell me. He and his wife are coming to dinner at our house in several days," Pope said. "I just received their response by mail."

"An interesting development, John. I will be eager to hear what his message is," Brewster said.

"Ask his beautiful wife if her father is still alive," Lincoln requested.

"Is she who I think she is?" Pope asked.

"Quite. The Booths seem to play heavily in my life. One killed my father, his brother Edwin saved me from sure death on a train platform a decade ago, now his daughter shows up. I simply cannot get away from them," Robert Lincoln said.

"Sarah came up with some news clippings about her. I will get her to go back and find some newspaper photos of her. Let's see how she has weathered. I had lunch with them near Charlottesville. She was quite lovely," Pope said.

"All of them were handsome. They had to be. They were America's leading thespian family," Lincoln said. "There have been reports of Booth sightings ever since the Ford Theater. Lafayette Baker said Vice President Johnson and maybe Secretary Stanton, in whose office I now sit, were involved. I never bought the story about the man killed at Garrett farm being Booth. It was just too clean and easy. Baker was the one who tracked them and even he thought so. Pinkerton, of course, denied the possibility. To me, Pinkerton was my father's great misjudgment. I think the Scotsman meant well but believed his own horse manure."

"I will keep my ears open, sir," Pope said, having no plan whatsoever to get into the assassination with his dinner guests.

After the meeting, he called Sarah on the telephone.

"We cannot get used to this. Wherever we settle will probably be a decade or two away from most folk's home having telephones," he said.

"I am sure, darling. Is this just for the experience or do you just miss me terribly?" Sarah asked.

"All of the above and one more," he said.

"Yes?"

"Before Tuesday, I would love to see as many pictures of Ogarita Booth Kane as you can round up."

"Oh, boy. I would not doubt it was the old librarian for the Library of Congress who took a shot at you. He seems pretty infatuated with me."

"Sarah, how could he not be? He's a man. And he is breathing. At least for now. If age doesn't get him, my friend Bowie here will if he keeps flirting with you."

"If I had a trustworthy friend left at Pinkerton's, I could get a real picture of her. But I don't. If Allan thought for a second, I had an angle on any Booth, he would climb out of his deathbed and be here on the next train," Sarah said.

"We have to keep this close to the vest. I don't even like speculating on the telephone. We don't know who is listening in," Pope said. As he said it, the central exchange operator wrote something on a notepad and slipped it into an envelope. She would be rewarded well, at least by her standards.

Later, a telegram was received in Scarsdale, New York. Sans the requisite "stops", it said, "Somebody named Kane has information for Pope. Will be delivered Tuesday by a person named Kane and his wife, Booth's daughter. Will advise when get time."

The edited response was, "Do not mess this up like last night. Hire better people or do it yourself."

Sarah went shopping with May on Monday to fill out the menu for Tuesday's dinner. They decided on roasted beef, potatoes and salad with cherry pie. Sarah selected a mid-range Cabernet Sauvignon and bought two bottles.

Once they got home and the housekeeper began cooking, Sarah went to the library and found several newspaper clippings with pictures of Ogarita Booth. She "borrowed" them quietly for Pope to look at, thinking she might return them the following day. Or perhaps not.

Pope returned in the evening. He looked at both clippings with photos of Booth.

"I swear I don't think it's the same woman I met at the Kane estate. Her face was not as round and the shapes of both her eyes and ears seemed different. One can lose weight and the face changes shape a bit with fuller cheeks. Ears, especially, do not change shape. They just get larger with age. The shape stays the same. See what you think tomorrow. Kane is a mystery man. I don't distrust him; I simply don't know what to make of him. He is an enigma," he said. "A very dangerous enigma."

"Have you given more thought to the shooter situation the other night?" Sarah asked.

"I have. We need to apprise May without scaring her. Just tell her to keep an eye out for anybody or anything out of the ordinary. I don't think we need to tell her somebody shot at me to kill me. The bullet flew past my ear. It was a miss, not a warning."

"What could you tell about the sound?" Sarah asked.

"It was a heavier caliber. Probably .44 or .45. Definitely not a .32 or even a .38. Most folks are not good enough to intentionally fire a round past somebody's ear. He was aiming for my head."

"I wonder if he was from out of town? Wouldn't a .32 or .38 be more usual for an Eastern townie? To try to hide a big gun takes some experience."

"You are dead-on, honey. Look at what you faced in Chicago and I faced in San Francisco. Usually smaller, lower caliber guns which did not require

Buscadero-type belt holsters. I struggle to carry one of my .44s hidden under a suit, but I also have them backed up by a badge. Or, currently, three badges," he noted with a grin.

"If anybody sees a gun print on you or me, we just flip the vest lapel and the explanation glints back at them," she responded.

Sarah told Pope the menu for the dinner with the Kanes. He said she and May were the experts and he was just a carnivore. She was continually impressed with the vocabulary and knowledge of the classics of a man largely home schooled by a mountain man.

"How did Israel know so many classical things to teach you? And words like 'carnivore'," she finally asked.

"By reading. Even during nights after a long day of working a trapline for beaver, he would go back to camp and read by the light of his small campfire."

"Why a small campfire?" she asked.

"Let me answer by unintentionally misquoting an old Indian saying. It was something like 'white man builds a large fire, tells everyone where he is and his front burns and his backside freezes. Indian builds small fire nobody sees, leans in close and gets warm'. It's close to what he used to quote to me when I was a boy, and he was teaching me woodcraft and tracking. Ask him next time we're all together."

"I will. You know, John, this thing of having people

over to our house for dinner is kind of like being a normal, married couple."

"It is. I like it. I will bet you find this couple as fascinating as I do," he said.

May called them for dinner. Sarah asked her to join them as they often did.

"This is delicious, May," Pope said of the fresh Chesapeake Bay rock fish, called striped bass elsewhere, and rice.

"May," he continued, "not for mention anywhere outside of this house, but Sarah and I were brought in to investigate something for the federal government. She and I are both detectives."

May's eyes widened, probably at the thought of the beautiful, raven-haired woman being a detective.

"We are getting close, we think, in the investigation. The people we are after may begin to try to watch us and the house. There is nothing to be alarmed about but keep your eyes alert for strangers in the neighborhood. Particularly if they seem interested in us or the house. And let us know right away?"

"I will, Mr. Pope. I remember how careful we had to be in Washington during the war. I will be alert like I was then."

Pleased with her taking the words without expressing a great deal of concern, the three continued eating and chatting. They learned May's proficiency preparing fish came from growing up in Deltaville where her father was a fisherman. She talked about the beautiful, historic town on the Chesapeake Bay. Her father was still there, though ailing. They determined to try to take her to see him before cold weather set in and did two weeks later.

Tuesday proved another uneventful day from the standpoint of their investigation. Around six, Pope met the Kanes at the front of the Willard Hotel.

Kane beckoned him to climb into the carriage he had driven up from Charlottesville. It was pulled by a pair of beautiful horses. They were powerful white horses with gray manes and tails. Pope asked about them.

"They are Andalusians from Spain. My son brought them to me on his first visit to America two months ago. He's still touring the country. He may move here once he gets his stepsister comfortable running her late father's estate," Kane said.

The trip did not require a light fast carriage, being a matter of only several blocks from the hotel.

They stopped at the front and Pope walked them up to the front door where Sarah greeted them. She was more striking than ever.

Fearing the horses would be stolen on the street, Pope recommended putting them in the rear stable and feeding and watering them after the over hundred-mile trip. The former cowboy quickly unharnessed, fed and watered the animals as he chatted with his guest.

"Guess you've done this before," Kane observed.

"I grew up on my grandfather's ranch in Alameda County. It was small, so I hired out for roundups, taking beeves to the market and all," Pope said.

"How did you become a detective?"

"I joined San Francisco Police early as a patrolman. The rise to detective was pretty quick. Then, two years ago, I solved a big case for Wells Fargo. Their chief detective saw me do it and offered me a job. Later, I recruited Sarah and she became my partner. It has been a whirlwind to say the least."

"You've almost become too famous in the West to be a detective. A disguise might work."

"Mr. Kane, would you rather talk our business for a bit here, or over whiskey or brandy after dinner?" Pope asked.

"Please call me Michael. What is your first name, Pope?" Kane asked.

"John."

"John, I reached out very quietly to a number of people. People with influence and also who know things. My results are vague, but a bit unsettling.

"I spoke to several railroad presidents. They are not overly miffed about the president's stand on the Chinese. I spoke with some rather ardent expansionists. People who want to grow the borders of the United States. South and into the Caribbean both. Most are old men and realize their time to see fruition of their dream has passed. I corresponded with a professor in Virginia. His mentor knew more about ships, navigation, and running a navy than any man alive. He literally wrote the book.

"The mentor said shipbuilders are ramping up for the change to steel hulls and the final throes of the death of sail power. Most are looking forward to opportunity, not retribution.

"Now, for the alarming part. I picked up several whispers of some dissident group out for the president any way they can get him. I can promise you these people are definitely not associated with the Knights of the Golden Circle.

"I have been unable to determine their motives, leadership or funding. I will keep looking if you want. I admit to being disappointed in my lack of success with this angle of your inquiries."

"John, are you and Mr. Kane about ready? May says dinner is ready," Sarah called out the rear door.

"Yes, darling, we are coming."

They spoke quietly on the way in.

"Michael, thank you for all your work and interest in this. You have saved me a couple of dead ends. I have two cabinet secretaries who are aware of what is going on and will ask them about dissident groups. Neither has mentioned the possibility.

"I just returned from investigating the wood versus steel hull angle in Florida and Mississippi. They are the primary sources of wood for hulls. The next day—or rather night—someone shot at me on the way home. I was unable to identify him. Hell, I couldn't even catch him. He missed the back of my head by no more than a couple of inches. It proved one thing. I must be ruffling somebody's feathers," Pope said.

"It's damn troubling, John. Bushwhackers are cowards. I will stay engaged if you will allow me."

"I am most appreciative, Michael. I take it your efforts should not be shared with the cabinet members?"

"I'd prefer not. However, the maritime expert said he could be quoted. You might want to ride down and speak with him so you can claim the effort. He is Professor John Blake. He worked under the famous Matthew Fontaine Maury at the Virginia Military Institute. You may use my name to get in.

"Speaking to John Blake will just be due diligence. He can help you mark off some suspects but does not know anything about dissidents. Though I guess since Maury's electric torpedoes kept the Union Navy from participating in the battle for Richmond, he might be called a dissident himself," Kane said with a grin.

"I will get Sarah to research him and will go down as soon as possible. Thank you, Michael."

By this time, they were approaching the six-person dining table and seated the two ladies, as was proper custom.

May's dinner was not exotic. It was simple comfort food cooked well and was enjoyed by all. Her cherry pie and coffee capped off the meal.

It would have been usual custom for the men to adjourn to a parlor and drink and smoke cigars. These were two singularly different couples. All four went to the parlor and no cigars were smoked.

They continued the dinner's chat over coffee.

"Rita, what is it like being a famous actress?" Sarah asked.

"Not as exciting as being one of the few lady detectives in the whole world, I bet!"

"I guess it is exciting. My first detective job taught me a lot. My job with Wells Fargo and my new partner taught me more. It taught me how cold it is to camp in a blizzard without a shelter, and how scary it is to be shot at."

"Have you ever had to shoot anyone?" Rita asked.

"Yes, a number of times. Each in self-defense."

"How does it feel? Do you have regrets? Guilt?"

"No. I did not ask someone to try to kill me. I just defended myself. It was their choice every time. Train or stage robbers, kidnappers, attackers. All their choice."

Kane knew the listing of situations in which Sarah had killed suggested a minimum of four or five kills. Probably more. He wondered about Pope. The newspapers said twenty kills. Yet, he just said he killed over half the number at age ten. Kane suspected he was faster, but his record was perhaps half the detective's.

Pope watched quietly. Sarah was a good hostess. A good wife, no marriage ceremony notwithstanding.

Rita circled back around to Sarah's first question and talked about playing just off Broadway. She also talked about a different hotel every night, having to look her very best every moment, meals missed, gropes eluded.

"Michael rescued me. He came to the door in Richmond, and I fell in love with him at first sight," Rita said. Both Pope and Sarah knew to not press Kane's background or business. Though his contacts were at the highest levels, his world was shadowy to say the least.

Kane looked at his gold Waltham Premier pocket watch.

"Heavens! It is after eleven. We have enjoyed ourselves so much, we missed the passage of time."

"Michael, did you ever check into the Willard? I thought I saw luggage in the rear of your buggy," Pope asked.

"No, we didn't check in yet."

"We have a spare bedroom already set up. Please spend the night here. The horses are already put away. I will run down and get your bags," Pope said.

Kane looked at his wife who smiled and gave a little nod.

"Thank you, John and Sarah, it has been a long ride and a great evening. We'd be pleased to stay and probably be asleep within minute after our heads hit the pillow," Kane said. They all went to bed early. Sarah took a pitcher of well water and a couple of glasses with her, knowing the salty Smithfield ham biscuit appetizers would keep them thirsty all night. Pope had introduced her to the salty ham after his visit to Topping Castle.

Around two in the morning, Pope was awakened by the horses sounding agitated in the stable out back. He pulled on trousers, and barefooted and shirtless, eased out the bedroom door, his single action Colt in hand. He and Kane almost bumped each other in the hall. Pope glanced at the seven-and-a-half-inch barreled Colt Kane carried. Even in the dark, he could tell it was special.

Pope led the way, carefully taking a quick peek around each corner in the house. At the rear door, he silently unlocked the door. Overseeing the renovation of space in Cheyenne to be a new, large Wells Fargo office, he had become something of a lock expert. He had made sure this one was well-oiled for occasions such as this.

The two men, matching in height and build and a decade apart padded silently towards the garage.

They saw two men trying to bridle the horses to lead them away. Pope brought the stag butt of his Colt down on the closest man's head. As he dropped, the rapid four clicks of Kane's gun spelled out C-O-L-T.

"Deputy US marshal. You are under arrest for horse stealing," Pope said.

Pope had number two drag number one away from the stable. Kane checked his horses and pronounced them alright.

Both men turned as the rear door opened. Two striking women stood there in thin nightgowns, transparent backlit by the moon.

One was a detective, the other a former actress of some repute.

The detective was holding a sawed-off shotgun. Her handling of it demonstrated a high degree of familiarity.

"Honey, if you want to shoot him, I'll step way away to avoid getting doused with body parts," Pope said, attempting to sound serious. The only one who did not detect the humor in his voice was the man in front of ten-gauge barrels as big as sewer pipes.

"No, darling. Why don't you question them? I will decide on shooting them once we see how they cooperate."

The first man had finally regained sufficient consciousness to hear the scary woman's last sentence.

"Who do you work for?" Pope asked.

"Nobody," the second man said, looking at his soiled boots.

"Why were you spying on us?" Kane asked.

"We was trying to steal these horses," the first man said.

"Who sent you here to steal them?" Pope snarled in a gravelly tone which always excited Sarah.

"We seen the horses when you came up. Nobody sent us."

"Sarah, we are going to have a pow-wow. Would you two ladies watch these rustlers? If they try to get away, please kill them as cleanly as possible," Pope said.

He and Kane walked off. The latter covered his mouth to hide his restrained amusement.

"What a pair of inept horse thieves," he said. "I doubt they are involved in any scheme against you or the government. I'd just as soon not have to be a police witness. Want to just scare some more hell out of them and let them go?" Kane asked.

"I'm thinking the same thing. You want to give them the send-off?"

Kane nodded and they walked back. Kane got in their faces and stared malevolently at both.

"I take it personal when somebody tries to steal my horse. When they try to steal two of my horses, I want to shoot them. Or, maybe cut them." He drew the Bowie Pope had suspected he carried.

Kane waved it very close to their noses. Pope could tell he knew how to handle a blade. The first clue was the lack of severed noses hitting the ground.

"I had a long day yesterday and you also interrupted my sleep and my hosts' sleep. If the two of you will
take off running, I will ask the lovely lady with the
shotgun to not cut you both in half. I have memorized
your faces. If I ever see either of you again, you are
dead. Dead. Get it?"

They nodded and Kane yelled, "Git!" Their com-
bined sprint down the alley was admirable.

The four watched them go out of sight.

They went in, relocked the door and resumed the
remaining several hours of sleep left before daylight.

As the two were disappearing, a shot rang out.
The bullet flew between Pope and Kane, closer to
the former. Kane instantly fired at the flash. There
was a scream, the clatter of metal on cobblestone,
and footsteps.

The two tall men sprinted off in pursuit. Sarah
urged Rita and now also May, back inside. She had
May turn the gas lamp down to its lowest without
going out.

Pope spotted a revolver in the moonlight. There
were specks of blood near it. He picked up the revolver and handed it to Kane.

"A Smith & Wesson Scofield," Kane said.

They continued to track the spots of blood for
several blocks, but then they abated and there was
nothing to follow on the hard surface.

"I am surprised the shots did not bring Washington's finest running our way," Kane said.

"Me, too. Very surprised," Pope replied as they padded their way, barefooted, back to Pope's house. "Damn good shot in the dark, Michael!"

"Unfortunately, not good enough. A hit might have solved your mystery. I am convinced the horse thievery was aimed at getting us outside for the shooter. The two idiots were prompted but probably not party to the plan to shoot you, John."

"It almost has to be the case. I must be getting real close."

"If you aren't, at least someone fears you are."

******

Kane and Rita were awakened at daylight by the aroma of coffee brewing and bacon frying wafting up to their room from the kitchen. May already had four place settings at the kitchen table, where they usually had breakfast.

Kane found Pope sitting in the small back garden by the stables. Unknown to Kane, Pope had already fed the two Andalusians. Now, he was drinking a cup of May's rich coffee.

May got a cup of coffee for Kane and told him Pope was already outside. The day promised to be another Washington high humidity scorcher.

"Good morning, John," Kane said as he walked out

and sat beside his host.

"Hi, Michael. Did you all sleep alright after last night's interesting interlude?"

"It took me a few minutes. I think I am getting rusty."

"Well, you didn't seem rusty last night. Your Colt must be specially made and tuned."

"It is, John. I had a matched pair for years. Recently, I met a young Mexican officer leading a patrol of Rurales. It was like looking in a mirror twenty years ago. I knew he had to be the son I never knew about. He was. He knew instantly also. We bonded. I gave him my left-hand Colt. I've since replaced it, but the new one's action still has to break in."

"Where did you study fencing, Michael?" Pope asked.

"In Spain and some in Germany. My father sent me to Europe to learn the martial arts. How did you know about the fencing?"

"I saw you with the Bowie last night. Old Jim Bowie himself could not move with the precision you showed. It was clear you received training. And a lot of it."

"I notice you carry a Bowie hidden from the eyes of ninety-nine percent of the world. Have you used it?"

"I have. I learned from my grandfather who would give up his Colt Army before his Bowie knife. You'd like him. Mid-sixties and fit and tough."

"I'm sure I would. I heard of him even as far east as Dallas," Kane said.

"Michael, thank you for your inquiries on our probable threat."

"I'm afraid I only helped you to eliminate some potential threats, but not put you closer to the real one. Or ones."

"In investigations, one lists all the potential suspects and then studiously eliminates them. Usually, the one you end up with is the one you are going to arrest."

"Think it will be so in this case?" Kane asked.

Pope grinned at him.

"No, I think the bad guy will come out of the shadows and not be on our educated guess list. I just hope I can stop him before the president is harmed."

"I don't know you except by reputation and our brief, pleasant stay with you and Sarah. However, I have a feeling you will shut down the operation before Arthur is harmed. I just hope you will have the backup and legal wherewithal to do it the way it needs to be done."

"Me, too. Michael. For Sarah's sake as much as mine."

"She looked pretty much at home with the shotgun last night."

"Sarah has used a shotgun with deadly force for Wells Fargo several times. A revolver also. It you look at the probable actual kills Billy the Kid made, she is ahead of him."

Kane smiled at this as if he were enjoying a personal joke.

"I know you have to get back on the case. Rita and I will head out. I fear I will indulge your hospitality a bit longer having smelled May's breakfast for four."

"Of course. You and Rita are welcome anytime. I really mean it," Pope said.

"You all did not mention her maiden name," Kane said.

"We knew it before you arrived. We figured if you or she wanted to talk about it, you would."

"I appreciate your concerns. It's really not as touchy a subject as you might think. One day, we will fill you and Sarah in," Kane said.

"I will continue to poke around among my sources and let you know if I find anything."

"Thanks, Michael. I will give you my telegraph address at the War office and the telephone here before you go. Day or night is fine. You and I both seem to have the capability to awaken and be ready to operate, no matter the hour."

"We do," Kane agreed sincerely.

May called them out for breakfast.

Sarah and Rita were already seated, in robes but with hair fixed for the day.

They ate and chatted, then the men went out and harnessed the Andalusians for the trip back to Charlottesville. At Sarah's suggestion, May made a picnic lunch for their trip home.

They were off at eight, leaving Pope and Sarah to summarize events already sleepily mentioned.

"I need to tie up the maritime angle by going down to Lexington and talk with the professor there. I think what we have to concentrate on now is dissident groups. People perhaps unrelated to the original lists of suspects. Political dissidents," Pope said.

"I will start today on the idea of political dissidents and see what I can learn," Sarah said.

"I will head to Lexington. I am not sure what trains are available. I know it's down the Valley Road. It runs the length of the Shenandoah Valley, I think. Andrew Jackson's foot cavalry went up and down it during the war. Depending on transportation, I may be back tonight or tomorrow. I will call the War office and let Lincoln know where I am."

Pope put his notebook, toothbrush and some clean clothes in a leather satchel and headed to the train depot. Sarah had more time to prepare before the library opened.

He arrived at the newly completed depot in Lexington late in the afternoon. He walked the distance to Virginia Military Institute.

Pope located Professor John Blake in his office. The man was expecting him from a telegram from Kane.

"I have been the so-called expert in maritime

matters since the death of my friend Maury about a decade ago. No one will ever have his breadth of knowledge," Blake told Pope. "Matthew Fontaine Maury had both real and intellectual experience."

"Professor, I have been asked by Washington officials to look into impact on converting to a steel hull navy. One of the things concerning me is how the various participants in the construction chain are reacting. From the suppliers of wood and steel to the marine architects, to the workers and their unions," Pope said, stopping so Blake could answer however he wished.

"As I told Michael Kane, there is little discord which might cause trouble. At least, as far as I have heard. The marine lumber builders and transporters will still supply to commercial interests. Since the Navy owns the greater part of the lumber supply with their live oak reservations, there is only small commercial impact.

"Everyone involved knows steel hulls are the way of the future. The transition now may be inconvenient for some, but it's inevitable."

"Professor Blake, have you heard any chatter in the industry the government should be concerned about. Threats, for example?" Pope asked.

"None at all. I have attended meetings and conferences about the subject. Industry representatives from every aspect of what you correctly identify as the 'construction chain' were represented. I have read virtually every available article on the subject. For one reason, it will affect what and how I teach. There is nothing about which I have heard indicating threats or violence."

"Thank you, sir. I really appreciate your input."

There was not another train until the morning, so Pope checked into a hotel for the night.

He documented the conversation in his notebook to be used to transcribe into typed form at the War office.

While he was still concerned about Conkling, he was beginning to think he should actually go to New York and speak with the man. He was convinced he should beard the lion in his den by the time he arrived back in Washington the next day.

Pope met with Lincoln on his first day back in the office. While his report was being typed on the office's new machine, he gave the secretary his executive summary of the visit to Lexington.

"I'm about to write off the wood vs. steel aspects of the case, sir."

"Without reading your full report, I am inclined to agree. I will take it to Brewster and make sure he concurs. Where to now?"

"I keep coming back to Conkling. I think the best way to get a feel for him is a face-to-face meeting."

"The prospects of such a meeting will occupy much

of my—no, our—meeting with the attorney general. Conkling was confirmed to the US Supreme Court and just never showed up. His legal knowledge greatly exceeds mine or Ben Brewster's. He can be the most dangerous man I know of in politics. There are those who say he engineered the assassination of Garfield to put his buddy, Vice President Arthur in office. I doubt it, but who knows?"

Lincoln called in his secretary and had him call Brewster's office and set up an appointment for thirty minutes. It was set for after lunch.

Lincoln seldom left for lunch. Pope walked over to the President's House and checked the logs and spoke with the office corporal and returned in time to walk next door with Lincoln.

A forty-minute discourse followed about the positives and negatives of actually interviewing Conkling. Pope reiterated Sarah's findings from the journalist.

They agreed Pope should visit Conkling in New York and Brewster would send him a telegram setting up the meeting at his office. Both secretaries warned Pope Conkling would be tough and cagey. He was a lawyer, politician, probable gangster, and trained boxer. None of those characteristics bothered Pope in the least. He was confident he had taken on and defeated better street and gun fighters in the past. And, at just under thirty, he knew he had not even reached his prime yet.

"I will have someone in my office call you at home as soon as I receive a response from Conkling by telegraph. He may play hard to get and ignore us until he gets a second request. If he wants to play it hard, I will subpoena his ass," Brewster said. Tough talk from a man Pope did not consider very tough. After all, it was Pope, not Brewster who was going to invade Conkling's territory and interview him.

CHAPTER 5

Pope and Sarah discussed the case during dinner.

"While you are in New York talking to Conkling, I will study dissident groups. The ones causing the most stir in my initial look today is the Socialist and Communist Movements. While they are technically two different philosophies, it is practical to lump them together. My cursory study suggests socialism has, as one of the more famous proponents, an economist named Karl Marx. He just died a few months back. These current groups were preceded by the Utopian groups of socialist communities, such as the Shakers. I have found the key terms to look for and should have a good picture of who they are and what they believe by the time you return," Sarah said.

"Depending on Conkling, I believe dissidents will be our next inquiry," Pope said.

"I heard from the chief detective by coded telegram

the other day," Sarah said. "It was kind of addressed to us both."

"This is the first time since we were sent back East. What did Hume have to say?"

"He asked how married life was treating us. Wondered about our progress and when we thought we'd be back with Wells Fargo. He ended by wishing us the best," Sarah said.

"All good things. I take it he thinks we really did get hitched. Since his final salvo before we left was about getting married was still up to us, he is acting now like he thinks we did get married. I still wonder what effect marriage will have on our careers as Wells Fargo detectives. You did a great job as an interim office manager. I could not do it. I'd go crazy. Would you do it?" Pope asked.

"I have loved the life here, even though May has done most of the cooking and all of the housework. So, yes, I could be an office manager for Wells Fargo. As long as you were the regional detective and it was in a decent town like Cheyenne or Prescott," Sarah said.

"Then, let's go ahead and get married. I'd like to do it in a way so Grandpa can come," Pope said.

"Of course. I really don't have any folks to come anymore. Maybe the Kanes. I really liked them."

"I agree. We will do it on our and their time, not Wells Fargo's schedule," Pope said.

******

Pope was on the early train to New York, having received a message the preparatory telegram had been sent to Roscoe Conkling.

He took a hansom cab from the train depot to Conkling's office. His opinion was the office looked more like a gangster's office than a man who had served in the Congress and approved by the Senate to be a US Supreme Court Justice.

The feeling was supported by the secretary who showed him in. The man looked more like a knee breaker from the Bronx than an office worker.

"So, Mr. Pope, I received the telegram from the attorney general asking me to assist in an investigation of the greatest importance," Conkling said in the gravelly voice of a man who was used to giving orders. And, having them followed to the letter."

"It is, Mr. Conkling. I would appreciate any guidance you can give us," Pope said.

"My first thought is I must be the suspect in this inquiry and 'help' is just a word to deflect my attention."

"I can see why you might think so. I have been told I can be totally frank with you. It involves a threat against President Arthur. The threat is personal or to bring down his presidency. Since the two of you are old friends, it seems unlikely you would be part of this. It is more likely you would want to ally with us to protect him," Pope said.

"Quite. Where and how was this threat manifested?"

"A member of the cabinet heard two men arguing through the partition separating two roomettes on a train from New York City to Scarsdale."

"What were they saying?" Conkling asked.

"The member did not hear the conversation until they started arguing. This occurred just as the train was pulling into Scarsdale. By the time he gathered wits enough to look at them, they were gone. The conversation was about bringing down the administration, killing Arthur if necessary."

"Are you sure it was not a couple of blowhards mouthing off?" Conkling asked.

"No, I am not. The secretary thought they were pretty serious. He said nobody but well-dressed men in suits were on the train. He immediately reached out to the attorney general."

"Who exactly are you? A treasury agent?"

"No. I am a Wells Fargo detective on loan to Justice. I have been named provost marshal and deputy US marshal for the duration of my investigation." Pope knew in his gut Conkling was already aware of this.

"What do I call you?"

"Pope is fine, sir."

"Am I a suspect or not?"

"Should you be?"

"Don't pull any cop horse manure on me, son. Just

answer the question!"

"No. At this point I am looking into political dissident groups. Since both parties to the conversation got off the train in Scarsdale, I thought you might have some ideas," Pope said.

"Pope, there is a Marxist group in Scarsdale. I chased them out of New York City because they were infiltrating my unions there," Conkling said. Pope picked up on the possessive used to describe New York unions, apparently of all types.

"How widespread are these Marxists in unions?"

"Too damn widespread! They believe the government ought to control everything. You work hard, a chunk of your pay goes to somebody who didn't work hard. Or, maybe, didn't work at all. It makes no sense."

"This one in Scarsdale," Pope began, "Do you think I could infiltrate it?"

"Not a chance. You scream cowboy gunfighter or copper."

"You're pretty perceptive. I have been both."

"I possibly already knew you were."

Pope smiled.

"Could a woman infiltrate the group in Scarsdale?"

"I don't know. I have a man who is in the know up there. Let me reach out to him. How can I get in touch with you?" Conkling asked.

Pope gave him a business card with his Navy office

contact information.

"Pope? How's my friend Chet Arthur?" Conkling asked.

"I hardened the protection on both him and the President's House. He seemed to appreciate it. He's unaware of the threat situation. We'd like to keep him in the dark about it for now. I have only met him once. He seemed alright. I think he liked my wife better than me."

"Haha! Sounds like my boy alright! Try not to shoot him yourself! I should take the rail down to Washington and have dinner with him. We need to mend bridges. He thinks I am mad because he appointed somebody else secretary of state. I was for a about a day. Then, I figured out how much money being out of this city would cost me. Hell, I am the worst at diplomacy. I'd tell the foreign kings and all to take a long walk on a short bridge."

"Then, it sounds like you were what we needed as secretary of state," Pope said, meaning every word.

"I have another meeting. Give me a day. I will check out the crazies in Scarsdale and let you know what I find," Conkling promised.

Pope left. He headed for the train depot and found a southbound was coming through in a half hour. He bought a ticket and knew he would be home tonight.

******

The next day, Pope met with Lincoln and Brewster.

"I went into this interview thinking Conkling was a gangster, crooked politician and enemy of President Arthur. I came out thinking he is a gangster, probably a crooked politician, friend of the president's, cunning, smart and a man who told me the truth."

"John, a lot of people fear Roscoe Conkling. He fosters such an image. He is a power broker in New York. I cannot imagine how he could wield such influence without dipping into the wrong side of the law occasionally. However, I have never known him to be a liar. He feels he's so untouchable there's no reason to lie.

"I am sure he will report back to you about the communists or whatever they are. And, will come down and have dinner with the president who he mentored as a politician in New York," Lincoln said.

"So, you all agree I should strike him from the suspect list?" Pope asked.

"At this point, yes. So, we have the Chinese issue with the railroads, the wood versus steel hulls, expansion and immigration all stricken. Since we are not too worried about the South rising again through the action of Southerners in Congress, the dissident groups and odd crazies are all we have left," Brewster summarized.

"Once I get some indication about infiltrating the Marxist group in Scarsdale, I will formulate a plan.

I do not believe in coincidences in an investigation. Robert hearing the argument between two men who got off the train in Scarsdale, and Conkling identifying a worrisome group in Scarsdale firm up the possibility to me," Pope said.

He left, checked in at the President's House security office and went home mid-afternoon. Sarah was still off conducting research on the Marxists and other groups.

When she returned, she filled him in on her findings and he told her Conkling had been candid and an all-around surprise. He said Conkling told him he would not be a good choice for insertion into the group undercover, but Conkling would find out if there were any women in the group.

True to his word, Conkling sent a somewhat vague, but useful telegram two days later. He said the group (he did not mention what group) had some women. All had Eastern European last names. People with a knowledge and interest of the subject were apparently welcome.

Sarah worked for two more days developing a cover with name, fictitious but non-verifiable family, country of origin and work experience.

She decided on Vera Petrov, a second generation Ukrainian whose late grandfather immigrated and became a coal miner in Pennsylvania. Vera did not know much about his past, nor did she speak Slavic.

The grandfather would not talk about the old country, except the system was horrible and people slaved and were killed by it. She grew up thinking there was a better way for governments to treat their people, drawing her to socialism and communism. She always wanted to live in a Utopian community but could not afford to move to one.

Sarah bought plain work dresses at a department store in Washington and heavy work shoes. She bought a used satchel and cheap personal items, like hairbrushes and night gowns. May colluded by washing each several times to help age them.

After looking at some photos in books, she decided to put her long black hair in the most conservative, tight bun possible. She would carry her smaller .38 in a small purse with a few dollars. Her backup choice was a paring knife. Luckily in mid-summer, she would not need a coat.

Sara, as Vera, met Pope at the door, a smiling May behind her waiting for his reaction. He expressed his only doubt was her beauty was hard to hide, but he agreed the cover was otherwise perfect.

The next morning, Pope packed a small carpet-bag and put on his workingman guise from his trip South. They headed to the depot and bought seats for Scarsdale.

Once they arrived, a cheap hotel was quickly located. While the area was generally upscale, there was a blue-collar area on the edge of town where workers, shop clerks and unemployed lived.

Logically, it was also where they found flyers posted for meetings of the New York Workers Association, the name Conkling told him the Marxist group used. A meeting was advertised in a hall two nights later.

Sarah and Pope used the time to familiarize themselves with the town. Sarah, in keeping with her cover, bought some basic cleaning items. They also purchased a new sheet, not wanting to sleep on the questionable one on the bed.

They stuck to their cover roles, living and eating as transient, out of work people might.

Two days later, the two detectives walked over to the meeting hall. There was a saloon across the street. Pope ducked in and ordered the first of what would be two draft beers.

Sarah went in and stood in the rear of the hall, acting hesitant.

A man in the front motioned her to the first row of wooden chairs. As Pope feared, her beauty would make her stand out, even in disguise. It also made men want to talk with her and worked in her favor. She did not have to volunteer any of her backstory. The man seemed more interested in keeping her speaking with him than anything else.

Finally, he called the meeting to order. He was

clearly the head of the organization.

"Welcome to new comrades in our fight against oppression! I see some new faces," he said looking at Sara specifically, "and welcome you all. I am Roger Nelson, the president of the chapter.

"First, I would like to report on our successes since the last meeting. We have continued to convert union members in all trades in New York to the Marxist enlightenment. These new Marxists are also voters, you know. We will be heard, no matter how long it takes.

"This chapter is leading the way in a project of national implication. I cannot talk about it further. But trust me. You will read about our success in the newspapers within a week!" Nelson said.

With this, Sarah knew more than ever, she needed to probe Nelson and get his total confidence.

Nelson spoke vehemently for another hour. Several times, he received applause. Sarah always clapped louder and was first to stand when he made a point, she read to be crucial to him.

After the meeting, working people left. Dawn was only six hours away. Several lingered, including Vera Petrov. Nelson seemed to be ushering the others off.

Finally, the two were alone. He made a halfway pretense of rearranging chairs and turning off unnecessary gas lamps.

"Mrs. Petrov, or should I say Miss Petrov," he began.

She interrupted with "It's Mrs., but you can call me Vera. I am just a cleaner. Nobody of importance."

"Vera it is then. Is your husband here with you?"

"Yes, Mr. Nelson. He works as a handyman where he can get jobs. I am looking for a cleaning job. We were in Virginia but could not find employment. He let me come here tonight. He does not care for political things. I do because of what I think my grandparents suffered under in the Ukraine. I think changes need to be made.

"If it was up to me, I'd blow up those politicians!" she said.

"Well, when we get to know one another better, I may tell you something which will excite you. A lot!" Nelson said. "And it is Roger to you, Vera."

"Good. I like to be excited. Tell me about you. How did you come to lead such an important group as this?" she probed.

"I lived at John Noyes' Oneida Community for a while. It was a Utopian socialist village. We studied communism and complex marriage, among other things. Oneida is where I became convinced communism is the true path."

"What is complex marriage?" Sarah asked, truly having no idea.

"It is a form of polygamy. It may be illegal in many places, but we believe mankind is not monogamist. Other cultures thrive with widespread polygamy."

"I see," Sarah said.

"Does the idea appeal to you?" he asked.

"I need to think about it. A tumble in the hay every now and then certainly does," she lied.

He smiled broadly.

"I live alone. Perhaps you can visit soon?" he said.

"Tomorrow night is Monday," she said as if thinking.

"My husband has a job. Perhaps then? You could tell me more about your special project. I take it you will have to go out of town for it?" Sarah asked.

"I am available tomorrow night. When might you be able to come?"

"Oh, say eight o'clock to be safe?" she asked, knowing the smile signaled success for an entrapment.

He wrote the address on the back of a flyer and handed it to her.

"And yes. I will have to go south for a day or so next Wednesday. The event will happen Thursday. But, with all luck, I can be back Friday night," Nelson said.

Sarah caressed his cheek and gave him a kiss on it, backing away before he could reciprocate.

"I am so very glad I came tonight. I really believe in your objectives, too," she said leaving him to pick whether she meant his personal or group objectives. She suspected he would think she meant both.

"Gotta go! I will see you at your house around eight tomorrow night. What should I wear? I'm afraid my monetary situation does not allow a large wardrobe."

"Clothes may be a temporary issue, my dear," he said. She smiled seductively, thinking *what a self-absorbed little man,* to herself.

Sarah breezed out the door before anything further might occur.

Pope was watching for her from the saloon. He waited for her to pass, then fell in step fifty yards behind her.

She turned the corner. Seeing nobody was behind her, he hastened. As he approached her, he saw she had the .38 Smith & Wesson break open revolver in her hand, hidden by the other hand.

She recognized the tall handsome figure and slipped the gun back into her purse.

"Success?"

"Oh, yes! The event will happen at an undisclosed location south of here on Thursday. We need to find out the president's plan for Thursday. Like right now!"

They went straight to the Western Union office at the train depot and sent an urgent telegram to Lincoln in care of the War office. Pope knew it would be delivered directly to him at home as soon as it was received.

He wished the War office had a cypher system like Wells Fargo had. If it did, he was unaware of it or its codes. In plain language he said they had new information about an event happening Thursday south of his current location. He asked what the "Chet's" itinerary was on Thursday. He said he would check back at the telegraph for the reply upon opening tomorrow morning. He also said he hoped to have more information tomorrow night.

"If we need to take Nelson to Washington under duress, I think getting a couple military policemen from West Point Military Academy might be prudent. I am jumping ahead, but if this is an assassination attempt in several days, we don't have much time to plan how to stop it," Pope said.

"It is coming down to the wire, I believe," Sarah said.

"How did you get this far so fast?"

"Feminine wiles. I dangled a big juicy orange carrot under the jackass's nose and wouldn't let him get near it."

"Don't you think what you did was pretty dangerous, Sarah?"

"Not at all. I could take him with my bare hands. Or gun, or knife. All without getting out of breath," she said.

Pope had a great deal of confidence in his partner. He also knew most men were stronger in the arms, shoulders and legs than most women. It was possible for a highly trained and motivated smaller person, man or woman, to succumb to being caught off guard and overwhelmed. He did not argue the point. He knew it was not productive from experience.

The next morning, Pope checked for a response

telegram at the Western Union office. There was none at nine. He found a nearby café and had coffee until ten. The second check was fruitful.

President Chester Arthur was scheduled to cut the ribbon at the dedication of a new monument in downtown Washington at two o'clock Thursday afternoon. Pope had never heard of the person depicted on the monument. All he cared about was Arthur would be a viable target, both traveling and at the dedication ceremony. There had been notice in local papers and a small crowd was expected. It would be a perfect time for the Marxists to strike.

Pope decided to wait until he had a chance to interrogate Roger Nelson before telling either Lincoln or Brewster more. He simply did not have enough of the plan to share yet. He did, however, know this was it. The threat. The case. He had a very dependable gut feeling. He sure hoped he was right. So much depended on it.

He walked back to the room.

"Arthur is dedicating a new monument in Washington at two on Thursday. There will be a crowd. I am sure the Marxists will attempt to hit him then," he told Sarah.

"Then, we have to get the information tonight from Nelson," she responded.

"Yes. We will need the plan and names of all participants."

They formulated their own plan and help phrase for Sarah. Pope did not like the chance she was taking at all, but she remained committed to it.

At seven-thirty, they walked towards Nelson's house. It was a long walk, but they did not want to take a hansom cab and have a witness to them being at the location.

Sarah fixed her hair so she could free it with a quick pull on a hairband. She wore a simple cleaning woman dress. While Pope checked the telegraph office, she bought a new, plain cotton shift to wear underneath it. Pope had not seen it yet. She suspected he would not like it for tonight's use. It was thin to the point of almost transparency. Sarah thought they had one opportunity to find out enough about the attack to save the president. Modesty was the least important part of the case to her.

It was dusk as they approached the house and getting darker by the minute. They decided to wait until it was completely dark.

Once dark enough, they went over their plan. Most people did not bother to lock their home doors. Sarah would knock and go in. They would eventually go upstairs. Windows were open on the hot summer night, so Pope would be able to hear her signals.

He hid in the bushes as Sarah knocked on the front door.

Nelson answered the door in some sort of satin

robe and clearly nothing else.

"Well, don't you look ready for a night of relaxation!" Sarah told him.

The door closed and Pope heard the lock click.

"Damn!" he said silently. He did not have his lock pick set. It was in the investigative bag in Washington. He had the Bowie and a Barlow pocketknife. Maybe one could slide the lock bolt aside.

Then, he heard the bolt click open, yet the door remained closed.

Sarah watched with surprise and horror as Nelson locked the door. She had to do something quickly.

She leaned her back against the door and smiled seductively. She unbuttoned her dress and let it drop to the floor. Nelson saw through the thin shift in the parlor light and smiled.

"Lead the way to wherever you have some wine, Roger," she said.

He turned and she unlocked the door with the hands hidden behind her back.

Sarah followed Nelson up the stairs and into the bedroom. He had a bottle of wine and two crystal wine stems beside the bed. If ever there was a seduction scene, this was it.

Pope slipped into the door and relocked it as they disappeared up the stairs. He noticed the carpeted steps did not make any noise as they climbed them. He hoped it would be the same for his larger frame. It was.

He waited, crouching at the top step out of sight.

"What kind of wine do we have?" Sarah asked.

"It's a Pinot Noir. A '71. I understand it was a good year."

"I've never had expensive wine before. I hope it does not make me act unladylike."

"Oh, I'm sure it will have a wonderful effect on you," he said trying to smile, but pulling off a face better described as leering.

She sat on the bed, ugly shoes still on. Sarah showed a shoe to hip length of long, beautiful white leg and Nelson spilled the wine he was pouring. The work shoes were hideous, if Nelson even saw them. They would be useful if she had to kick him. She suspected she would, even with Pope backing her up.

Sarah accepted a glass and took a sip. It really was a good year.

"You look like you are ready for a romantic evening, Roger," she said signaling Pope to make his appearance.

Pope stood and burst into the room, yelling, "What are you doing here?" to Sarah.

He had the .44 double-action Smith & Wesson out, but Sarah was between him and Nelson.

Nelson realized his only opportunity and dived for the nightstand drawer.

Suspecting he had a gun there, Sarah tackled him

and they both went down, her shift around her waist and her bare bottom up in the air.

Pope stuck the .44 in Nelson's ear as Sarah moved to straddle him.

He rolled the big revolver so his hand was on the frame and smacked Nelson in the jaw with it. Pope intentionally did not hit him hard enough to either knock him out or damage his ability to converse. Nelson had a lot of important talking to do tonight.

Sarah stood as Nelson tried to clear his vision. She went downstairs and brought her dress back over her arm.

By the time she returned, Pope had handcuffed Nelson's hands behind him with Wells Fargo nippers.

"Stand up!"

Once Nelson was standing, Pope shoved him into the single chair in the bedroom.

"I would like to straighten my robe!" Nelson demanded.

"Not much to see anyway. You will stay like you are for now. How you answer our questions will determine how you are treated," Pope said.

"Who are you people? Robbers?"

Pope backhanded him across the face with his left hand.

"I will ask the questions and you will answer."

Nelson frowned at him.

"Do you have a bathtub?" Pope asked.

"What a stupid question! Do I look like some sort of unclean savage?" Nelson said.

"Where is it?"

Nelson frowned harder and Pope slapped him open-handed harder, bringing tears to Nelson's eyes.

"The mud room just off the kitchen."

Pope glanced at Sarah, who headed downstairs immediately.

Pope stared at Nelson, saying nothing. After a few minutes, he heard Sarah dragging something. The next sound was apparently a kitchen pump. The two upstairs heard water hitting galvanized metal.

Nelson looked quizzically and Pope continued to glower at him.

"Okay, honey," Sarah said.

Pope jerked Nelson to his feet and shoved him towards the stairway. When he was two steps from the bottom, Pope shoved him, and he fell. The shove was carefully staged so the fall would be painful, but not debilitating.

Pope grabbed him by the hair and helped him onto his feet. He pushed him into the kitchen where Sarah had almost filled an oval bathtub.

"Darling, would you close all the windows in the house? We don't want the neighbors bothered by the screaming and crying," Pope asked.

"Are you the couple from hell?" Nelson asked.

"Your personal hell. Yes, we are. Now shut up and

answer my questions."

Sarah returned having closed windows upstairs and down.

Pope moved Nelson to the end of the tub on the floor.

"Kneel right here!" he ordered, grabbing the back of Nelson's robe and jerking it off and tossing it on the floor.

Sarah removed a pad and pencil from her purse.

"Now, answer our questions and this will be easy. Refuse to answer and it will be hard. Very hard," Pope told the naked Nelson. The night was hot and the temperature was exacerbated by the increasing heat in the house with no ventilation.

"What are you going to do on Thursday?"

Nelson looked at him and said nothing.

Pope grabbed him by the back of the neck and pushed his head under water. Nelson tried to hold his breath, but finally gave up and began choking and gurgling.

Pope pulled his head up before he lost consciousness. He let the Marxist cough for a minute and then resumed.

"As I was asking, what are you going to do Thursday? No need trying to delay. I will get my answer." Pope dunked him again for about ten seconds.

"What are you going to do?"

"Kill Arthur, damn his capitalist soul."

"How?"

"Shoot him. All three of us. At the same time," Nelson said.

"Where will this happen?"

"At the unveiling of a new monument in Washington."

Pope and Sarah looked at each other. They had called this one right.

"The names and locations of the other two?" Pope asked.

"I'm not a rat."

The statement earned him a longer period underwater to reconsider his answer.

He came up sputtering and vomited pure water.

"Have you decided to tell us the names and location of your coconspirators yet?"

"Go to hell!"

This time was the longest time yet. Forty seconds, Pope estimated. Nelson was struggling so hard Sarah had to help hold him down.

Pope was soaked. He grinned at Sarah.

"Now I know why you didn't put your dress back on. Besides, I know you like walking around with just your shift."

"And you hate it?" She smiled. He shook his head.

"Nelson, once again: Who are your associates?"

"Harvey Johnstone. Head of the Dockworker's Union located in the Bronx. The other is Bob Romano. He owns a liquor warehouse in Queens."

Pope made sure the terrified man had not excluded other conspirators. He also obtained detailed descriptions of both men and found none planned on wearing a disguise. The three were going to shoot fast and disappear within the crowd. They were going to hide in a fleabag hotel in Washington for several days, then take a train back to New York. The hotel was the Cherry Blossom Hotel on 15th. The plan was simple and would have been effective.

"I've told you everything you asked. Now, let me go."

"Let you go? You are planning an assassination. We can't let you go. We are going to have to arrest you," Pope said. "Honey, you can get dressed now."

She slipped the shift off and stood for a minute before donning the work dress and shoes.

"You really missed out, Roger," she told the prisoner. Pope just shook his head.

"Bitch! Whore!" he screamed at Sarah.

Pope instinctively throat punched him. He hit too hard and crushed Nelson's larynx. They were unable to help as Nelson choked to death in front of them.

"The situation is now simplified. I don't guess he has any rope laying around?" Pope asked.

Sarah looked, but to no avail.

Pope took out the Bowie and cut five two-inch strips from the top sheet. He twisted each and tied them securely. He made a noose in his makeshift rope and slipped it around Nelson's neck. A hanging would also explain the bruise already starting to form on his throat.

Pope used his height to reach a rafter. The two struggled to lift Nelson's dead weight and used the sheet rope to loop over the rafter. Sarah slid a kitchen chair under his feet to measure for height, then kicked it aside after Pope tied the rope.

"John, should we have put his robe back on?" she asked.

"Most of the suicides I investigated in San Francisco were naked. I have no idea why people strip to kill themselves or why they slit their wrists in a tub of water. People are weird, honey.

"While I check out the house and empty the tub and put it away, will you see if you can find two things? First is anything incriminating about Thursday. The second is samples of his handwriting. On checks, anything. I need to write a suicide note."

"For him, I hope. I've gotten used to having you around. And, you haven't even made me an honest woman yet," Sarah remarked. Pope assumed it was in jest but was never quite sure with his partner.

A half hour later, the crime scene was perfect. The note was written in a hand close enough to Nelson's.

The two detectives reopened windows and were able to lock the rear door on the way out. It was ten o'clock and nobody was up and about in the back alley. They walked three blocks in the alley, then cut over to the main street and walked to their room.

Since both of their remaining suspects were in New York City, they headed there.

On the way to the platform Pope dropped the text for a telegram to Lincoln stating a suspect had outlined the threat to his boss in detail and it was at the Thursday event.

Perhaps more importantly, he dropped off the text of a telegram to Conkling about the warehouse owner and union chief in New York being involved in a Thursday attack on his friend. Pope said he was on his way to New York and would be there late in the morning to see Conkling for assistance.

The cleaned up, well dressed couple riding the train bore no resemblance to the workers who had been in the rough edge of Scarsdale. They got off the train in the city and took a hansom cab. Sarah went straight to the New York Wells Fargo office with a cypher message to the Washington office, detailing exactly what was scheduled to happen two days hence on Thursday. Pope went directly to Conkling's office.

He and Conkling met immediately. Conkling knew both the suspects from his days running the Customs House and running New York in general. He told Pope he had men watching both. Neither had departed for Washington. It looked like they planned to leave Wednesday as Nelson had.

"What is this Nelson's status?" Conkling asked.

"He spoke to us and later committed suicide."

Conkling smiled.

"He just up and killed himself?" he said.

"Pretty much. He left a brief note about being upset over participating in a plot to assassinate the president and decided to end it all. He finished with a stupid statement about Marxism infiltrating unions."

"Sounds like a good piece of work," Conkling said.

"The situation was very clean. No loose ends hanging."

"Let's send a note to both, to meet me at ten tonight at Pier 15. It's largely unused and a good place to have a nice, private chat. I'd like for you to go. There is sure to be a gunfight when you try to make an arrest. You will win, which I suspect would be the case even if we didn't set it up," Conkling said.

Conkling outlined how his plan would go down. Pope liked it.

Pope and Sarah spoke about the plan. Both agreed, she would stay in the background out of sight of everyone. If Pope did not appear fairly soon after, she would approach. Each had his function. Conkling was a good Samaritan identifying the two men to be arrested. Pope was the deputy US marshal to arrest them.

Being summoned by the most powerful and perhaps one of the scariest men in New York worked.

Pope, Conkling, and two very big Conkling associates showed up at the pier. Romano and Johnstone were waiting.

"Hi, boys," Conkling greeted them.

"I understand you have a plan to kill my old friend, Chet Arthur. Some sort of Marxist crap. I cannot allow you to do it. The tall man beside me is a US marshal assigned by the attorney general to interrupt the plan," Conkling said.

Pope had the silver badge pinned in clear sight in the light shown by a gas streetlamp.

"Romano, Johnstone. You are both under arrest for plotting to kill Chester A. Arthur. Throw up your hands right now!" Pope ordered.

His coat was open and loose. His only doubt was using the heavy pull double-action revolver instead of his usual Colts. He need not have worried.

Without help from Conkling's two men, the conspirators looked at each other.

"It's coming now," Pope thought to himself.

They both drew revolvers. Before they had their guns anywhere near pointed in Pope's direction, there were two cracks.

Each man was hit in the upper torso. Two more cracks from Pope's gun as insurance. Again, these two shots were fired before their draws were completed.

Romano and Johnstone fell dead on the wooden planks of the pier.

Sarah breathed a sigh of relief from the shadows. And a smile of pride. Pope emerged victor again. Against uneven odds. *Damn, he's good*, she thought as she smiled more broadly.

They heard New York police whistles in the distance.

Conkling sent one of his two giants to direct the responding officers to the pier.

Of the first three to arrive, one was a sergeant who Conkling seemed to know well. Pope suspected he was on Conkling's payroll.

"Sean, this is Deputy US Marshal John Pope. He is investigating a plot to shoot the president. His investigation has implicated these two, who I think you will recognize as Marxist conspirators. They are two of the three men involved. My men and I came to assist by identifying them.

"When the marshal attempted to take them into custody, they pulled guns. He pulled faster and killed them both. I've never seen anything like it. Never.

"Sean, it was as clean a shoot as anyone could imagine. You write it up and the marshal will come downtown in the morning and give you his statement. Then, he has to get back to Washington and report all clear to the attorney general.

"Marshal, please give the sergeant one of your unfired rounds so the coroner can compare calibers. Sean, you will see it's a .44-40. Not something you will see around the city. It's a Wild West cartridge carried by a Wild West lawman."

"Yes, sir, Mr. Conkling. Marshal Pope, report to Detective Fusco at headquarters tomorrow morning after nine. I will make sure he is expecting you and will get you in and out real fast," the sergeant said.

The four men walked slowly away from the scene. Pope reloaded his Smith & Wesson as he walked.

A woman with glossy black hair and blue eyes joined them after a block. Taking everyone but Pope by surprise.

"Mr. Conkling, this is my partner, Wells Fargo Detective Sarah Watson Pope," Pope said.

"An honor, Mrs. Pope. How is your old employer, Allan Pinkerton doing? I've known him for years, but lost contact," Conkling replied.

Was there anything or anyone this man didn't know, Pope thought, saying nothing.

Sarah did not miss a beat.

"I am afraid Allan is doing poorly. He had a stroke last year and seems to be on his last legs. I have not mentioned it to John yet, but I need to stop in Chicago on the way back West and see him. Probably for the last time."

"Please give him this card and express my best wishes for a good recovery."

"Yes, sir, I will."

"Mr. Conkling, thank you for your help on this.

The president will be made fully aware you were instrumental in breaking up this cabal."

Conkling gave two more cards to Pope. One for the president and one, he said, for the two detectives to keep in case they "ever needed anything in New York".

Sarah and Pope knew Conkling's definition of "anything" was very broad in their case.

Conkling had a carriage waiting conveniently a few blocks away from the scene. He gave them a ride to their hotel and rode off into history. A great friend, a bad enemy.

"Honey, we need to get to Washington as soon as possible. But first a telegram to Lincoln. On the outside chance we've missed a member of the Marxist group, we need to have Arthur covered heavily at the statue event. I cannot leave until I sign a statement with this Detective Fusco person."

They checked out of their hotel. Pope met with Fusco quickly and made the southbound train to Washington just after the one Sarah had taken just in case he was delayed. He arrived well before the dedication of the new monument.

The telegram to the secretary of war preceded them by hours. They had time to stop by the house and clean up. Pope found a saw with May's help and sawed the butt off Sarah's shotgun, leaving only the pistol grip. The result was a powerful weapon which would fit in her largest purse. She took it to the dedication when they left to scan the area hours before any dignitaries arrived.

The Washington police officers were putting up rope barricades. One stopped Pope, who showed him the deputy marshal badge and explained his presence.

Pope and Sarah identified several windows which would offer good shooting points for a sniper with a target rifle.

They entered the buildings, one commercial, one residential, and interviewed residents. The asked the commercial building to lock off the floor with the offending windows once they found the floor was storage only.

The several residential windows were in the apartment of an elderly couple Pope and Sarah did not feel offered a threat.

They checked trash receptacles and around the monument itself for any type of explosives, such as dynamite. Nothing was found. They were being careful though Nelson said the plan was for all three to shoot Arthur at the same time.

The two detectives remained on station until the dignitaries arrived. Pope was glad to see his President's House security team escorting the president.

There was one protestor with a sign. It said, "Share the wealth," which the two detectives thought might have been a subtle socialist or communist saying. He was a fairly well-dressed man of about forty with wild hair.

Sarah walked over to him and flashed her gold Wells Fargo badge so fast he could not read it. She then stood beside him.

"You have the right to protest. But the president has the right to speak without you interrupting. Do so and you will suffer dire consequences," she told the man.

In case he was a decoy for a real shooter, Pope stood back and studied the crowd. He saw Lincoln and Brewster. Neither would have usually attended a statue dedication. This was special though as the original site of the threat. They saw Pope in the crowd and Sarah next to the sign carrier.

Chester Arthur gave a short speech and looked into the crowd. He saw the sign and the woman standing next to the man holding it. He recognized Sarah instantly and beamed at her.

I might have to shoot him myself, Pope thought.

Lincoln and Brewster had advised the president of the threat and who had investigated and mitigated it prior to their departing for the monument.

He was stunned but appreciative to them, the Popes, and his old friend Conkling.

Arthur was not dismayed the Popes took permanent action against his would-be assassins. He had his secretary begin to do a complete dossier on the two out of curiosity. Especially about Sarah. He had no idea what dangerous ground he was treading.

After the dedication and ribbon cutting and the usual butt kissing which follows such an appearance, the president mentioned to Brewster he would like to have him, Lincoln, and the Popes join him for lunch. Brewster, suspicious of motives, immediately said, "Mr. President, I believe the Popes are leaving directly for San Francisco. I'm afraid it may be too late to catch them."

He was an observant man. He saw Arthur looking at Sarah. And, more importantly, Pope's cold stare back at him in return. He did not know exactly what Pope was thinking, but he hit pretty close.

Pope and Sarah had virtually no packing to do at the house in Washington. They spoke with May.

"How would you like to come back West with us? We are not sure where we will end up, but you are welcome to have a job and home for life," Sarah offered.

"Oh, Sarah. You two are so sweet. What you don't know is I already do. The owner of this house is my nephew. I am his only kin. He has willed it to me in the tragic event he dies abroad with the military. But he is a confirmed bachelor and needs me to take care of him like the mother I have been for the rest of either of our days. Otherwise, I would jump at the chance to go with you and John. You feel like family and have treated me like a family member instead of a housekeeper or employee.

"Do you know where you are going with Wells Fargo?" May asked.

"May, we have not got a clue," Pope said in true detective fashion. It was a bit worrisome to him. He did not want to get too far from his grandfather as Israel aged. Sarah only had several surviving family members and did not speak often or fondly of any of them.

Before leaving Washington, Pope went to a jeweler with one of Sarah's rings and bought another ring to quietly hold for her.

Both stopped at the secretary of war's office late in the afternoon.

"Is there anything else you need from us? Further report elaboration?" Pope asked.

"No, John. I think the case is closed thanks to the two of you. The president wanted you two, Ben and me to join him for lunch this week. Ben feared he might have an ulterior motive and said you had already left. Hope you concur with Ben's gut reaction."

"I certainly do, Robert," Pope said. Sarah nodded.

"Our train leaves in the morning. I'd like to say goodbye to my team at the President's House, but just as soon avoid bumping into Arthur. So, I will write to them."

"As will I to my little friend at the Library of Congress, such as it is," Sarah said.

"What's on the agenda for you two now?" Lincoln asked.

"We honestly have no idea. If you would, telegraph Lloyd Tevis and copy James Hume at Wells Fargo and tell him we fulfilled what you needed and are on the way back."

"Of course. Your investigation was thorough and brought to a permanent conclusion. More than Ben and I could have asked. As a bonus, I am keeping you on the payroll for another three months but releasing you at your leisure."

"Thank you, Robert. It's most generous of you. Here is your provost marshal badge. And here is the deputy US marshal badge to give to Ben," Pope said.

"Ben already addressed the matter of his badge. He would like for you to stay sworn and keep it. It will be good as long—or short—as he is attorney general."

"Please thank him. It has been a pleasure working for both of you."

Both detectives shook with Abraham Lincoln's son and departed.

Not trusting Arthur's probable amorous attempts, Pope suggested they find a hotel near the train depot for an early start. Sarah knew exactly what he was doing but said nothing. He suggested she start her night in the new little shift. She did not require more urging than a mere suggestion. Soon, it was in a pile at the foot of the bed.

The next morning, their sojourn in the East ended. They were steaming towards the west coast and totally unaware of what turn their careers might take.

CHAPTER 6

The trip certainly had not sped up since they went from California to Washington. Both enjoyed train rides. Though Pope loved to be on the trail with Caesar, trains were better than his trusty horse for crossing vast expanses.

They talked a lot about life. At least as much as they could not knowing where Wells Fargo would send them.

"Sarah, I think we should get married. We could tell the general world we want to go back and have a church wedding. People could make their own assumptions.

If we took this approach, we could have Grandpa and Millie, Hume, Thatcher, Morse, maybe the Kanes if they wanted to travel so far, and whoever from your family outside of Chicago you want."

"Is this a proposal, John?"

"You have an open proposal. This is just the next discussion about it. I figure if we don't do something, we will miss a perfect opportunity."

"So, a business decision?" she asked. He was not sure whether it was in jest or serious.

"No. It is a plausibly deniable opportunity to speed up what we both want," he said.

She thought about this for a few minutes as the train rumbled across the southern part of Illinois.

"I think you are right. I love you totally. Do you have a question to ask?"

"Sarah, will you marry me?" he asked.

"Yes, I will happily marry you."

Then, he shocked her with a diamond ring set. She was speechless. Something he would gloat on for years. He had finally made her speechless.

"John, it's beautiful. I love it! It fits perfectly."

"Of course, it does. I took one of your left hand rings with me," he admitted.

"Handsome and brilliant. And still the fastest gun in America, if not the world. Do they have fast guns outside of the US?" she asked.

"Maybe. I doubt it."

"Where would we have this wedding?" Sarah asked.

"San Francisco? Wherever you want."

"What denomination church should we use?"

"Any church whose pastor or priest or whatever will marry us," Pope said. "But we should, as a current couple, know where we are going to live and buy a house first. Even if it's not in San Francisco," he added.

"You know, John, Wells Fargo has a horrible reputation of moving its employees around the country."

"Yes, it has been worrying me. A lot, actually."

"What could we do?"

"One option is to take over Grandpa's ranch. He and Millie seem to like the cabin in the woods in Marin County better. Maybe I could run for sheriff and you could run the ranch. Along with me, of course."

"So, you think we are destined to leave Wells Fargo?" she asked.

"I fear so, honey."

"John, what do you think of the ranch?" she asked.

"Well, I grew up there. But I am tied to Israel Pope, not the land. If I were to have land and raise anything, I would prefer it be a little more remote. Alameda is growing way too fast for me."

"Let's keep considering options. We will plan the wedding in San Francisco. There is nobody in my family I care about coming to it. We will see what Hume offers us and take it or not. Probably not. We will see what Israel wants to do about the ranch. He might want to sell it and split the money with you. Or he may want to sell it and buy a big piece of land adjacent to his Marin cabin. We could put a cabin on it. One day, you will get his land anyway. I think we should ask his advice. He's pretty wise and several of our alternatives depend on what he does anyway," Sarah said.

"You sold me," her partner responded. "I really do like where Grandpa is across the Bay. I don't know what their sheriff situation is. I may still be a Deputy US Marshal, but even if Arthur had me appointed the US marshal for the district, I'd have to work in San Francisco. And my job would disappear as soon as another party took the presidency."

CHAPTER 7

A day later, their northbound connection stopped at Chicago and they climbed down from the train. Baggage including long guns secured at the train station, they took a cab to 80 Washington Street, the headquarters of the Pinkerton National Detective Agency.

They took a chance the stroke-stricken sixty-five-year-old founder was in the office.

As Sarah suspected, he was and agreed to see one of his favorites immediately.

"Sarah," he said in his Scottish brogue. Pinkerton tried to rise from his desk but could not.

Sarah walked over to the famous detective and kissed him on the cheek. He beamed like an adolescent.

"Who is this over tall young man you have in tow, Sarah?" the short stocky Scot asked.

"My husband, Detective John Pope, Allan."

"I have read about you, Detective Pope. You are

a gunfighter detective. Killed more men than Billy the Kid or Jesse James. Both of them, thank heavens, have met their rewards. So, you won the hand of the second-best woman detective in America?"

"No, sir. I won the hand of the first best."

"Well, you are right. Kate Warne was the best and saved Abraham Lincoln. She's gone now, God rest her soul. So, Sarah is, as you say, number one.

"What brings you two to the Windy City?" he asked.

"Just to see you, Allan. We were so close."

"Aye, I'm glad you came. Time is running out for me, Sarah."

"Oh, Allan. You will outlive all of us. You are far too mean to ever die."

"Ha! I wish. Were you back east?" he asked.

"We were, sir," Pope said.

"We were requested by the secretary of war and the attorney general to be transferred to the government. There had been a threat against President Arthur, and we were asked to mitigate it."

"An awfully big word for a young man schooled by a mountain man," Pinkerton said, proving he knew more than he seemed upon meeting Pope.

"He was a very well-read mountain man, Mr. Pinkerton," Pope replied calmly, not showing a whit of the anger he felt at the contemptuous older man.

"Robert's father would have contacted me. I guess the apple fell a ways from the tree. He will never be the man his father was," Pinkerton said.

"I suspect few could be the man your dear friend and admirer, Abe was, Allan," Sarah said softening the subject.

"So, what lies ahead for the two of you?" he asked, turning to Sarah and effectively dismissing Pope.

"We will find out in several days, Allan. Right now, we have no idea whatsoever," Sarah said.

"Well, tell Hume I said look after you, Sarah. Tell him when I go, he might be the number one detective. Him or Morse. It would be a big jump for either."

"I trust he will. He has always been fair to John and me both."

Seeing just these few minutes were tiring the great detective, Sarah bid her adieus and the two left.

"Is it the stroke, or has he always been an ass?" Pope asked.

"He always was a bit of an ass, but today he was ruder and more argumentative than I have ever seen him. He was not even a gracious host. I am sorry I subjected you to him," Sarah said.

"I have dealt with far worse. Sad, though," he said almost pensively. "I have read all of his books. He was always a bit of a hero to me. No longer, I'm afraid."

"John, he did not save Lincoln like we saved Arthur. He did not get Jesse James. He lost a lot of credibility when Pinkertons became a strike breaker and beat or shot American workers. I suspect he looks back on his life as a failure. Kate Warne was very special to him. She died young and he buried her in his plot. He will probably be buried next to her. Something which did not thrill his wife and sons, I'm sure. Seeing him like this breaks my heart, John."

He nodded to her and squeezed her hand as they walked back towards the Northwestern Depot. He held her left hand up and the diamond sparkled in the sun. She smiled at him, momentarily getting past the sorrow over the decline of her old friend and boss.

Several days later, they pulled into San Francisco. A quick ride to their rooming house found the adjacent rooms safe, but musty from weeks without ventilation.

They aired the rooms out, took clothes to the Chinese laundry down the street and prepared to see Hume the following morning.

Chief Detective James Hume got to work early. He was always in before seven. The two detectives knew it was always better to see him before everyone else darkened his door.

He was expecting them and had a coffee pitcher and three cups on his desk. Coffee poured they sat and waited for him to open the conversation.

"John, the New York papers said Deputy Marshal Pope killed two conspirators on a dock of some sort in New York City. I am assuming it was you solving the threat against the president?"

"Yes, sir. The third conspirator had remorse and hung himself in Scarsdale. All concerned consider the entire matter to be closed. The president and two secretaries were pleased, and we were dismissed with appreciation," Pope said.

"Tevis got a telegram from Secretary Lincoln saying much the same. He is happy. From my standpoint, anything happen which will cause repercussions to Wells Fargo?"

"No, sir," Sarah said neglecting to summarize their kills. They set up one fake suicide, she killed two attackers, and Pope had to gun down two conspirators. She was aware Hume knew about the latter.

Pope continued to shock her with his esoteric knowledge when he described their case on the train by saying *veni, vidi, vici* or they came, they saw, and they conquered. As Pope had said to Pinkerton, his grandfather was well-read.

"I guess you are wondering what's next for the pair of you?"

"It has been a bit of a topic of discussion, Boss," Pope admitted.

"You seemed to like Cheyenne. I spoke with the superintendent and he concurred with assigning Sarah as office manager of the new office you all built and John being the regional detective. This would be at least a two-year assignment."

"May we give it some thought?" Sarah asked,

shocking Hume who thought they would be thrilled.

"A week or two off to rest and think about it would be appreciated," Pope added. "We have been going hard. Sarah was undercover and had to beat off an attacker, I have added to my list of kills. We need some time to visit family and think. Sarah and I dropped in on Allan Pinkerton. His condition is bad and has added to her worries."

"Alright, take two weeks off. You have earned the time. But, let me know about the assignment within several days," Hume said, not pleased at all.

They left, walked downstairs without checking their desks and walked out the front door to Wells Fargo & Company. Sarah took a cab back to their rooms. Pope went to the livery stable where he kept Caesar.

Pope had sent his grandfather a letter. The older man had delivered Caesar back to the livery before Pope's arrival. The pleasure between man and horse was mutual. The bill was up to date. Pope had a stable hand saddle the big horse and he rode him home.

Sarah had packed for both of them. In a riding skirt, she mounted the horse behind the cantle, and they rode the short blocks to the port. They took the ferry to Sausalito. Caesar was glad to get off San Francisco Bay. The extra hundred twenty pounds on the back of the saddle did not faze the sixteen-hand horse. The bumpy ride across in the ferry did not please him. They headed north from town and soon were at Israel Pope's cabin.

Pope hailed his grandfather, "Grandpa! Put two more cups of water in the soup. You got company."

The first one out the door was Pope's dog, Scout. Hearing the voice made him about the happiest dog in America. The blue tick hound put both paws up on Pope's leg while he was still on Caesar. The horse was even glad to see his canine buddy.

The handsome older version of the detective walked out of the cabin and put his rifle against the wall. His pretty wife, lately the housekeeper of the family whose kidnapped daughter Pope and Sarah had rescued, followed. Both were smiling with genuine pleasure.

Pope embraced his grandfather.

"This is a wonderful surprise, Sonny. C'mon in and tell me what's going on. I know you better than anyone. When you pop in, you need to talk."

"You are scary smart, Grandpa. Always have been." Pope could not help but to draw a comparison between this robust, mid-sixties man and the one he and Sarah had visited in Chicago.

"Millie, you have hugged the girl long enough. It's time her soon-to-be grandfather in law hugged her!" Israel Pope commanded to his lovely new wife.

"Sarah, my boy and I built this cabin ourselves. He was only about twelve then but could swing a mean axe. Was before he had to worry about keeping his hands in shape for fast gun handling. You done anymore shooting, John?"

"Yessir. A few on the way back to Washington in a robbery and three conspirators trying to kill the president. One was a suicide if anybody asks. The others were justified shootings."

Israel Pope, in his mountain man days and since, had amassed a long list of kills. He understood there were bad men and sometimes killing them was required. What he worried the most about with his grandson was the growing newspaper coverage. Notoriety led to wannabes. Wannabes were usually people who had big ideas and little skills. People like the Kid Taos fellow from their Cheyenne case. Sometimes they got lucky. Which was a source of worry to the grandfather.

"This talk you and I need to have. Is it just us? Or a family pow-wow?" Israel asked Pope.

"Family for sure. We have some big decisions and sure would appreciate your and Millie's advice."

"Let's hold it for just after dinner. We'll talk on full stomachs," Israel said.

Pope and his grandfather put Caesar out in the small pasture. The big horse ran and frolicked like a colt, Scout behind him barking in support.

"It's sure nice up here, Grandpa," Pope remarked.

"I like it better than the ranch. I promised I'd leave you the ranch. Do you really want it?"

"It's about the only home I remember. But soon it's going to be all settled in around it. You are certainly welcome to sell it from my standpoint. Assuming you and Millie would rather live up here," Pope said.

"I may have mentioned there's another hundred acres of woodland adjacent to this seventy-five acres," Israel said.

"I remember you said there was some available land. I don't remember if you said how much."

"What if I sold the ranch and bought the land here. I would leave the whole hundred seventy-five acres to you. Of course, Millie could live here, looked after, the rest of her life."

"Grandpa, I'd look after Millie without any type agreement. We both love her. Besides, then, she'd be all I have left of you."

"I had to spill it out, boy. But I already knew the answer. It's how you were raised."

"Have you talked about this with her?" Pope asked.

"I have. She's good with it. She saw you in action saving the girl she damn near raised in San Francisco. The one who is planning on stealing you away from Sarah."

"She actually is a sweet kid. I don't want to hurt her feelings but have to be real careful what I say to her."

"Yep."

"Sonny, was this part about the ranch and up here in any way related to your visit?"

"Yessir. It is partially related. We have some marriage and job things for our pow-wow."

"While we are talking, I reckon I'm ready to tell you more of my story before I took over raising you. There's a part I left out. Millie knows it. After dinner, you will, too."

******

Dinner was venison stew with doughy rolls fixed in a Dutch oven. Millie capped it off with a mixed berry pie from fruit she and Israel gathered.

Sarah retrieved the black coffee pot from the fireplace and topped their mugs.

"First off, Sonny, tell us as much as you can about the case you resolved in Washington," Israel said.

"The president of Wells Fargo was summoned to Washington. Once there, the attorney general and the secretary of war—Abe Lincoln's son—asked to borrow us to investigate and make a threat against President Arthur go away. He came back and met with our boss, Hume, who you both know from the Mattie Lane kidnapping."

"Two good things came out of the kidnapping," Israel said. "You got the young lady back safely and I met and stole their housekeeper!"

"You did. And we all benefitted when Millie joined the family," Sarah said. "And, the young lady is still sending love letters to John," she added unnecessarily.

"Well, of course she would. I'm a couple years too old for her," Israel said breaking the uncomfortable silence.

Pope said nothing.

"Sarah did a lot of research and we came up with a number of folks who might have a legitimate grievance against Arthur. A big worry was it might be an illogical nut group. They would have been virtually impossible to find. One of our primary suspects, a New York politician and probable crime boss, became our most valuable resource.

"We finally narrowed it down to a small dissident group of communists. Sarah went undercover and confirmed them. I interrogated the leader harshly and he sang like a robin in spring. He prompted me to hit him. The throat punch killed him. We staged a suicide. Of course, nobody but the four of us know about it. The police in Scarsdale investigated and bought the suicide without question.

"Knowing who and how the attack on the president was going to happen, we used the New York politician to set up a meeting with the two remaining shooters. Neither knew their friend was already dead.

"I told them, I was a deputy US marshal and they were under arrest for conspiring to kill the president. They both pulled and I killed them on the spot. Right in front of a former US senator. He knew the police sergeant who was first on scene and recounted the incident. I filed a report at police headquarters the next morning. We came back to Washington and attended the event where the shooting was supposed to occur. It looked like we eliminated the threats. We ducked out of town to protect Sarah from an amorous president."

"I concur except for the last. I could have handled him. John also left out I had to kill a couple of attackers in New York City. Probably just thugs," Sarah added.

"Sounds like you two had a successful and exciting stay in Washington," Millie observed.

"All in all, I guess we did. Which brings us to now. We were pretty mad when the president of Wells Fargo sent us on a case and required us to get married. We have every intention of getting married. But to be ordered by an employer?" Pope said, obviously still bothered by it.

"A helluva lot of nerve is what I'd say. Does he think he is God or something?" Israel asked.

"Sounded like it to us, Israel," Sarah said.

"Hume kinda gave us a half-hearted pass, but now thinks we are married by a justice of the peace or somebody. We plan to have a church wedding soon. The invitations will say, 'We missed out on a church wedding, so want to have one now.' Let people use their own imagination about it," she said.

"Smart!" Millie said. "Marriage is very personal and

something not to be made part of your continued employment. I don't know who people think they are."

Sarah held up the new rings, which she put on at the table.

"I'll loan the wedding band back to John for the marriage ceremony," she said.

"Did Hume say anything about what he had in mind for you two as a couple instead of just detective partners?" Israel asked.

"Yessir. What he said was assigning Sarah to be the manager of the new Cheyenne office she opened and me as regional detective out of Cheyenne," Pope said.

"Not too bad, I guess," Israel said pensively.

"He gave us a couple days to answer him on it and was peeved we didn't jump at it. Sarah and I talked long and hard on the train. Our family is important. And it's all sitting here at this table. He also said it would be at least a two-year assignment. Then, we could be sent anywhere. So, we are looking at our options if we both resign."

"You wouldn't know this, but the sheriff here just got all broken up when his buggy turned over. He rolled down a rocky hill and won't be able to walk right, or ride at all again. His chief deputy is a nice fellow, but no leader."

"Who will appoint his replacement?" Sarah asked.

"The governor. I'm betting you could get some pretty powerful folks in Washington and even in

Wells Fargo to write him a letter. And, how about the sheriff you helped out in Cheyenne?"

"Grandpa, it could be a solution for me. How far is the county seat in San Rafael from here?"

"About four miles. I don't think I ever took you over there. You kinda blew in and out of the cabin for visits. San Rafael is a nice little place. It started as a Spanish mission long ago."

"How about Sarah? It kind of leaves her out in the cold."

"I ran a tax office in Prescott. Maybe I could do something like it in San Rafael," she said.

"I propose we all ride over there tomorrow and scout it out. Then, if you like it, get on the telegraph and get some letters going into the capitol," Israel suggested.

Pope looked at Sarah and she smiled and nodded. She had not said anything, but between Pinkertons and Wells Fargo, she was tired of traveling all the time. A job, or no job would be just fine with her and they had sufficient money saved between the two of them, saving salary and living on expenses, for her to take her time.

"Alright then. I think we have a plan, family," Pope said. His grandfather beamed. He wanted nothing more than to have his only living kin back near him.

The next morning, the four rode into San Rafael and had breakfast, then walked around the town and visited the old mission. Israel knew the sheriff and he and Pope visited him. The sheriff was in pain and their visit was short. The man was familiar with Pope's law enforcement background. He asked whether Pope had interest in being appointed his replacement. He was concerned his office had coverage for daily patrol but feared a void if a serious robbery or crime against persons occurred.

Pope indicated he was tired of the constant travel with his current employer. The sheriff said he would be willing to wire the governor and suggest Pope be appointed. To Israel's question about other wires from famous people, he replied, "Yep. He's a politician first and foremost. Famous politicians and others would have a lot of influence. But move fast before he does something stupid and appoints a big political donor."

Based on the information, Pope and his grandfather went directly to the telegraph office and sent telegrams to the attorney general, secretary of war, sheriff of Laramie County and Roscoe Conkling.

Due to the urgency the sheriff said existed, Pope and Sarah left immediately for San Francisco to meet with James Hume. On the way, they agreed to not bring up their irritation at how the last case was assigned and to stay positive.

They arrived at the headquarters and found Hume was meeting with his friend and frequent contract detective, Harry Morse.

They finished their discussion and invited the two in.

"Well, Popes. Do you have an answer for me?" Hume asked. Neither Hume nor the Popes minded their friend Morse being present.

"We have some concerns. I may also have a possibility offering us a solution," Pope said.

"Keep talking."

"Sarah and I do not want to move to Wyoming. Not now. Since our marriage was virtually mandated by Mr. Tevis, we want to establish more than a two-year home. My grandfather is the only kin I have. He is not getting younger and needs the occasional bit of help now. I have to be near for him. Other than Sarah, he's the most important thing in the world for me."

He saw Morse nodding in agreement. Hume did also. Morse was Hume's primary decision sounding board.

"John, I appreciate your dedication to Israel Pope. It's quite laudable. Where does this leave us?" Hume asked.

"I don't know if you've heard, but Sheriff Mahoney in Marin County was seriously injured in a riding accident. He is partially crippled and advised the county commission and governor he cannot perform his duties any longer. He does not have a strong number two and has said he would support me being appointed as his successor until the next election.

"Both of you have been county sheriffs in California. I'd like to take a shot at it, gentlemen. Especially with your support."

Hume paused, clearly in deep thought. After a full minute or two, he spoke.

"John, you have done everything I ever asked you, up to and including saving the president. I still feel Tevis ordering you to get married for a case was unconscionable.

"I'd be willing to support you in the sheriff appointment."

"I would too, John," Morse added.

Hume swiveled his desk chair to face Sarah.

"Which leaves us with you, young lady."

"I would make you a wonderful regional detective for the counties north of the Bay," she began. The idea had arisen during their trip across San Francisco Bay on the ferry.

Hume stopped again. Pope knew he was thinking about whether the volume of cases in Marin, Sonoma, Napa, Yolo and others would support a regional detective. He decided they would. Pope saw the almost imperceptible exchange between Hume and Morse. *Good old Harry!* he thought, *He's backing our play to the hilt.*

"So. You would be stationed out of San Rafael, assuming John's appointment went through?" Hume asked Sarah.

"Yes, sir."

"John, I'll hate to lose you. But I think you've earned the right to stay in one place. I suspect any office job, even here, would drive you crazy in a week.

"I will telegraph the governor immediately. Harry and I helped him out not too long ago, which is a good thing. John, hold on to your badge and any company equipment until this goes through. If it does not, we will revisit your situation then.

"Sarah, your assignment commences at the end of your two-week holiday."

"One other thing for both of you," Sarah began.

"Due to the urgency of getting to Washington, we missed having a real church wedding. We are going to have a small one and hope both of you and your wives will be our guests?" She omitted the fact they missed having any wedding at all.

"Let us know when and where," Hume said.

"I wouldn't miss it for the world. I'm almost disappointed Jim agreed to you being a regional detective, Sarah. I was prepared to hire you on the spot to do the very thing for my company," Morse said.

"I'm honored, Harry. I would have accepted here and now."

They parted with handshakes, as was Hume's way.

At Pope's desk, he took a telegraph form and penned a wire to the governor asking for the sheriff appointment in Marin County. He mentioned he had the support of the current sheriff, some key California law enforcement notables and some folks back east with whom he had worked. He said they would contact him separately. The telegram was gone before they left the Wells Fargo building.

Now, hurry up and wait.

They stopped on the way to the return ferry for a celebratory lunch. They loaded Caesar and one of the several cow ponies Israel had left and had moved to Marin when he vacated the ranch.

The next day, Israel and Pope went to the ranch. They had a nearby lawyer who specialized in land deals. He listed it for sale. Even a low bid would more than cover the acquisition of the new, adjacent land in Marin.

"Sonny," Israel began once they started the ride to the ferry from the ranch, "I never got a chance to tell you the story I wanted to after dinner the first night. How 'bout now?"

"Sure, Grandpa. Unless it's something Millie and Sarah need to hear with me."

"Millie already knows. You can tell Sarah if you think it's important.

"I was married after your grandma. Married to a beautiful Indian princess. We lived with the tribe then in a cabin for several years. It was a good marriage. One day I was trapping and a small war party from another tribe out of the area came by. They killed her and savaged her badly. I had already lost one wife and I was filled with hate.

"Boy, I tracked them down like you and I did those who killed the rest of our family five years later. I killed all six of them in one fight. Four were hand to hand. Or Bowie knife to body or throat would be more correct. I took their scalps to her father. He was a big chief. After a period of mourning, and he was as sad as me, he put together a war party. I didn't go. They rode into the camp of the other tribe and killed every soul there.

"He was an honorable man and knew I wouldn't hold with killing women and children and old folks. So, he spared me. First and foremost, he was a chief. He had to do it his way as a sign for every other tribe.

"We had a burial ceremony for my wife when he got back. I gathered her ashes and gave them to the four winds. She's out there somewhere, smiling down.

"Her spirit animal was a hawk. Every time I see one soaring, I think it's probably her, checking on me.

"With the bad luck I had with wives, I was scared to marry Millie. But I knew now there was two of us, you and me, to protect her. With you living close now, I feel calm. Calm for the first time in years, Sonny Boy."

Pope looked at his grandfather. He thought Israel Pope was the most dangerous man alive. Even in his mid-sixties. He had no idea his grandfather was convinced Pope himself was. Even so, together, it would have been difficult to find a more fearsome pair. Add Sarah, and they were stronger yet.

Not beginning to think about this, they rode on, lost in their own thoughts. Happy to be riding together. Riding home. For the first time in a while.

*****

With letters from famous lawmen, the attorney general and secretary of war, and a former US senator, the governor was swayed to appoint Pope sheriff for the remaining several years of the current sheriff's term. The telegram from the president, a man of his own party, sealed the deal. Robert Todd Lincoln decided to call in a favor. Arthur was aware the two detectives had probably saved his life. His telegram to the governor was eloquent and would have been hard to ignore.

He telegraphed Pope and told him to come to Sacramento immediately.

Pope boarded a train and went in the suit and white shirt he was wearing at the time.

He went to the state capitol and presented himself at the governor's office. With his telegram from the governor, he was given an appointment an hour hence. He took a seat in the lobby and waited.

The bearded former Union officer whose West

Point roommate had been Stonewall Jackson, greeted Pope at the precise time scheduled.

"Governor Stoneman, it's good to meet you," Pope said, offering his hand.

"And you also, Mr. Pope. Your telegram proposing, I appoint you sheriff was actually preceded by some pretty interesting people. Just after yours, I received a letter of endorsement from President Arthur. He claimed you and your partner saved his life recently.

"I'd like to hear the details."

Pope gave him the summary of the case.

"Interesting. James Hume and Harry Morse are well-known to me. Both said you are the top detective at Wells Fargo."

"I respectfully disagree, Governor. They are the two top detectives in America. No question about it. My wife, Sarah, is the best detective otherwise."

"I had some interaction with Allan Pinkerton during the war. She is better than him?" the governor asked.

"Maybe not in his heyday, sir. He trained her. We visited him in Chicago a week ago. He has slid backwards badly after a stroke. I fear he won't be with us much longer."

"What did you think of him?" Stoneman asked.

"I read all of his books as a young San Francisco detective. He was like a hero to me. When we met, it was clear he cared a lot for Sarah. He was resentful to me, though I gave him no reason. I reckon it was related to his failing health."

"Don't be too sure. I found him an irascible cuss twenty years ago," Stoneman said.

"I would have been surprised to hear it a year ago. After last week, I'm not surprised at all. Sarah always said he was testy. Nonetheless, he advanced criminology farther than anyone up to Jim Hume, who has taught me so much at Wells Fargo."

"I understand Hume had developed some court-approved tests for bullet ballistics," Stoneman said, perhaps testing his interviewee.

"He has. I used them in Cheyenne, Wyoming recently to prove a case against some stage and train robbers," Pope said.

"Hume said you have solved every case he has assigned you. Either by good detecting or good shooting," the governor said.

"Even a blind squirrel finds an acorn sometimes, Governor."

Stoneman smiled.

"You realize if I appoint you for this job in Marin, you will have to run in an election to keep it in about two years?"

"I do, sir."

"Would Israel Pope be your campaign manager? He is a not a Californian by birth but by choice. And a state treasure."

"I have not thought about running, but I cannot

think of a much better advocate."

"I don't know, your telegram advocates set a pretty high bar. Other than at San Francisco, have you ever been a sworn officer?"

"I was provost marshal to the secretary of war and was sworn as a deputy US marshal reporting to the attorney general during the Washington case. The attorney general asked me to keep my badge in case he needed me for something else during his term. So, I am sworn right now."

"Might be helpful for a sheriff chasing a fugitive around the state. Or, out of it."

"I was thinking the same thing, Governor," Pope said.

"Do you have any questions for me?"

"No sir. I am ready to serve at your pleasure."

"I have a judge standing by. Give me a moment."

The governor called his secretary and asked the judge to be located in the building and brought into the office.

After introductions, Pope raised his right hand. He held his left on a Bible.

"Do you, John Pope, solemnly agree to uphold the ordinances of Marin County, the laws of the State of California and support the Constitution of the United States, so help you God?" the judge read.

"I do."

"Then, by the powers invested in me by the State

of California, I appoint you Sheriff of Marin County for the remainder of the elected term of your predecessor. Congratulations, Sheriff Pope."

"Thank you, gentlemen."

"Sheriff, I don't have a badge. You will have to get one from the man who was sheriff or have one made. I will give you a court order, under seal, commemorating this swearing in. It will be your official proof of being sheriff," the judge said.

"If you gentlemen have nothing further, I better get back down to Marin and start enforcing the law," Pope said.

"I will telegraph the Marin Sheriff's Office and local Marin papers and advise you have been sworn in as sheriff. No need for you have to show up yourself and explain it," the governor said.

"Thank you, Governor. I appreciate the courtesy."

He was on a southbound train an hour later.

******

Pope sent an advisement of his new status to Hume from San Rafael. Hume responded he would be there for the wedding or Sarah's start as regional detective, whichever came first. Pope could turn in his Wells Fargo badge and resign then.

After the telegrams were sent from the train depot, Pope went to the sheriff's office and introduced himself.

He liked the chief deputy, a man named Bill Isakson. He was a man of good administrative skills, knew everyone in the county and was well-liked. He just did not want to take the responsibility of being sheriff and was glad to welcome Pope.

"We have ten patrol deputies and ten jailers. The only deputy other than me with supervisory powers is Jason Hinkley. He's the chief jailer. Running a jail takes a lot of work with repairs, food, and staffing. Whenever you want, I'll take you over for a look-see. We have a firing range and a garden over at the jail. I guess you know it's just outside of town on a couple acres."

"Let's plan to go over first thing in the morning for a tour and to meet Jason and whoever he has on duty," Pope said.

"I have some personal stuff to take care of over the next couple of weeks, Bill. A lot of the weight will stay on your shoulders like it has been since the sheriff's accident. Sarah and I have to move from San Francisco, get a house near here, and get a church marriage added to our nuptials." The sixty-year-old nodded with understanding and sympathy. He would not want to have to cram a lot of things in the short period of time the new sheriff allotted himself.

Pope sat down in his new office and drafted letters to Hume, Morse, Brewster, Lincoln, Conkling, and

President Arthur thanking them for their supportive telegrams. He advised he was sworn in today and ready to begin enforcing the law.

He went to San Francisco later in the day and met with Hume, who still seemed a bit miffed at his leaving. Pope turned in his badge and a shotgun Sarah had checked out of the armory. He went on to several jewelers until he found one which would craft a sheriff's badge for him. He chose a five-point star with balls on the end of the points. It would have Sheriff across the top of the circle in the center and Marin County, CA below. He chose to have it hammered out of a gold Mexican cinco peso coin like the Texas Rangers used. The jeweler promised to have it sent to him via none other than Wells Fargo within a week. In the meantime, he had his deputy US marshal badge in case he needed to show authority or make an arrest.

Pope gave some thought about how he would approach the job. First off, he would wear a suit, except on a long trail. His experience suggested a California sheriff was a bit more formal than one on the frontier.

He would use his single action Colt .44 with a smaller revolver as backup in an inside the waistband holster. He chose a .44 Webley short, barreled Bulldog revolver, infamously carried in a longer version by Custer seven years earlier, and Garfield's assassin two years earlier. It was not a bad backup, short range weapon and oddly accurate for a short firearm. Pope decided to wear it on the left under his vest.

Remembering the horrendous recoil of Sara's pistol grip-only sawed-off ten gauge, he picked up a used Greener twenty-gauge and had the gunsmith saw off the barrel several inches in front of the fore stock and the butt just behind the pistol grip. It would be a lighter, but friendlier gun to shoot. Like the heavier one, she could carry it in a large purse.

Hume had told him he wanted to meet with Sarah about assignments and reporting schedules during the coming week. He seemed to ignore she was on holiday. Pope would ask her to check on his new badge at Marks and Co. in San Francisco while in the city.

The following day, he and Sarah went to the Presbyterian church in San Rafael and planned a small wedding for ten days hence. Sarah was Protestant but did not bother to tell Pope which particular denomination. Pope believed in God, but most of his religion from his grandfather was slanted to Indian beliefs. They kept quiet about all of this and planned the service with the pastor without any theological discussion.

Within a week, Sarah had met with Hume in San Francisco and Israel Pope had received a lowball offer on the ranch. After discussing the offer with his grandson, he decided to accept it without countering. It was in gold, which had a lot of appeal. Further, it was more than enough to buy the adjacent hundred acres and build a cabin for Pope and Sarah as a wedding gift.

Sarah returned with a portfolio full of cases for primarily Marin and Sonoma Counties. Most were investigating the validity of lawsuit claims against Wells Fargo. One was a stage robbery at the farthest end of her territory. Hume, who did not seem to be angry with Sarah, said he reserved the right to expand her territory whenever needed.

Both Sarah and Pope knew what he was doing was slipping one more experienced detective into Hume's and Morse's longstanding case against Black Bart. The robber had been single-handedly robbing Wells Fargo stages since 1877 and was the only blot on the reputation of the two great detectives.

Sarah also brought Pope his new gold Marin sheriff's badge from the jeweler.

Israel and Millie Pope left for the ranch to be present at the closing. He took the gold and, at his grandson's suggestion, converted it into a negotiable bond. He folded it up and stuck it inside the top of his long johns, somewhere a robber would be unlikely to look for it. He would convert it back to close on the adjacent woodland when it closed several days later.

While the senior Popes were gone, Sarah and Pope met with a local builder. He gave them the price on building a two-bedroom log home with a tin roof. It would have a main room, a storage cupboard, a privy out back and a well. Pope decided to save money and build his own stable for Caesar and a horse for Sarah. The builder would also clear any trees necessary to use a horse-drawn drag to scrape a primitive road in from the main road.

The last thing they needed to do was invite a few people to the wedding. After much discussion, they invited the Lanes. Joe was the Wells Fargo executive whose kidnapped daughter Mattie they had recovered. Millie Pope had served for years as their housekeeper and virtually raised Mattie and her older sister, Martha. Israel came into the investigation and proved a valuable asset. He, Sarah, and Pope all liked the family except for the wife and mother. Harriett Lane was a tough person to like. Millie, who virtually ran the household, was able to moderate her disposition.

Sarah's comment as soon as they found Millie would be marrying Israel was, "The poor family. How will they get along with such a horrible woman without Millie?" Her gracious feelings were somewhat lessened when the pretty young Mattie began to write love letters to John Pope which would have embarrassed a San Francisco Tenderloin madam. Sarah planned to smile directly at young Mattie as she said, "I do." She only shared her plan with Millie.

Millie, who had virtually raised the Lane girls did not say anything initially. Later, she cautioned Sarah against it. "Why add avarice to what should be the happiest day of your life?" she asked.

Sarah thought of the close relationship she and older sister Martha established during the kidnap investigation. Martha had come into her room and climbed into bed to talk and be assured her sister would be returned alive. Sarah realized her action would be unnecessary and hurtful to more than just young Mattie. She also realized it would be petty and beneath her.

Towards the end of the two weeks, their wedding occurred. It was quiet.

Guests included the chief deputy, Hume, Morse, the Lanes, the Kanes.

Young Mattie, now a pretty woman, cried during the ceremony. Nobody but Sarah and Millie took notice as crying at weddings was not unusual. Her mother scowled as was her habit most times. The older sister schemed on how to become one of Pope's deputies.

Weather allowed an outside meal and reception at the cabin.

Kane took his new friend Pope aside.

"John, I have a problem which has just arisen. I may need your help. I don't know whether your assistance will be professional or just personal. But it is highly confidential. I need to swear you to absolute secrecy and ask you follow my lead and not let any law enforcement zeal decide your efforts."

"Michael, it's a pretty tall order. But I will abide by your conditions to help you," Pope promised.

They had walked away from the wedding party and were out of hearing of everyone.

"My wife is not Ogarita Booth. She is an actor who is her best friend. My 'Rita' is really named Sally Hemsworth. The real Rita wanted to drop out of sight and asked my Sally to assume her identity. They look enough alike to be twins. Friends of Rita never picked up on the differences. It gave Sally the opportunity to be a famous actor," Kane said.

"What happened to the real Rita?" Pope asked.

"She is happily living with a new husband out West as Rita with a new last name. What it is does not matter."

"So, Michael, I have not detected what's worrying you yet."

"Herein lies the biggest secret you will ever know but cannot share.

"A reporter in San Francisco spotted and recognized my wife. He wrote an article about Ogarita Booth and her new husband being in town."

"How does it worry you, Michael?" Pope asked.

"Because her father saw it and realized my 'Rita' is not his 'Rita'. He even looked us up and watched us without our knowing it. He knows for a fact I am not married to his real daughter."

"Do you mean John Wilkes Booth is alive and reading San Francisco papers?" Pope asked incredulously.

"Yes. I do."

"You must have been aware of him not being killed in Virginia after he killed Lincoln, then?"

"I was. I reckoned wandering the world, waiting for a bullet in the back or a knife across the throat was a far worse punishment than a hangman's noose. He is virtually a man without a country or without a life."

"If he was identified, could it come back on you?" Pope asked.

"Not if some gunsel or copper in some town identified him. If I identified him to you to arrest, it probably would prompt many questions I wish not to answer in a court of law. It would ruin me. And, ruin Sally," Kane admitted.

"I trust you have a plan."

"I do. I propose meeting with him alone, but with you outside the door. I will tell him the truth. His daughter and her best friend cooked up this identity switch to let Rita disappear. Yet, if the popular actress dropped out of sight, it would cause too many problems. So, with their plan, Rita could marry her beau and Sally, as Rita, could act for a year or two, then marry and drop from the public eye. The plan was better than it may seem on first reflection. Until the troubled Booth showed up. He was an unstable tool used by Lincoln's administration."

"Michael, Robert Todd Lincoln told me much the same. He and General Lafayette Baker believe members of the Cabinet supported Booth and facilitated his getaway and intentionally buried an imposter."

"I am pretty sure it's exactly what happened. Now, don't mistake this—Booth did kill Lincoln. But I think of him as an 'accidental assassin'. He does not have the skills to be a spy as he fancied himself. Shooting an unaware man in the back of the head from a foot away did not take any skill.

"However, in the ensuing eighteen years, he has to have developed skills to avoid being recognized and captured," Kane said.

"What is your opinion of Booth?" Pope asked his friend.

"He is an egomaniac, he is mentally unstable, misguided politically, and has a miserable personality. I was there when he and his daughter met for the first time in her adult life. They did not seem to like each other and parted on less than warm terms."

"I won't ask how you got involved in all of this," Pope said."

"Good. Then, I won't have to lie to a friend."

"When will your, or maybe our, meeting with him happen?"

"It has to in next couple of days. I told him we

were going back to Virginia soon and if he wanted an answer, it would be at our convenience not his."

"If he does not gracefully accept the truth, I fear I will have to kill him in self-defense," Kane said.

"I had the same thought. The problem is he would be identified and how you came to have to shoot him would be a question asked you in court. If you have to kill him, you will have to dispose of his body in such a way it will never be found."

"Then, I will have to plan the meeting in a dark, deserted area."

"Yes," Pope agreed, adding, "You will need at least a buckboard with a big enough bed to handle a body. Is he a big man?"

"He's not as tall as you or I, but still tall. He is medium build. Not an easy body to hide."

"Your story is true. He should accept it."

"He's a nutcase though, John. We will have to play it by ear."

"Let me know when. I will be available."

"Thanks, my friend, I appreciate it," Kane said as they walked back to the wedding party.

"Sheriff, are you hiring any girl deputies?" Martha Lane asked.

"I'm not sure, Miss Martha. I have not really started yet and gotten the lay of the land," Pope replied pleasantly.

"How are your trail riding and shooting skills?"

he asked.

"I can ride. Astride, not sidesaddle. I need to learn how to shoot. Will you teach me?"

"You come out here one weekend, and Sarah and I will do a trail ride and some shooting. She's the better instructor."

"I'm almost nineteen now. What should I buy?" she asked.

"Try some of ours before deciding. It's all about what feels right to you," Sarah answered.

Mattie stood back listening. She was behaving. It was obvious she was going to come along on this jaunt, though it was Martha who had spoken at length with Sarah about going into law enforcement. Pope remembered the two in summer nightgowns in Sarah's bed, talking and giggling. Mattie could be a problem, he feared. Less so since he was not employed by Wells Fargo. She must be almost eighteen he thought.

Both had partnered for the night shift when he was in the hospital recovering from two bullet wounds gotten rescuing Mattie. They had been a godsend with the hours Sarah had spent. Grandpa had sat out front of the hospital with Pope's dog, Scout, on guard all night. They had coalesced like a family. Then, Mattie's teenage infatuation matured into something more graphically serious. She knew Pope had Sarah. But they were not married. They were only ten years different in age. She gave it her best effort. Her frequent letters were informative and mature. They were also lusty as hell. Pope was in a bit of a spot. He hoped the letters would subside with the marriage. Time would tell. The looks she was giving him did not seem to bode well for it to happen anytime soon.

Scout adored Mattie, so at least he kept her busy scratching his ears and telling him what a handsome pup he was. Pope determined to give him some additional beef or venison for a treat tonight. It was not the first time Scout had saved Pope's bacon.

The Kanes were staying at a guest house in San Rafael. Israel took them back in the buckboard. Kane and Pope agreed to meet in the morning. Booth had already come to San Rafael, but Kane was unaware of his whereabouts. The town was small, but he was nowhere to be seen. Both Kane and Pope kept a sharp eye around the church and later the woods near Israel's cabin for the reception. Neither saw the fugitive assassin. Pope decided it would be injudicious to make any inquiries in town and raise curiosity.

Normally, Pope would have enlisted Israel to help watch. Nobody could have been better. But he did not want to involve his grandfather in what had every indication of becoming a criminal conspiracy. One which might end in murder.

People began to leave after the Kanes. The Lanes were next. They were staying in town. The last ferry across the Bay had left hours ago.

Pope and Sarah felt for Joseph, or Joe, Lane and his two daughters having to travel with Harriett Lane. Her expression had become more pinched and intolerant in the months since the kidnapping.

Millie spent some time talking with her former employer. She told her husband, stepson and daughter-in-law later she thought Mrs. Lane was ill. She remembered her as being a stern but tolerable woman. She had gotten much worse in the last two years. Millie ended with saying she felt sorry for her and the people around her but did not miss her mood swings and narrow-minded comments at all.

Pope wondered how a narrow-minded woman could bear such an alarmingly open daughter.

A night deputy came riding fast into the Pope spread around midnight.

"Sheriff! Somebody has shot up the small hotel where your guests are staying. Nobody is hurt, but the shooter got away!"

Israel came out in his night shirt, shotgun in hand.

"Grandpa. There is somebody with a grief against Kane. He told me about it. They could come here. Could you saddle Caesar and one other horse. Saddlebags and canteen, please. And would you kindly stay here and watch out for Millie and Sarah?"

Before Sarah could raise the expected objections about not arming up and riding, Pope was riding at full gallop with his deputy. They cleared the four miles back to San Rafael.

He found Kane patrolling around in the dark with the long-barreled Colt.

"Was it your friend?" he asked Kane.

"I didn't get a good look. I would guess so. Who else is crazy enough to shoot up a guest house in the middle of the night?" he said between clenched teeth.

Pope checked around. Kane said the reports sounded like revolver caliber carbines. Probably one man, but he did not know for sure. The guest house was small and only rented a total of three rooms for guests, with the owners living in it and using the other two bedrooms. It was a Victorian style home and bore the pockmarks now of the shooting.

The sheriff gathered the owners and guests. Most were in night shirts or gowns.

"Mr. Kane and I are going after whoever did this. I am going to leave the night deputy on patrol. Mr. Lane, are you armed?"

The Wells Fargo executive nodded.

"We are seriously understaffed here. All adults are going to have to pitch in. Would you guard your family, except for Martha? Martha, you say you want to be a deputy? Take this backup .44 of mine and go to the Kane's room. I am deputizing you to stay with Miss Rita until we get back. As a famous actress, she may be the target here."

Pope took Martha aside, though her sister accompanied them.

"This is a .44 British Bulldog. If you have to fire, hold it in two hands and squeeze the trigger. It holds five rounds. You do not have to cock it for each shot. Just pull the trigger. It is for close-in work. Mattie, you will be deputy next time, alright?" She beamed and mouthed a kiss in the dark. Pope spun around and left.

He made sure the saddlebags had some coffee and he got biscuits from the guest house. Both Caesar and the spare horse had carbines. Pope had stuck his Dietz police lantern in his saddlebag as well as a pair of nippers before leaving home.

Pope cleared out everyone who had meandered over to the guest house because of the shooting. The lantern showed him what he feared. The onlookers had obliterated any usable tracks. He and Kane found .32-20 brass scattered in the grass outside the house. Most were under a tree. It was definitely the shooting point. There were no additional piles of empties, suggesting one shooter. He found a few prints in a spot where the lookers had not been.

"Michael. Shoe prints. Not boots. Either a hired gun from San Francisco or our man, I'd venture to say."

Pope circled the tree in increasingly wider revolutions until he spotted what he sought.

"Here! There's grass bitten off and some horse dung. This is where he tied his horse. Probably a livery horse since most folks trust their animal to stand, reins down. I can't be absolutely sure, but I think the indication is strong for the livery horse.

"We need to ride over to the livery stable and scout around. If there's a horse there with a saddle still on it thirty minutes later, we need to look for a man trying to hide in the dark and wait until time for the ferry in the morning. The trip around the whole Bay is a long, arduous one. I doubt either a San Francisco thug or your man would want to try it in the dark. If nobody is there, we come back here and take the road northeast. It leads to the next town."

"Let me offer an option to save time, John. You go to the livery and look for clues. I will start on the road north. If I don't see anything before I get to where it also veers off to Sonoma, I will leave you a sign as to whether I went north or east. The only fear is if you are right about him being around the livery, you are searching alone."

"It's a good plan, Michael! Searching alone is what I do. Darkness is my friend. Maybe if you get to the cutoff, wait an hour. If I have not caught up by then, ride on back. It should mean I have somebody in custody."

"It's a deal, my friend. Ride safe and shoot straight!"

Kane spun the horse around and rode at a gallop out of town.

Pope had a shorter distance and rode slowly,

watching for signs the man had been his way. The town street was well-traveled and too hard for Pope to cut sign. He slipped his Winchester '73 out of its scabbard and rode with it over the saddle horn.

When he approached the town's livery stable, he dismounted and left Caesar reins down under a tree.

Pope moved forward furtively, scanning side-to-side before each step.

He heard a horse knicker behind the stable. The sound came from the back corner on the side where Pope was standing. So, he edged around the far side, encountering nobody on the way around. From his new corner he spied a horse standing, still saddled. He eased his way up to the horse. The brown gelding was not winded. He had not been ridden far enough or fast enough to give any sign which would be helpful to the lawman.

What the horse did indicate to Pope, was the probability of his suspect hiding in the immediate area.

He looked around. Pope had completely circled the livery stable and had not seen a soul. It was raining now. The man would want to seek cover. Where? The stable was locked. The rear door leading to a small, fenced corral was also locked. He looked down the alley behind the stable. The next building was a café.

The rear of the café had some boards leaning against the wall of the building.

Pope stood totally motionless and listened. His

sense of smell was hampered by the garbage smell behind the café as well as the smell of used grease. He would have to rely on sight and sound.

He levered the Winchester in the wet silence. The metallic sound of the action opening, the bolt going back cocking the hammer, the lifter raising a cartridge and the bolt being levered down to chamber it carried loudly in the night.

"This is the sheriff. I can fill the area where you are hiding with .44 bullets and kill you deader than hell. Won't take but a couple of seconds. Now, you slide your .32-20 out and crawl out and you will have a nice hot breakfast down at the Marin County Jail.

"Otherwise, your blood will mix in the puddles in the alley as you bleed out. What's your choice? Smart or stupid?"

Pope saw a rifle slide out on the dirt alley. A man came out on all fours.

"Now, lay on your belly and spread your arms out. I am going to approach you and put the nippers on you. You move and you die. No damn questions asked. Die right where you are laying."

The man nodded up and down. Pope approached. He left the carbine leaning against the wall. He knew he could draw his Colt in much less than a second. He pulled the nippers from behind his gun belt.

As he approached, he put one knee down diagonally across the man's shoulders. Pope took one hand and put the clasp of the handcuff on it. Then, he did the other.

"Roll over on your side. Now, get up!"

When the man was standing, Pope patted him down and removed a folding knife and a two-dollar revolver. It was a .22 or maybe a .32. Pope would look at it later.

He whistled and the big horse walked up. Pope recovered his carbine and put it in the scabbard. He looped his lariat around the handcuffs or nippers and did a double wrap around the saddle horn once he was mounted.

"Now walk!"

He walked the man to the sheriff's office and took him inside. The night deputy was there, having just finished one of his several nightly patrols. Pope set the .32-20 rifle, junk revolver, and pocket4knife on the table as the deputy uncuffed the suspect and put him in one of four temporary holding cells.

"Know who he is?" Deputy Honus Rasmussen asked.

"Not yet. Wanted to get him unarmed and in here before it started raining cats and dogs," Pope replied.

He walked over to the cell.

"What's your name?"

"None of your damn business!"

Pope reached between the bars fast as a rattler and grabbed the young man's collar. He pulled him into the bars and punched him with his left fist between the bars. The man staggered back against the cot as Pope let go of his collar.

"Let's try again. What's your name? If you don't answer, I will come inside the cell and lock the two of us in and make you answer."

"Thomas Maupin."

"Where are you from, Thomas?" Pope asked pleasantly.

"San Francisco."

"How old are you?"

"Old enough!"

"Yep, Thomas, you are old enough. Old enough for me to smack hell out of you if you don't answer my question," Pope snarled.

"Eighteen."

"Why did you shoot up the San Rafael Guest House less than an hour ago?"

Silence.

"The offer to come in and lock the cell door and make you talk is still on the table. You have already interrupted my sleep and gotten me soaking wet in the rain. I'd kinda like to question you up close and personal," Pope reminded him.

"They were in there," Maupin said.

"Who is 'they'?" Pope asked, not as pleasantly.

"The Lanes."

"Why did you want to kill the Lanes?"

"I didn't want to kill anybody. I shot to just hit the building with a little .32-20. I knew it wouldn't go through. I just wanted to scare them."

"Why was it you wanted to scare them, Thomas?"

"I asked Mattie out and she said 'no'," he responded. Mattie again.

"So, you wanted to scare them because she did not have interest in you?"

"Yep. Bitch. Said she had an older boyfriend who'd beat me from here to Sunday."

Oh, boy, thought Pope. *the 'boyfriend' kinda just did.*

"Wrap up in the blanket. I don't want you to die of a cold before the judge sees you."

"You gonna arrest me?" Maupin asked.

"Yep. I'm going to wait until I talk to the district attorney to see how tough he wants to make it on you first, though."

Pope walked over to the door and saw Kane, soaking wet, riding into town.

"I was just going to send a deputy after you. I just put a man in custody. It's unrelated to the matter we feared, Michael. Thanks for your help. Try to get some rest. I'll see you in the morning," Pope said to his friend as he dropped him at the guest house.

Pope rode Caesar back to the cabin. He led Grandpa's spare horse Kane had been using.

It was almost dawn. Sarah was still asleep. What a honeymoon night, he thought as he slid in beside her.

******

Sarah had gone to bed alone, something she would have never dreamed would happen on her wedding night. Strong or not, she cried herself to sleep. Their cabin was still not finished. She was in what used to be Pope's bedroom. Israel was sitting on the front porch in the dark, his Winchester across his lap. He was standing guard as his grandson asked, Scout alert at his side. Under the questionable circumstances of parts of the wedding party being shot up, he would have anyway.

Millie heard Sarah and tapped on the door before going in.

"Are you alright?" she asked.

"No, I'm miserable. It's my wedding night and my husband is off working."

"Honey, he has a hotel in his generally peaceful county shot up during his first week or so as sheriff. Of course, he had to go. You of all people should understand it."

"But I usually gun up and go with him!"

"You were his detective partner. Now, you are not a deputy sheriff. You are his wife. He wants to reduce your risk to danger. I think it's a pretty sweet thought on his part. If you think it has anything to do with your ability to shoot or your bravery, you are wrong. You have different jobs. If you get a call about a stage robbery and it's outside of Marin County, he won't go with you. He will trust you to be careful and professional and do your job. You'll see," Millie said.

Sarah smiled. For the first time since the ceremony.

"Thank you, Millie. I know you are right. I guess because Mattie is where he is going worries me too."

"I can tell you, knowing John and Mattie both, he loves you and not a little seventeen-year-old girl. She is with her parents who can control her. You need to work on some trust. You have trusted your life with him, why not your heart?"

Sarah was quiet and thought a while. Millie was right. At the end of the kidnap recovery, the villain pointed his gun at Sarah and was going to pull the trigger and kill her. Pope, with two bullets in him, forced the will to shoot the man in the back of his head and kill him instantly before losing consciousness. He saved her even though it could had caused his own death. Thank God, she thought, it had not, but it was very close. And, the girls, including Martha who she thought of as her little sister, had taken care of her John so she could get much needed rest. Taken care of him during very controlled hospital conditions. Done it very professionally for kids. So the young one cared for Pope. Was she any competition for Sarah? Hell no! Sarah committed herself to worrying about things worthy of her concern. She hugged Millie who then padded silently back to bed. Sarah was asleep soon.

She awoke on a strong shoulder. With a strong arm around her. She smiled before even opening her eyes.

"Good morning, husband. Or should I say Sheriff Husband?"

Pope, still asleep with the two hours he would get for the evening, mumbled something. She kissed him on the cheek. His mustache tickled her nose and she giggled. She took off her nightgown for some real, skin to skin warmth and went back to sleep herself.

Pope awoke later. Sarah was still on his shoulder but had lost her nightgown. He hoped he had not missed something important on this special night. He stroked her back and she purred. Purred in contrast to the Blue Tick hound snoring on the floor beside him. Could it get any better than this? He wondered for a second. Then, he realized it absolutely could not.

He patted Sarah gently on the bottom and went back to sleep.

******

The next morning, it was still raining. He put on his suit and a slicker and rode into his office at San Rafael. The Lanes, minus Harriett were waiting.

"Hi, folks. Long night."

"Are you serious about hiring my eldest daughter as a deputy sheriff? I have plans to send her to college."

"She has spoken with both Sarah and me about

policing. We've tried to give her straight forward answers. The talks have not progressed any further."

"Did you get the shooter, John," Mattie asked, changing the subject away from her sister.

"We did get the shooter. Your shooter, as it turned out. A former suitor named Thomas Maupin." He looked at Lane first and Mattie second. The latter turned crimson.

"I know the young man. He comes from a good family. Will he go to prison?" Lane asked.

"His sentence is up to the judge. He will be found guilty. We have his confession. I expect to dig a bullet out of the guest house and compare it forensically to the rifle I took away from him. I'm glad it was not more powerful. He could have accidentally killed one of you. He did say he figured the little .32-20 would not penetrate walls. I know it can, so he was lucky. So was everyone in the guest house."

"Should I get his father to send a lawyer over?"

"Everybody is entitled to the best defense they can get," Pope said.

"We will be leaving on the first ferry in the morning," Lane said.

"Thank all of you for coming. Sarah and I feel you all are special to us after the kidnapping and helping after I stepped in front of a couple bullets."

"Is Miss Harriett alright?" Pope asked.

"She's in one of her moods," Martha responded

before her father could stop her.

"I hope she gets better," Pope said, concluding his thoughts with the simple sentence.

"We have really missed Millie. She gave a sense of balance to our household," Lane said.

"She is truly a gem beyond compare. She seems very happy living in a cabin in the woods, collecting berries for pies, growing a small vegetable garden, and looking after my grandfather. Trying to keep him from climbing tall trees and jumping wide creeks is a full-time job, and she does it like nobody else could," Pope said.

"Certainly, the impression all of us got seeing her yesterday," Lane said, the two daughters nodding their agreement.

"Does Mattie have to be at the trial to testify, since she knows Maupin?" Lane asked.

"No, I doubt it. I think we have a tight enough case. Of course, anyone is welcome to come and watch it."

"No, I think we have seen quite enough of Thomas Maupin for a lifetime," Lane said as they left. His youngest daughter was quite subdued. Pope reckoned the two girls would sway their father to bring them back, albeit for different reasons.

Maupin was moved to the jail before Pope arrived. He went over to the prosecutor's office and introduced himself. The prosecutor seemed young, but Pope realized he was approaching thirty like Pope himself. They hit it off well.

Pope warned him a likely big shot San Francisco attorney might be coming across the Bay to represent him. They spoke about the fact he was a smart aleck but did not truly resist, said he was trying to scare the Lanes and not hurt anybody and thought his lower power rifle would not penetrate the walls of the house.

The prosecutor suggested aggravated assault and holding drunk and disorderly as a plea agreement with the defense attorney. Both knew he did not appear to be inebriated but thought it may be an acceptable compromise.

A magistrate heard the charges later in the day and sent it "upstairs" to the higher court for adjudication. Not much crime was happening in Marin at the time, so the case was set for a week hence. Pope sent Lane a telegram advising him.

When Pope got back to the office, Kane was waiting for him. They went into Pope's office and closed the door.

"Anything new on your 'father in law'?" Pope asked.

"Yes, actually. He left a note for me at the guest house this morning. He said he hoped we were not harmed in the shooting last night. He may have been in the crowd. Remember, as an actor, he is a past master at disguise.

"He said he would meet us two miles north of town

today. I have already gotten a horse from the livery stable for the ride. Unless you think we need a buggy."

"The use I had in mind for a buggy or buckboard was more of a body disposal nature than we could do in daylight," Pope said. His friend grinned evilly.

"John, he wants to meet at three o'clock. He was insistent I come alone. I don't know how we will hide you."

"Don't worry. I will ride out before two and hide myself. Was he specific about the location beyond just two miles north?" Pope asked.

"Yes, he said by a big oak tree with a branch going all the way across the road."

"I suspect I can find it with no trouble. Just in case, take this police whistle to signal me if you don't want to signal by Colt," Pope said as he handed the whistle from Washington to Kane.

"Sarah is coming into town today to stop by her new office. She should be here anytime. Why don't you go get Rita and we'll eat lunch together? Mind you, I have not told her any details about your matter."

"Sounds like a plan to me!" Kane said and left to pick up his wife. Pope picked up on the Colt and the butt of his Bowie knife printing in the back flap of Kane's suit coat as he walked out of the office. With the badge pinned on his lapel, Pope did not have to worry much about such things anymore. Of course, he never had anyway.

Sarah rode in on horseback a few minutes later, instead of driving Grandpa's buckboard. She tied up outside the office next to Caesar.

"Seen your little girlfriend yet?" Sarah said with a mischievous, though not malevolent grin.

"I have, in fact. She was a bit subdued since the shooter I put in jail last night is one of her disappointed suitors. Stupid kid. May have ruined his life over a teen romance."

"Well, I'll be! The little minx."

"Harriett did not come. Lane all but admitted his wife's moods were sickness related. He said they really missed Millie."

"Well, they have to get past me to get her back," Sarah said.

"You, me, Grandpa, Scout and Caesar you mean."

"Do you have a big day planned?" she asked.

"Not really. I have to ride north on business after lunch. Otherwise, continue to become oriented to the job and the citizens. I still don't know my way around too well. All my visits here to Grandpa have been local to his property. Things like building the cabin, hunting with him and all. I need to know where things are. I have to be able to respond quickly if something happened," Pope said.

"Exactly. Who would have ever believed somebody would shoot up a guest house in San Rafael? Amazing the effect Mattie has on men," Sarah observed.

"Well, boys at least. Soon, I suspect her wiles will affect men. We will see significant effects then." Sarah held her response.

"Is this your official first day at the office?" he asked.

"No. We are still on holiday. But your holiday passed when you resigned. Thank goodness, Hume does not appear to hold the grudge now he did earlier."

"Especially for your sake," Pope said.

"He never seemed agitated with me. Only you. I suspect he was grooming you to succeed him one day."

"I think I'd have to wait thirty years to succeed him. He will signal retirement when his lifeless head hits the desk," Pope said, unaware how prophetic his words would prove to be.

"We have lunch with the Kanes later this morning or early afternoon," Pope said.

"I'm glad. You going to pick me up?" she asked.

"I will. See you shortly actually."

"Well, I am going to arrange my new desk and see what supplies I might need. I have my new, small twenty-gauge sawed-off scattergun in my purse. It's awfully handy. I didn't know they even made buckshot for such a small gauge," Sarah said.

"They do. It's more popular than you might realize. With the reduced recoil, you can get your second shot off faster. And, if you need to touch off both barrels at the same time, it won't fly back and knock you unconscious like the old ten gauge could. I almost wish the ten was a loose powder and shot percussion. Then, we could reduce the powder charge. It was fine when it was four feet long. Whacking off the barrel and stock was a mistake. Made it almost unusable."

Pope's comment gave Sarah an idea. She would look into it later in the day. Perhaps when Pope rode north on whatever mission he had. A similar gun might be handy for a county sheriff. He was a difficult person for whom to choose gifts.

She went on to the office and set up her desk. She had assembled an investigative satchel like Pope's. It had a magnifying glass, sketch pad and pencil, tweezers, small evidence sacks, ruler and measuring tape and more. Pope had surprised her with a Dietz police lantern and metal fuel bottle upon her appointment to the regional detective position. He also urged her to keep her saddlebags filled with coffee, rudimentary cooking gear, a knife and hatchet, ammunition, and a blanket. She already had the shotgun, carbine, and poncho. She was ready to hit the trail. Sarah had watched and helped Pope pitch camp under various and often bad circumstances. She knew how to survive. The weather in Northern California in her counties never got as bad as they had faced on the plains and mountains further east.

She went through her case file at the office. She had six investigations related to claims, either false or exaggerated, against Wells Fargo. Though boring, these legal matters to be investigated were the bread and butter of Wells Fargo detectives. They kept her in a job between stage and train robberies.

Pope walked around town, greeting merchants as they unlocked doors and flipped their signs to "open". He planned to go to each town in the county at this time of day and do the same thing. The two years before the next election would come quickly and he wanted to start off right. More importantly, he thought, it was simply good policing. Even at Martha's age, patrolling San Francisco, he had done the same thing. It paid off for him many times.

During his patrol, he spotted Kane and Rita coming out of the café where they had breakfast.

"All set?" Kane said.

"All set. I'll be heading out before two," he responded, not sure of what Rita, or rather Sally, knew. Kane nodded.

They picked up Sarah for lunch. An hour later, Pope told Chief Deputy Bill Isakson he would be riding north some this afternoon and rode out of town.

He found the tree described as the meeting place. There was a small, but thick copse of trees about a hundred yards further on. He tied Caesar in the middle. Pope took his poncho and carbine. He set up behind a tree facing the meeting place. He was sure Booth, now going as David E. George according to Kane, would not be able to see him or the horse. He put a feed bag with some oats on Caesar. It all but guaranteed the horse would not snicker or whinny.

Pope settled into his hide and waited. Twenty minutes before the appointed meeting time, he saw a small rental carriage called a shay. It was approaching from the direction of San Rafael.

One man was in the two-seater. He wore a black suit. It matched his hair and thick mustache. Pope had seen newspaper photos of Booth. In them, he was a handsome young man with dark hair and a thin mustache. This man was just an almost twenty years older version. He was surprised the man had not used his theatrical talents to disguise himself. Under cover during the kidnapping case, he and Sarah had both used professionally applied disguises. Pope was made to look older and Sarah to look pregnant. Why wouldn't, ostensibly dead or not, the most wanted man in America not disguise himself?

The man climbed out of the shay and tied the reins to the tree. He walked in a circle, checking for watchers hidden by nearby trees and undergrowth. He walked part way to Pope's hide but turned around before getting there.

Almost exactly at three, Pope saw a tall man in black approaching on horseback. He knew from the way he was sitting in the saddle it was Kane.

Kane dismounted and shook hands with Booth. Pope could not hear a word of the conversation.

******

"Wilkes, I came. What's all the hurrah about?"

"I want to know why an imposter is pretending to be my Ogarita!"

"Then, you need to talk to your Ogarita. But I will save you the trouble."

"Go ahead, Kane."

"After the rescue in Mexico, your daughter asked me to help her drop out of sight. She had an idea. Her best friend was an actress who looked passably like her. Her friend was willing to assume her identity and act for a while. After, she planned to fade away. As it ended up, fading away was marrying me. Your daughter is happily living in Texas. She is with the young man she met from the posse."

"Where in Texas?" Booth demanded. Kane was getting more riled by the minute at his demeanor.

"Send the Circle in Dallas a letter for her. They will make sure she gets it. It's not up to me to tell you."

"You sure as hell will!" Booth screamed, almost loud enough for Pope to hear.

"Or, what? You'll make me kill you dead right here, right now?" Kane asked.

Booth reached inside his suit and Kane drew the long barrel Colt and smacked Booth's hand hard with it.

Kane reached into Booth's coat and removed a

Remington revolver. He tossed it into the bushes.

"You had your one chance to draw on me and live. You don't have another. You are looking a gift horse in the face and are too damn crazy to know it. I am helping your daughter hide from the horrendous legacy you laid on her.

"You have three options to consider right this second. One is to consider yourself lucky and ride away, never to contact me again. Two is for me to kill you, make it look like a robbery and I'll ride away. Three, my friend the sheriff could make the greatest arrest in American history and put the man who shot Abraham Lincoln on the gallows. He's just the man for the job. He worked in Washington for Robert Todd Lincoln. The secretary of war would say your trial is an extension of the ones for the conspirators hung at the Navy Yard. He'd pull the lever himself.

"Think fast, Wilkes. I am giving you far more than you deserve. My choice would be to just kill your ass right now."

Booth turned and untied the shay. Booth favored the sore hand. He would return and get his revolver later. Without a word, he rode out of Kane's life.

*****

Once Booth was out of sight, Pope joined his friend.

"I guess it went alright. You didn't kill him."

"No, John. But I wanted to. Really badly. This way he suffers every day the rest of his life for what he did for history. Removing the man who was the hope of America. One day, they'll find his corpse in an alley. Knifed by a thug who wanted his wallet. I doubt he will be identified. He will just be stuck away in a pauper's grave until hell freezes over.

"He is meeting his reckoning now. This will be his hell. And he deserves every suffering minute of it."

"I agree, Michael. Will you ever see him again?" Pope asked.

"Hard to tell. I told him to never contact me again. He's crazy. He may or may not. I'll probably kill him next time."

"I'm sure it will be self-defense," Pope said.

Kane just gave Pope a smile which made even the tough sheriff's blood run cold. They rode back to town and had a whiskey at the local saloon. Kane and Rita left for the train depot shortly after. Pope knew he would see his friend again soon. He had an ominous feeling when he did, it would be to ride against an enemy. An as yet unknown enemy. He did not think it would be Booth. Despite Booth's notoriety, he was not a worthy enough adversary for the two of them.

Pope went by the Wells Fargo office. Sarah had already ridden home, so he followed.

CHAPTER 8

The judge heard testimony carefully guided by a high dollar San Francisco defense attorney. He found Mattie Lane's former suitor guilty of aggravated assault. It was his first criminal offense. He had rounded his age up a few months during questioning. Maupin was still seventeen, so he could not be tried as an adult. The case would be sealed, and he would not carry a criminal record into adulthood.

Pope was fine with the results. A hefty fine was paid by his father. The man gave every indication of planning some serious corporal punishment of his own. Justice would be served, if not even-handed, then hard-handed.

Lane brought both daughters for the trial. Despite Lane's earlier words, Pope was not surprised. He knew the girls would convince him. Mattie was on good behavior, partially because Sarah stayed close during their entire visit.

Martha still wanted to go into law enforcement. Her father still wanted her to go to college, a rare but not unheard of thing in 1883.

Pope, with Sarah close at hand, guided a trail ride on Saturday. They urged the senior Lane to accompany them, and he did. It was the first time the Wells Fargo executive had traveled on a horse instead of behind one for years.

Israel Pope led the procession on a ride through the hills. Then, they headed to the Pacific beaches. Millie did not go, but she saw them off and her picnic lunch accompanied them.

Israel taught the girls how to cut sign. Pope and Sarah rode ahead and out of sight. His grandfather showed them how to recognize broken horse-high twigs and to see hoofprints. He pointed out a slight irregularity in one of Caesar's horseshoes. Israel explained how such details allowed a tracker to differentiate among prints when the trail got "busy", as he called it.

He asked the girls if they smelled anything. Neither did until they concentrated. Both picked up a faint hint of wood smoke in the air.

Israel let them lead the way tracking. Soon, they came to a steep bank, leading down to the ocean. They smelled the smoke stronger, then saw Pope and Sarah below sitting at a fire. Millie's picnic was laid out and the faint whiff of coffee was added to the smoke, beached seaweed and salt air.

The four riders picked their way carefully down the slope to the beach. They dismounted and Pope complimented them on identifying smoke smell.

"Why, John? It's just smoke," Mattie wondered aloud.

"It is just smoke. The key is it's just not a strong smoke smell you were following. We built a Dakota fire pit in the sand. It has a small hole connected by a tunnel to a larger hole with fuel. The fire sucks air through the tunnel from the small hole.

"The air feeds and superheats the fire. The resultant efficiency makes the fire burn with less smoke. It not only makes for a better fire, but one with less giveaway smoke for predators to smell. Especially, two-legged predators," Pope explained.

"Notice John could not dig a tunnel connecting the two pits. So, he dug a trench and covered it with driftwood branches and covered them with seaweed. He accomplished building what the sand would not let him. A tunnel," Israel explained.

"I learned about them early as a trapper. I was trapping in Indian country. Most were my friends, but not all. A small, efficient fire without a lot of telltale smoke saved me many a time, I 'spect," the former mountain man said.

"Did you ever have to fight Indians?" Martha

asked, not knowing much about the famous mountain man's history.

"Ha! I did, lass. When they killed my wife. When they attacked me on the beaver trapline. And, when my boy here," nodding to Pope, "and I rode the retribution trail after the ones who killed his ma and pa and baby sister."

"How old were you, John?" Mattie asked.

"Ten," he answered simply, not wanting to intercede in the master storyteller's yarn.

"John and I tracked a party of about twenty. We knew they were the ones from watching the tribe for a while. We set up an ambush and killed them all. Split pretty evenly between the boy and me. We scalped them and took the scalps back to the tribe. We presented them to the chief.

"I watched my boy. He was looking at the scalps hanging on the tent. One was reddish. It was his ma's. He couldn't tell his pa's. Then, I saw a change come over his face as he spotted a small, long blonde haired one. His little sister. He looked at me.

"I didn't have to nod. We already developed a way to communicate with looks and nothing more. You might have noticed we still do it.

"My boy raised his Henry rifle and shot the chief between the eyes. Then and there. Stone cold dead."

Sarah felt a cold chill as she heard the term "stone cold". She had described Pope with it several times during their relationship.

Neither the girls nor the father spoke. The story struck them hard. Pope had heard this story recounted more in the last few weeks than in the ten years preceding added together. He reckoned it was the legacy which made him Pope.

"Sarah and I both have had to fight Indians, even in the past year. There are good Indians and bad ones. Just like any group of people. I do not hate Indians at all. I respect them and particularly the way their religion revolves around nature and faith and trust. Overall, I might even like them more than my own people.

"Except for the ones sitting around the fire here, right now. Add Millie and you have the ones most special to me," he said quietly in an admission so unlike the stoic, taciturn gunfighter.

Sarah had not thought she could love her husband more until then. The same was true for both young women drinking in the story and hearing his last admission.

They had fried chicken, cheese, fresh rolls and Millie's wild berry pie for lunch. Sarah made strong, rich campfire coffee rivaling the coffee of her two favorite men sitting there.

After lunch, Pope found a driftwood log and lined it up along the bottom to the slope. He placed some empty peach cans he brought on it, spaced a foot apart.

Sarah placed her .38 S&W and the .44 Bulldog Martha had used to protect Rita Kane on the picnic blanket. Pope surprised her when he added his finely tuned Colt Frontier Model beside them after removing the cartridges. He sat a box of .44-40's beside the .38 S&W cartridges and the .442 Webley ones.

"Now, we are going to have some basic marksmanship instruction. I had the honor of being the female shooting instructor for Pinkerton's," Sarah began.

"A couple of ground rules first. Always assume a gun is loaded when you pick it up. Don't let the muzzle or end of the barrel cross anything you don't want to shoot. Keep your finger off the trigger until you are ready to shoot. And make sure you know what your target is and what's behind it if you miss or penetrate it. Makes sense?"

"It seems automatic to put your finger on the trigger when you pick up a gun, doesn't it?" Mattie asked.

"It does, honey. You just have to overcome the tendency. Now, for aiming, line the front sight bead up even in the rear sight groove. Some people like to put the bead in the middle of the target. I always put it at a six o'clock position. I don't like anything to hide my target.

The two smaller guns are double-action. Double-action means pressing the trigger both cocks and fires them. For more precise shots, you can manually cock each. The benefit is it reduces the pressure necessary to fire and the time during which your front sight can sway off the target. However, in a gunfight, unless the person is pretty far away, you generally don't have time to do it. So, you press the trigger straight back until it goes 'bang'."

She taught the two how to check to see if each gun was loaded and got them to handle all three. Though Mattie gravitated towards the big Colt for less-than-subtle reasons, the smaller two fit their hands far better and were simpler to operate.

Sarah had Martha load the .38 first and fire five shots single action. She came close to each target but did not knock a can over.

Mattie went next. She hit two of the three cans.

Sarah offered Joe Lane the opportunity to shoot, but he was having too much fun watching his daughters. She coached each girl until both could knock over all the cans.

Sarah then graduated them to the British revolver Pope carried as a backup.

"Sarah, the barrel is so short. It won't be as accurate will it?" Martha asked.

"You've made a very logical assumption, Martha. Let me answer it in two parts. One, a short barrel makes it harder to shoot, but no less accurate. Second, Webleys are known for being uncannily accurate. There's just something about them. To our American eyes, they are kind of awkward looking. But, somehow, they shoot like a barn afire. Try and see."

Martha, then Mattie, proved Sarah right. Both shot the larger caliber English gun slightly better than the .38.

They graduated to Pope's single action. Sarah made them use both hands, due to the grip size and additional recoil. Both loved it, though neither shot it as well as the Webley.

"John and Sarah, won't you all shoot?" Mattie asked.

Sarah picked up Pope's .44 and fired five times as quickly as she could. She knew she was literally seconds behind what her husband could do.

"What a fantastic display, Sarah! How long have you been shooting?" Joe Lane asked.

"I started hunting food for the family in Illinois when I was about twelve or so. Revolvers were much later. Actually once I joined Pinkerton's," she added.

"John, how about you and Mr. Pope?" Martha asked.

"From my standpoint, it's Sarah's show, Martha. There's nothing I could show you she hasn't already."

The group turned to Israel Pope. He whipped out his large Bowie knife and threw it from the same distance they were shooting. The blade penetrated the sixth can and pinned it against the dirt slope.

"Just remember, a gun is not your only option," he said as he retrieved the Arkansas masterpiece and wiped the blade clean.

As Sarah repacked the lunch containers and put the food out for seagulls, Pope poured seawater in the fire pit and covered both pits with sand.

"Some folks say 'leave nothing but footprints'," Israel Pope cautioned the girls.

"I say, 'don't leave anything for somebody tracking you to find'!"

"John, can I be a deputy?" Martha asked. "A full-time deputy on the payroll," she clarified.

"You and your father need to work out your future. Education is important. You all need to figure out if college is what you need to do and the rain and long trails and danger of being a peace officer is truly what you want," he said gently.

Sarah walked between the two young women and hugged them both at the same time.

"You listen to John. He's not just the handsomest gunfighting sheriff in America, he's pretty wise, too." She did not get any argument from her fellow distaff pistoleers.

They mounted and returned to the town. Along the way, Israel pointed out types of trees and birds and potential water sources. Sarah kept silent, learning many new things herself.

They parted at the guest house in San Rafael, its bullet pockmarks now filled.

Each Pope led a horse back as they rode home, concluding it was a good day.

Sarah felt better about her attitude regarding Mattie. She and Martha had bonded during the kidnap investigation and today's experience just drew them closer.

******

Progress continued on the cabin. Pope picked up an iron swing arm for the fireplace and a cookstove with a small oven. He and Sarah took the buckboard to several nearby towns and found a rope bed, mattress, table and chairs and a pair of wardrobes. A couple of braided rugs completed their purchases. They brought cookware and plates from their rooms in San Francisco.

Finally, a week and a half after the Lanes' visit and ride, they moved into their cabin. It was close enough to Israel's to share the corral.

The last addition was a mare for Sarah. They carefully chose a mid-size gray with endurance, no reaction to close gunshots, and good obedience. It was a lot to expect from a very young horse, but with a little guidance from her former cowboy husband, would fill the bill.

Sarah named her Kate, after Kate Warne. Warne was the first female detective in America, if not the world. She ended as the supervisory female detective for Pinkerton's She died at only thirty-five years old.

Sarah never knew her. Warne died twelve years before Sarah joined Pinkerton's. She always thought Allan Pinkerton wanted her to be the next Kate Warne. Sarah just wanted to be herself and not a reincarnation of anyone.

Sarah often wondered about the judgement of her brilliant former leader. He buried Kate Warne in the family plot. It was not a precedent, though, as other Pinkerton detectives had already been buried in there.

Sarah learned of Pinkerton's last big project during her visit to the Pinkerton offices in Chicago with Pope. He was organizing all the criminal records he could amass into a national database. He made great headway before his death and the massive file was continued by another odd little man in Washington less than fifty years later.

Despite Pinkerton's eccentricities, Sarah held him in high esteem due to his brilliance and the opportunities he gave her.

New houses, especially cabins, have their own particular smells. Sarah took a long sniff and picked up strong cut wood and leather. Smoke from the fireplace would add to it as the weather got cooler. When she cooked in the cabin, she did with all the windows open for the saving cross ventilation. Sarah did not plan to keep them open in cold weather. A little smoke smell beat freezing, she thought.

This was both her and Pope's first home deeded in their names. Over the weekend, she and Millie worked on curtains. They got Pope to hang them. Maybe one day a fancier duvet would cover their wool Hudson Bay blanket on the bed. But neither Sarah nor John cared. They both had the right partner, right home and right job. They lived in the woods, but reasonably close to work. The weather was temperate. They had enough land, as part of Israel's total holding, to keep neighbors at bay.

Millie had already started a garden. It was larger than she wanted to handle, so Sarah agreed to work half, and they would share the crops equally.

Sarah felt she had finally slipped into the fulfilling life she always wanted. She knew she was a pioneer as a woman detective. She did not even consider she was also as a housewife and professional woman.

******

Pope was comfortable in his new life also. He worried he would get bored because the pulse throbbing adventure of riding after outlaws was missing. The challenge of besting them in a draw down on the street or trail. He missed setting up camp and surviving under the harshest circumstances. He loved the outdoors and the cold, the snow and rain and being trail weary did not concern him. He just considered it what he did. Who he was.

Pope mentally kicked himself for lamenting the lessened excitement. He had more adventures in less than thirty years than most men in a long lifetime. Pope knew he should be content riding patrol, training deputies and serving the public. He could not have had a more wonderful wife he came home to every night. He got to spend his non-working hours with his legendary grandfather. Nobody ever had a better best friend than the two Popes.

He kicked himself again as he talked with Caesar. They were riding west towards the ocean. Caesar was not terribly supportive of his feelings. He was just supportive of being with his master and having his friend, Scout, running along beside him. Pope had started taking Scout with him most places. The dog proved to be one of the most popular members of the sheriff's office. Children and adults alike stopped to pet him and talk to him. Little did they know the gentle, sometimes comical canine, had saved his master's life and was an outstanding trail dog.

Like old times, Pope rode along munching a piece of jerky. He tossed part down to Scout. He was on the trail with two of his best friends. It was shirt and vest weather with a cool wind as fall approached Northern California.

A whitetail doe crossed the trail ahead of them and Scout took off in hot and loud pursuit. Pope grinned.

He loved the sound of a good hound on the trail. And fresh venison. He let this one go and decided he and Grandpa should go out and bring home a couple bucks soon. The season was almost right for hunting, though he knew the mountain man preferred tracking dinner in the snow.

Pope whistled for Scout, who returned disappointed his pursuit had been cut short.

They stood on the precipice overlooking the Pacific. It was the spot where everyone carefully rode their horses down during the trail trip with the Lanes.

Pope did not give any particular thought to the frisky younger Lane as he looked out. He was here for a reason.

A constituent told him there was odd activity in this area. Small boats rowing in from larger ones offshore.

Offloading materials on the beach, where other men waited. Then, the men on the beach hauling the probable contraband up the steep slope and away.

With ports nearby, this practice was surely some sort of smuggling. Drugs perhaps, more likely items bypassing trade tariffs. He would like to catch them in the act.

Pope had his deputies stop by here on a frequent basis patrolling.

So far, the beach had been empty, on everyone's checks. Pope doubted the deliveries would be made during darkness. The landing of a small boat in the surf was treacherous on a bright, calm day. As was transiting the steep clifflike slope up from the beach. Especially when one was hauling a load uphill.

The sheriff determined he and his deputies would continue watching. It would come together when it was time. Patience would pay off. Pay off as it did with most things legal and illegal.

Pope enjoyed the solitude. He took in and savored the smells and sound of the surf for a while. He had to force himself to turn Caesar back towards San Rafael.

He wanted to swing by Sausalito before calling it a day, so the three headed southwest. Pope stopped at a spot on a high cliff. It was at the northernmost Marin Headlands and overlooked San Francisco. He saw the ferry coming and Alcatraz Island between the point and the city beyond. Turning seaward, the view was magnificent as the Pacific stretched out, seemingly to infinity.

Pope turned Caesar towards Sausalito and rode on, doffing his hat in town as they rode through. He liked the job Marks Jewelers had done crafting his new gold sheriff's badge. It glinted at every speck of sunlight as he rode down Caledonia Street slowly before leaving the town and heading for San Rafael some eight miles away.

He checked in at the office. There was nothing of great importance for him from the chief deputy regarding goings-on in Marin County. Pope headed for the hills and home.

******

The next morning, Pope rode to Tiburon after court.

Sarah went to her office and began laying out a route for investigative trips related to claims against the company.

Midmorning, the telegrapher called out for her and said she had a "Most Urgent" telegram coming in from Wells Fargo headquarters. She knew it would be from Hume.

"Should I decipher it?" he asked.

"Yes, please," Sarah replied.

Several minutes later, he brought the plain language version over. He had transcribed it in readable cursive. Telegraph operators were required to be able to always write in a clear hand so there were no mistakes.

"Black Bart robbed stage halfway between Schellville and Napa on the Napa Road. The driver thinks he winged robber. He hacked a mark on a tree close to the road at robbery site. Respond with all due haste and begin crime scene review. Unknown whether location is in Sonoma or Napa county. Do not advise sheriffs. Morse and I are on the way. Hume."

"This is it," she thought. "My big one. Alone." Sarah felt very odd in not asking Pope to accompany her. She knew, though, it was a credibility moment for her. Despite her experience as a detective, this was a major opportunity to prove herself.

"Wire Hume back. Say I am on the way now." She looked at the big Northern California map on the wall. It was twelve miles between the two places.

The trip up to Schellville appeared to be about twenty-four miles. It would take her two or two and a half hours with Kate going as fast as Sarah would want to push her for the distance.

She changed from her dress to the riding skirt, blouse and vest she kept at the office. She put on both guns and pinned her badge on the vest. Going out to the hitching rail, she placed the new sawed off in the front holster she had a tackle maker craft for her.

Sarah knew she had her investigative kit, Dietz lantern, and extra ammunition in one saddlebag and camping and cooking gear and some food in the other. She stopped at the café and picked up some biscuits and sliced meat.

Riding past the sheriff's office at a fast trot, she saw Caesar was not there. Pope must have left for Tiburon already.

She picked up the speed a bit once she got out of town. Like Pope, she had begun to talk with her horse and planned her strategy aloud for the next two hours and fifteen minutes.

Schellville was small enough she passed through it without slowing down. She calculated she should start looking for the scene in about half an hour.

She slowed Kate a bit and began to watch for a man on foot as well as the scene.

Morse and Hume had developed a profile of the man known as Black Bart over the past seven years.

The stage robber always operated alone, though he used painted, tapered sticks as fake rifle barrels pointing at the place where he stopped his stages. These were the illusionary rifle barrels he claimed were covering passenger as well as Wells Fargo jehus and shotgun messengers. Nobody in twenty-eight robberies had ever seen his face. He was a short man, dressed as a workman. He always had a feed sack over his head. It had cutouts for eyes and mouth.

He left or recited a poem several times during his robberies.

Though he wielded a full-length double-barreled shotgun, he had never fired a shot in his many robberies. He preyed almost always on Wells Fargo stages. His *modus operandi* was to break off the green treasure box's padlocks.

Sarah scanned the road and left and right as she rode. She slipped the new twenty gauge from its holster hanging off Kate's saddle horn. This would be the arrest of a lifetime, she thought. Sarah was unaware Pope had turned his back on the opportunity to make the greatest arrest in American history only a week ago. He would never tell her. She did not have a need to know.

Soon, she came to a place with rifle barrels behind a tree and several bushes. She knew they were a ruse, but dismounted Kate and circled around the clump with two barrels and approached, shotgun at the ready.

As she thought, they were fakes. Props used to scare victims into thinking they were surrounded. Sarah circled the area and began her search for clues and evidence.

There was every possibility the famous robber and his shotgun were still in the immediate area. She did not know what transportation he had or how badly he was wounded. Or, if his wound was just a hope on the part of the Wells Fargo driver or jehu. She wondered why it was he instead of the shotgun messenger. He may just want to be known as the man who shot Black Bart. One of the detectives needed to ask him why he shot the robber.

It took Sarah a while to clear the area and feel confident Black Bart was nowhere close. She put her shotgun in the holster since the description was more apt than scabbard.

Removing her notebook, she began her crime scene sketch. She wrote the location as closely as she could in the upper right corner and drew the road and, using her compass, included the direction. Sarah left the box undrawn until she searched the area. She did not want evidence to fall outside the box she drew around the main scene. She put an X where it appeared the stage had stopped. A clue was one, ten-gauge empty shotgun shell. The shotgun messengers always reloaded as soon as possible after firing, having only two rounds before resorting to less effective revolvers.

She made a note to ask if the jehu had handed the shotgun back to the shotgun messenger who had reloaded.

Sarah placed the empty shell in a small evidence sack and continued her search. The treasure box was not there. Apparently, either the driver took it onwards with the stage to Napa or the robber took it. There were no other horse tracks in the area. Black Bart had never been identified with using a horse to reach or leave a robbery. Sarah deduced the driver took the treasure box on the stage. Had Black Bart actually gotten any treasure, or valuables carried in the treasure box? Or had he been shot, and the robbery interrupted?

She did find a broken padlock. The lock answered her question. She noted its position beside the road on her sketch and put it into an evidence sack also.

Sarah circled in a fifty-foot radius of the stage's position. She found footprints. The shape of the toe and heel suggested shoes to her rather than boots. They were not deep, even in a patch of soft loam. She noted the man was not very large, which also fit the profile for Black Bart. She tried to track him but lost the trail after a hundred feet into the scrub. Where were the two Popes when you needed them?

At the point where she lost the footprints, she found what would prove the greatest clue of all. A handkerchief with specs of blood on it. It was still twisted as if it had been bound around something. She surmised it had been used as a bandage wrapped around a hand, wrist or ankle.

She marked the find and used a rock to hold it in place until Hume arrived. Sarah noticed a laundry tag safety-pinned to one corner. This one clue, she knew, was how they would find and end the stage robbing career of Black Bart, whoever he was.

Sarah could hardly contain her excitement.

Using the paced off distance from the find to the stage, she drew a line between the two. Sarah then scribed the outer boundaries of the box for her sketch. She carefully paced the length and width and included those measurements by the lines of the boundary.

She dated and signed the sketch and ate something while waiting for the two senior detectives.

They arrived in a rented carriage and she reviewed her sketch and walked them around the crime scene. They stopped and examined the handkerchief and its laundry mark. Hume told her it was important. Morse offered to track it down but asked for Sarah and perhaps five other detectives to assist. If Black

Bart was based in San Francisco like both Hume and Morse thought, they had to visit each of hundreds of laundries until the owner of the small rectangle of cotton was found.

Hume concurred. They stopped by the cabin on the way back to the ferry. Sarah told Millie what was going on. Millie told Sarah, Israel was on the way back from an errand and would unsaddle, rub down and feed Kate.

Sarah packed several days' worth of clothes in a valise and left with the very excited Hume and Morse in the carriage.

"I think, after all these years, we've got him, Jim!" Morse exclaimed.

"I do, too. Thank heavens you walked a wide perimeter, Sarah," Hume said.

"I did, but actually found the handkerchief at the point where I lost his trail while tracking him. It was frustrating losing his trail. As you have always maintained, he does not appear to use a horse or mule. There would have been some sign of dung, chewed grass or tracks. But there was nothing indicating a horse. When I was riding out, I watched both the road and the surrounding land for some sign of one man walking or hiding. Nothing. Not a thing at all. I believe he walked towards woods.

"He will probably lay low for a few days. I sure would like to know how hard he was hit and where,"

Sarah said.

"I would also. Changing back to the handkerchief, those tags are more indicative of a San Francisco Chinese laundry. Ones in Sausalito, Oakland, or other towns or cities on either side of the Bay are different, though I don't understand why. Your evidence, Sarah, will solve this seven-year case. I know it will," Harry Morse said.

Though they were late getting back to the office, Hume insisted they lay out a search grid on a San Francisco city map in his office. The grid would be for ten searchers. Morse offered additional of his men to add to Hume's. Hume would stay in the office and coordinate and Morse would be the senior person in the field for the search. Sarah would accompany Morse.

By ten o'clock, they had concluded their plan and Hume had the night manager flag a hansom cab to take Sarah to a hotel. She checked in for several days, suspecting she would have to extend her stay beyond her reservation.

She slid a small wooden wedge under the door to keep someone with a passkey from entering. Sarah placed her short shotgun beside the bed and stripped. She was asleep almost as soon as her head hit the pillow.

In Marin County, Pope proudly received her message from Millie as the two men sat down for dinner.

"Sounds like Missy did everything right," Israel commented. Pope nodded, wondering if he should take a day and go to San Francisco.

"I wouldn't, it's her play," Israel preempted Pope's question. "She was a Pinkerton detective going undercover and arresting people before you met her. She will be with Harry and with Hume. Don't worry. She's a big girl."

"She wasn't a wife then, Grandpa."

"Being a wife didn't make her lose her edge, honey," Millie quickly said.

Pope nodded and his thoughts drifted. He wondered how quickly he would solve whatever was going on over on the beach. He would go over there first thing in the morning.

"Another great meal, Millie! Scout and I are going to check the horses. Y'all have a good night," he said to Israel and Millie.

The sheriff and his dog walked outside. The night was cool. He checked on his grandfather's four horses and mule as well as Caesar and Kate.

He built a small fire in his cabin fireplace, let it burn a while as he stared into it.

Eventually, Pope banked the fire for the night and climbed into a cold bed. He still watched the glowing embers until he drifted off to sleep. The place was really starting to feel like home. The only thing missing was a raven-haired beauty.

The next day, he checked in at the office and rode out towards the beach to see what may be going on. As he approached, he saw a bald eagle. His spirit animal. It soared high. He heard its call. Pope took it as a good omen.

He arrived at the beach and saw it was deserted. Knowing no pick up team would approach with him there, he and his horse and dog slipped into the woods and waited.

After an hour, he rode out and went back to the office. He checked the reports for yesterday and last night. The deputy on day patrol checked the beach and did not have any sightings either. Pope wondered how frequently drugs would be delivered by ship. He assumed the largest market and probable end point would be San Francisco.

"Why not bring them directly into port?" he wondered. The port security was not extremely tight. Or at least it wasn't a few years ago when he was with the San Francisco Police Department.

He telegraphed his old boss, now Detective Lieutenant Howell.

"Ships dropping off contraband on Marin coast. Using small boats to bring in to deserted beach. Heroin? Ideas? Sheriff John Pope, Marin County."

Howell did not reply until late in the day.

"Sheriff? When did you leave WF? Supplies of heroin and hashish are way up here."

Pope grinned. Howell was a good man. He fully believed he taught Pope everything he knew about being a detective. More was about how to wrap up cases solved or not and how to make money off the job. The latter, at least, did not involve being on the take.

Not conclusive, but supportive, Pope thought.

******

Sarah completed her first day of interviewing laundries. Mostly Chinese. Many did not speak English, or at least not very well.

Hume had a photograph made of evidence laundry tag FXO7 Sarah had found. He had copies printed of it and distributed to his detectives on the case and those of Harry Morse.

Even in situations where the laundry owners Morse and Sarah were interviewing did not speak English, they communicated effectively by shaking their heads when shown the facsimile of the tag.

Hume maintained a master sheet on the laundries interviewed.

On the fourth day, Morse and Sarah hit pay dirt. It was the total teams' three hundred fifty-seventh laundry interviewed.

They got a nod instead of a shake of the head.

While Sarah waited, Morse found the only Chinese

detective he employed. A man he considered his best detective.

Morse hoped the laundry owner spoke Mandarin like Detective Lee.

They quickly found out the two were able to communicate, though not easily. Their dialects were different.

Lee turned to Morse and said, "This tag is one for a Charles Bolton. He lives at a hotel where Mr. Wong delivers his laundry. He does not know the name but will take you there."

"Tell him it will be worth his time."

Lee told the man, who took off his apron and made ready to leave.

"Harry, this has been your show more than anybody's for about eight years. Why don't you make the arrest? You deserve the glory. Lord knows John and I owe you for the way you have supported the two of us since we've known you," Sarah said.

Lee asked the laundry owner to describe the customer. Lee told Morse and Sarah he was a small, older man perhaps in his sixties and dressed extremely well. He said the suits he cleaned for Bolton were of the highest quality.

"With the money he made robbing stages, I damn well bet they are!" Morse said, immediately apologizing for cursing in front of a lady. Sarah shrugged and brushed it off.

"Why don't you two go with us to the hotel? If he's there, I will arrest him and take him to Jim Hume. If not, we'll work out a stakeout plan to catch him when he returns." Both agreed it was a good approach.

They walked four blocks. The laundry owner stopped in front of the Webb House Hotel and pointed.

"I guess we're here," Lee noted.

"Let me go in and inquire about him," Sarah said. "I will pretend to be his niece."

At the very moment, a man walked out in a suit and bowler hat. He had a walking stick, diamond stick pin, diamond ring, and they were to later find, gold watch.

The laundry owner became very excited and started saying, "Bolton! Bolton!"

Bolton turned to go back in, but Sarah drew fast and yelled, "Freeze, Black Bart!"

Shocked, the man froze in his tracks and Lee handcuffed him.

Bolton flinched as the handcuffs were put on and Lee found a wrist was heavily bandaged from where jehu McConnell had fired and nicked him on the wrist with a rifle.

Lee proceeded to frisk him as Sarah put away her .44. He was completely unarmed. Not even a penknife. The laundry owner returned to his business, fifty dollars in gold richer from Harry Morse. The three detectives walked the man, who looked like a wealthy businessman, to Wells Fargo headquarters.

Sarah made sure Hume was in his office and congratulated Harry Morse. Lee returned to Morse Detective Agency and its owner walked the man known as Bolton into James Hume's office.

"Chief Detective James Hume, may I present my prisoner, Charles Bolton. He is otherwise known as Black Bart, the poet stage robber," Morse announced.

The door was open, and the detectives present in the bull pen let out a cheer. Almost eight years of investigating. Now an arrest was made by one of the nation's most respected detectives.

Hume rose in his seat and approached Bolton.

"Mr. Bolton, I have been looking forward to this moment for a long time. You have been a thorn in the side of Wells Fargo and to my friend Morse and myself. Specifically, since July of 1875. You have robbed some twenty-eight of our Concords.

"Please sit down so we can get to know you."

The prisoner sat and the three conversed for several hours. He was not interrogated. The talk was more the nature of three old school friends getting caught up after not seeing one another for some time.

They found the man's name was really Charles Boles, he was a fifty-five-year-old war veteran and great poetry fan. He carried a shotgun yet never used it. Subsequent searches of his room and storage found the shotgun. It was a breech loader whose hammers were permanently frozen in the cocked position and totally inoperative. The only thing working was the barrel wedge which allowed Boles to break the old gun down to carry in a duffle bag when walking to robbery sites. He admitted he was terrified of horses. He rode the ferry across San Francisco Bay and walked to each robbery site. Sometimes, he said larger hauls of gold coins were difficult for him to transport back to the city.

After advising the district attorney's office who they had in custody, they turned him over to the San Francisco Police to hold until trial.

Boles, because he was sixty (he had lied about his age) and had never harmed anyone, was sentenced to six years at San Quentin State Penitentiary. His charge was one count of armed robbery. He was not charged with the other twenty-seven. No treasure from the robberies was ever recovered. A model prisoner, he would be released four years later and would literally drop off the face of the earth.

After considering him the spawn of the devil for eight years, Hume and Morse candidly admitted to each other over whiskeys the night of the arrest how charming a gentleman Charles Boles was.

Sarah felt good about Harry Morse getting all the credit. He devoted eight years to chasing Black Bart. He deserved the addition to his already national fame sure to follow capturing the stage robber. There would be other stage robberies and train robberies, but Sarah thought, there would never be another Black Bart.

Morse Detective Agency expanded greatly from the fame of its founder. Probably far more than Harry Morse wanted. He did not want to be a large business owner. He loved solving crimes. No one would be more famous at it until he was surpassed worldwide by a fictional London detective with an odd hat four years later.

CHAPTER 9

Sarah was glad to come home, especially with a feeling of a job well done. She had ridden hours alone, found her site, done a perfect crime scene sketch and search and had found the clue resulting in the arrest of one of the most sought-after outlaws in the West.

To cap it off, she had assured the credit went to the detective who deserved it the most. Nobody had put in the work to capture Black Bart like Harry Morse.

Pope agreed with her when she shared the story over dinner with the rest of her new family. He got up and hugged her with pride.

She couldn't help tease her husband by quoting Morse who said, "When you drew on Boles when he was heading back into the hotel, I'm not sure even Pope could have whipped out a .44 any faster!"

Instead of taking it as a jab, he was filled with even more pride. She truly was one of the best detectives in America. Not best woman detective. Simply one of the best. Period.

For the first time, he shared his case about potential drugs coming in from offshore. He was stumped as to the frequency cycle of deliveries and how the contraband was being moved from the remote cliff to San Francisco. Until he was able to watch the operation unseen, there seemed little he could do to stem the flow.

Slightly bored without a ranch to run, Israel offered to ride out and "take a look see", every other day. Pope accepted the offer and made sure his deputies knew who the new player in their surveillance game was.

By the time something broke, they were all wearing coats to combat the chill coming off the Pacific.

It was Israel who rode to the coast and saw a wagon and team sitting unattended near the spot they had ridden down with the Lanes several months before.

He made sure nobody saw him when he rode into nearby woods and dismounted.

Israel furtively moved to the edge of the woods and crawled to the cliff and peered down. He saw four men waiting. A wooden longboat was being rowed in by two men. It had packages piled in the stern.

He saw the four waiting men offload the packages. Israel counted twenty. The men carried them two at a time up the steep slope and piled them at the top.

It was clear to the elder Pope they did not want to

put them in the unattended wagon a hundred yards away from the edge.

As the men passed, he saw they were Asians. He guessed Chinese but could not be sure. He had heard about Tongs running crime in San Francisco and thought this may be an example.

He watched as the boat rowed half a mile offshore to a waiting ship and was cranked aboard davits. The ship, which Israel thought must be about a hundred fifty feet, steamed off as the men on the beach completed their job.

Moving through the woods like the frontiersman he was, Israel watched the men throw a tarp over the bed of the wagon and ride off. They went south.

He followed close enough to not lose them and far enough to not be seen. He knew trailing like he was constituted a slippery slope of risk.

The wagon went into Sausalito in late afternoon. He saw it disappear behind a restaurant.

Israel tied his horse to a hitching rail and casually walked down the street. He noted the name of the restaurant and returned to his horse and rode to San Rafael.

"Got your smugglers, Sonny. Watched them unload from a ship and haul twenty packages to Sausalito. They went behind this restaurant," handing Pope a scrap of paper with the name.

Pope and his grandfather went straight to the

district attorney. He went with them to the judge on duty and they secured a search warrant.

Pope knew darkness was falling shortly. He took a deputy coming on night shift and they rode down to Sausalito. Horses tied down the street, Pope and deputy, Will Nickels, found a good place to watch and set up surveillance from a hundred feet away. Nothing happened during the night.

Knowing the contraband was still intact, they watched for the manager and a couple of employees to arrive.

Pope sent Nickels around back in case there was a runner.

Pope knocked on the locked door. The manager came and Pope showed him the search warrant.

He pushed through the three men and headed for the storeroom. Before he got to the door, he heard a revolver cock.

Pope ducked to the side and spun to face the noise. He saw one of the men his grandfather described aiming an old Colt converted to cartridges at where he had been.

Pope drew and fired before the man could re-aim.

Off balance, Pope's shot hit the man in the shoulder. He dropped the gun and went down. The other two froze.

Nickels kicked in the back door and came in, revolver at the ready. They restrained the two men and let the wounded one lay for a minute.

The bundled contraband appeared to be hashish for the illicit hookah dens in San Francisco and a large amount of heroin.

Pope arrested the two and had them carry the wounded man out the front door. Pope guarded them while Nickels went for a doctor and the chief deputy. Later, he sent Howell an advisement telegram about the arrest and the contraband.

The next day, Detective Lieutenant Howell arrived from San Francisco. He had a US attorney and two deputy marshals in tow.

"Hey, Boss!" Pope greeted his old mentor. "What's with the cavalry here?" he asked Howell.

"Looks like you broke up something big. The customs folks and US Attorney Bey here have been trying to catch these fellas for a while."

Bey shook hands and introduced the two deputies.

"Sheriff, have you arrested these men?" Bey asked.

"Only for custodial purposes. I have not specified a particular crime pending searching the restaurant where we found them when serving a search warrant. One tried to get funny and he's recovering at the doc's office. We don't have a hospital in the county yet."

"We might have to re-arrest them on federal charges."

"Go ahead, but I'm still sworn as a deputy US marshal," Pope said.

"To whom? The Northern District of California US Marshal?" Bey asked.

"Nossir. To Attorney General Brewster."

"What? How did he swear you?"

"I was a special investigator for him on an attempted assassination of the president. He asked me to keep the badge and stay sworn in case he needed me for another case."

Pope reached into his wallet and showed Bey his badge and warrant as deputy marshal.

"Well, I guess we don't have to re-arrest them. Just specify the charges of conspiracy to distribute narcotics and importing without customs stamps.

Did you get a look at the ship?"

"No, my grandfather did. We have been watching the coast for a month or so now based on a tip about suspicious activities on the beach. He said it was a small steam powered ship. Maybe one hundred fifty feet in length."

"Would your office be interested in helping us get the ship?" Bey asked.

"We sure would. But how?"

"If we could offer a deal to get these men to talk, we could find out the next delivery and get them to set it up. I can have a Navy ship standing by out of sight up the beach and when the men hit the beach with the next load, we could disable their small boat and fire a flare to alert the naval vessel to come and intercept the smuggler's ship."

"I believe I could disable the wooden rowing vessel with some bow shots with a couple of buffalo guns. Then, you could fire a flare, and the marshals and my deputies could move in on the men stranded on the beach.

"I think we have a plan, assuming these Tong members will rat out their friends. I have found they are pretty loyal to their organization. Loyal so their family members won't be raped and executed in front of them," Bey said.

Pope took the party to the jail and full charges were made. Then hours of questioning, threatening and cajoling followed.

By the end of the day, the prisoners broke, and a plan was set to fake a telegram to the distributor and have the ship return early.

"We are good except for one thing," Bey told Pope.

"We cannot trust the prisoners to serve as pickups. But we don't have any Chinese deputies."

Pope had an idea based on Sarah's recantation of the Black Bart case.

"Go ahead and set it up. I will take care of the Chinese part."

He telegraphed Harry Morse and told him he needed Detective Lee. Pope then tapped Howell who he knew had access to several Chinese patrolmen he could recruit. They had four smuggler impersonators on call after an hour of telegraphing. Pope thought how much easier the Washington phones were for matters like this. There were a few phones in San Francisco, but none connected with San Rafael.

The telegram was sent to have another drug run made sooner due to "extremely high sales".

The response was for the run to occur at the same beach four days later. Little time was left to put the final touches on the operations plan.

A hitch appeared when the US Navy did not have a ship it could send in time. The US Revenue Cutter Service, which was operated as an anti-smuggling marine agency anyway, had a Revenue Cutter, the US Grant in San Francisco. The Grant had bark rigged masts and large steam engine. It could go thirteen miles per hour under power. The hundred sixty-three-foot cutter carried seven officers and thirty-four enlisted men. It had four twenty-four-pound howitzers and could outrun the smuggler's vessel or sink it, if needed.

Pope was excited. This was going to be fun. He made Israel a special deputy and asked him to bring his Sharps Big Fifty buffalo rifle. It was the same .50-90 caliber model as fellow mountain man Billy Dixon had used to drop an Indian chief seven eights of a mile away. Dixon made this shot at the Battle of Adobe Wall in Texas during a siege of the trading post. Dixon fired his nine years before the two Popes planned theirs.

The night before, Howell showed up with several detectives and three Chinese police officers. Bey and his deputy marshals came. Harry Morse came with Detective Lee.

Bey and Pope briefed the men in detail. They were instructed to not discuss the operation anywhere someone could hear them and to report to the sheriff's office at dawn. Pope rented several small carriages from the livery and Israel drove his buckboard at his grandson's request. With luck, they would have lots of contraband and a number of prisoners.

At dawn, the men filled themselves with strong black coffee and piled into the carriages and wagons for the trip to the beach. They left Israel's buckboard at the woods and hid the rentals in case some other smuggler familiar with the transfer showed up. The two Popes led the men down the hill carefully as the sun began to rise.

They took branches and driftwood and built a barrier to hide the lawmen.

The US Attorney stayed on top of the cliff. He had borrowed a Very pistol and three red flares to shoot to signal the Revenue Cutter. Bey climbed to the tallest point so the cutter hidden around a point could see the flare and steam towards the smuggler's ship.

A small ship approached at nine-fifteen. Israel said it appeared to be the one he saw earlier.

Pope brought his small brass binoculars from the

investigative kit in his left saddlebag. He watched as crew members loaded bags onto the small boat. Three crewmen climbed aboard, and it was winched down to the water.

As it was rowed up to the beach, Lee and the Chinese policemen, all dressed as workmen, waved at the incoming boat. They waved in a manner Israel had witnessed. The officers thought the wave must be some sort of all-clear signal.

The bow hit the beach and the crewmen jumped out and dragged it further up into the sand.

The two Popes, one with a massive single shot Sharps and the other with his fast-firing Marlin .45-70 lever action opened up. Within seconds the bow of the wooden boat was holed and wooden laps in the hull were shattered. The three would not use it to escape.

Pope handed the Marlin to his grandfather and led a couple of his deputies and the deputy marshals from behind the makeshift barrier, guns out. The Chinese officers pulled their revolvers. Soon the three smugglers from the ship were surrounded.

Bey fired the Very pistol at the Popes' first shots. A red meteor flare soared high into the blue sky.

The ship offshore was building a head of steam to leave the three crewmen to their fates.

Then, the sleek US Grant Revenue Cutter came around the point at full speed. It veered seaward to intersect the ship. The ship began to run.

The men on the shore saw a waterspout appear off the ship's port bow. Several seconds later, they heard the concussion.

The Grant had fired a warning shot with one of its twenty-four-pound howitzers. The boat gave no intent of stopping and the next shot took off the smokestack.

The men on the beach cheered, except for the terrified crewmen.

A fire started on the ship. The Grant came alongside and shot heavy streams of water on the ship to quell the flames and save both lives and evidence.

Pope watched through his binoculars, then handed them to Israel. A boarding party was gathering the captain and crew and handcuffing them at gunpoint.

The fire knocked down, the smuggler ship was taken under tow and the cutter pulled it around Golden Gate Point and towards the Port of San Francisco.

US Attorney Bey and his marshals wanted to be there as soon as possible to search the ship and question the captain and crew.

"Sheriff, would you hold these prisoners for me? Don't question them, just feed them and keep them locked up. I will send the deputies back to pick them up as soon as possible.

"Thank you for your help. Your office will get full credit in our reports and probably the news rags. We will drop off one carriage at the livery before getting on the San Francisco ferry."

The federal men left and Howell, Lee and the San Francisco officers left in another carriage, also promising to drop it at the livery.

Israel Pope slid his Big Fifty into the bed of the buckboard and grinned at his grandson and the deputies.

"Boys, we saw some action here today unlike any I can think about. The cutter chasing the ship, sending a round across its bow...the fools didn't stop and the next one hit them in the breadbasket! I've never seen such a thing! Don't suppose I ever will again."

"Grandpa is right. I'd like to add how proud I was of you today. You upheld the finest tradition of the Marin County Sheriff's Office. I believe we will find we participated in bringing down a very major smuggling operation. Most use wagons, these people used a ship. A lot of money was behind this. These people will talk. The entry level crooks might not know much, but the captain of the ship sure will. Very few people will go to prison for somebody else. We have only seen the tip of the tail of this cougar.

"Let's ride into town and dinner is on me. You, too, Grandpa. There are mountain man tales these fellas have not heard yet."

They rode in. There was a new sheriff in town, and he was stirring things up.

******

Pope let the US attorney handle his case, and his deputies and Howell did the interrogations and deal making.

The sheriff was happy to read in the San Francisco Chronicle about the case as it developed. The US attorney was clearly politicking. He brought some others he thought might be helpful along. One was Pope. Pope got a lot of press, mostly good.

The case proved to be one of the most major drug cases in California history up to then. The number of arrests and crime families put out of business was surprising even to Pope and Detective Lieutenant Howell. It was gratifying to them it was across all ethnic lines.

Out of the whole thing, Pope's and Israel's favorite thing was the ship pursuit and the firing of the big guns to stop the pursuit. Pope was glad his office got credit for identifying the case and making crucial arrests. He truly did not care about more credit for himself. Until his grandfather reminded him of an election in two years.

Tevis at Wells Fargo organized a congratulatory dinner for the arrest and prosecution of Black Bart. Sarah was invited since she had found the crucial piece of evidence and was there with Morse for the arrest. Pope was a tagalong guest at the event, at what was apparently Tevis' favorite place, the Bohemian Club.

"John, I know you don't like him. I don't either. But you have the handsome tuxedo from Washington, and I have the blue dress you seemed to like. I have to go. You ought to go to support me. Besides, as Israel lectured you at dinner, every time you get in the paper as a hero helps your re-election. We have to start campaigning now. We cannot wait for six weeks before the ballot boxes open to do it."

"Honey, are you finished? I was planning to go anyway. Hume said Tevis was going to say something about us in Washington and I should be there to take a bow when you curtsy. Or whatever you are going to do while they are clapping."

She punched him in the shoulder. She had not done it for a while. He thought she must have been saving energy for a big one. At least he did not have a bullet wound like last time.

His big mistake was thinking these thoughts aloud.

My wife can be so damn volatile! he thought. At least silently this time as he rubbed his shoulder from the second punch.

Sarah booked a room at the Palace Hotel on Market Street for them by telegram from the office.

They went to the gala. Sarah was seated at the head table. Pope, who had nothing to do with the Black Bart capture was seated with strangers at a table near the front.

Tevis welcomed everyone and dinner was served. After, he stood and spoke for forty minutes, crediting Hume and Sarah and giving Harry Morse much less credit than he deserved. In speaking glowingly of Sarah, he mentioned her husband, a former Wells Fargo detective had recently been involved in breaking up a drug ring in the area, and additionally he had assisted Sarah in saving the life of the president. The person who led both of those investigations sat unnamed in his tuxedo twenty feet away.

Pope could see the shock on Morse's face to learn after eight years and arresting Black Bart, he had "assisted" two Wells Fargo employees. He looked off into the crowd and saw Pope scowling. He scowled on Pope's behalf as Pope's two major accomplishments were played down. Morse knew the company's founders. He would make sure they knew what transpired here tonight. He knew it would not do any good.

This horse was already out of the barn and out of sight, he thought.

After the dinner, a very upset Sarah and Morse left the head table as other people there spoke about what a wonderful speech Tevis made. The only other one still at the table, but extremely disengaged from the conversations was Hume. He knew the truth.

Further, he knew this would signal the end of the most beneficial business and friendship in his career at the company he served so long. He was crestfallen.

Sarah and Harry Morse took one look at Pope and knew he was dangerously angry. His look was fierce, yet he said nothing. He gave a glance at a beloved wife and a dear friend walking toward him but focused on Tevis and even Hume. Hume picked up on it and left the table. He knew he had to do something, but for once was stumped as to what.

As they approached Pope, Morse spoke. Both Popes heard him, but none of the dignitaries Tevis invited did.

"This night marks a sad change in the long relationship between my company and Tevis's."

"The move will cost you, Harry. Damnably, it will cost you too much to hire me. I, with John's agreement, am considering resigning from Wells Fargo Monday morning."

Hume caught up in time to hear a bit of his closest friend's comment and all his best remaining detective's.

"I cannot make up for what Tevis did and didn't say. Somebody," and they knew he meant him, "will make sure the Chronicle and every damn paper in the West hears about these slights. I just hope you both are just angry and not serious. We could not operate half as efficiently without the Morse Detective Agency as a partner and Sarah Pope as a detective," a very shaken Hume said.

"Jim, you've known me a long, long time. We have been through bullets and blizzards together. If anybody knows I don't say serious things through anger, it's you.

"I need to do some serious thinking," Morse said.

"Sarah, you have my full support on what you just expressed. With or without you joining our dear and respected friend Harry, we'll get by," Pope said.

She turned to a man she respected highly. One who she also liked.

"Mr. Hume, you have provided wonderful opportunities for John and me both. The slant put on our— especially Harry's and John's actions in the biggest cases in years worries me. A lot. I'd like to meet with you Monday and talk further."

Hume nodded at all three and turned. He walked away without saying a word.

"Just in case my friend is more of a gelding than I ever thought, my contacts in the media are even better than his. And I will get to them first. Jim is a politician. He plans to retire from Wells Fargo by dying at his desk there. There is no way in hell he will drop information in any way showing Tevis for the pompous ass we just saw," Morse said.

The headlines the next morning read "Tevis Slights Famous Detective Morse And Pope, Who Saved the President". The story had details what the speech should have said and did not. They had already done full coverage on Pope and the drug cartel earlier in the week.

Israel Pope, hearing the story, said, "Don't fret. People like him create their own hells. It will come back to bite him in the butt without any worry or action by you two or Harry. Good always wins out in the end. And you three are as good as it gets."

Tevis called Hume into his office on Monday. He wanted to know what the uproar was all about. Hume gracefully corrected items in his speech and reported the Morse Detective Agency was likely to reduce, if not sever, its long relationship with Wells Fargo and he expected Detective Pope to resign. The governor and the president were later interviewed and echoed Morse's version. They were not as angry as the founders of the company or its board. As a very major shareholder, Tevis was not affected other than by ridicule.

Sarah was sitting outside his office waiting when he returned from the top floor. She gracefully and sadly handed him her badge and letter of resignation.

"I wish you the best. You've been a great boss and have John's and my everlasting gratitude. It breaks my heart it ended this way." She proffered her hand, and he shook it. Sarah walked out of Wells Fargo, never again to re-enter what she knew to be a wonderful company.

For almost twenty years, Pope listened to and followed his grandfather's guidance. He did this time, also. Sarah tried, and did a pretty good job.

Harry Morse was a more serious enemy with powerful friends.

Harry Morse rented a one-room office in San Rafael. He had the door painted with his agency name and let Sarah select what went inside. She kept it simple and economical. It looked more like a smaller detective bull pen than a business office. Two desks, several locking files, a wardrobe and coat rack and a gun cabinet. She put a picture of the founder, Harry Morse on one wall and a large map of Northern California on another. Pope did the lock work to make sure it was impenetrable.

The Morse Detective Agency North Bay office was open for business. The first customer was a woman who thought her husband was poisoning her. Sarah jumped right on it. One of Morse's most famous cases was to be another poisoning. The co-founder of Stanford University, Jane Stanford, was poisoned in 1906. Harry investigated the first attempt. Mrs. Stanford succumbed to strychnine poisoning in Honolulu six months later.

As she got into the Morse cases, she felt at home. It was more like the variety of Pinkerton cases on which she had cut her teeth. Yet, without the questionable tactics of union and strike busting.

The Morse agency was on retainer to many insurance companies. Those cases paralleled the claims cases she and Pope had investigated for Wells Fargo.

In her first month, she closed seven cases. Morse was ecstatic. Closure meant cash flow and moving on to other retainers, then final payments.

Morse continued his friendship and assisting Wells Fargo with cases he selected after careful evaluation. The era of *gratis* work because of friendship or an interesting case seemed to have passed.

Pope had worried he would get bored with the sheriff's job. Having a guest house shot up, seeing John Wilkes Booth, and breaking up a large smuggling ring in which he saw a ship chase and fight...all in his first few weeks as Marin sheriff. He would have never guessed such goings-on. They held him in good stead. He knew over time he may miss the long trails.

With Wyoming and Washington back-to-back, Pope and Sarah rode some distant trails. Maybe enough.

Pope had to admit he liked coming home at night. Home to one of the most beautiful women he had ever seen. Being near Israel Pope almost daily. It was like the "old days" but better.

******

There had been a downside to the various papers' commentary on Pope in response to the Tevis speech and its omissions. While Morse saw a surge in new cases, Pope felt he was gaining unwanted notoriety. In 1883, there were a lot of wannabe gunsels roaming the Western United States. Notoriety with people like Kid Taos in one of the cases he and Sarah had worked in Cheyenne.

He thought he was fast because of the people with whom he picked gunfights. Pope found out after he took him down, he usually went up against drunks.

Kid Taos did not stand a chance against someone like Pope. Or Kane. Or any of the legends who tamed places like Dodge City. People like Masterson, Earp, or Tilghman, who was still marshal. They were real gunfighters, not make-believe ones.

Pope worried the publicity would draw them to San Rafael to show they were faster than him.

He spoke to the family at dinner about this. Millie did not have experience to contribute, other than her normal wisdom and ability to take things down to their basic elements.

Sarah said, "If I heard any other man alive suggest he was so fast, he would draw would-be gunfighters, I'd think it was pure male ego. In John's case, I am afraid he is exactly right. I wish he was not, for once."

"I been around some real hairy characters. Some were so scary nobody would take them on. Hugh Glass comes to mind. In the 1830's about exactly fifty years ago, he was mauled by a bear. He crawled a couple hundred miles, eating worms and grubs and anything he could find. Now, there was a man with bark on! Nobody messed with him."

"What ever happened to him?" Millie asked.

"Ha! An Indian shot an arrow in his back and killed him a year later in 1833, I believe!

"But, to get back to the discussion at hand, I think my boy has a valid point. A lawman wants to be respected, but not notorious. Notorious draws in a kind of fool we did not have to contend with in my day."

He turned to Pope.

"Sonny, you can outdraw about any man alive. But there's one out there you can't. And even the ones you can, get lucky sometimes. You can have a misfire, have the sun in your eyes, go up against a man with a shotgun like Sarah's cocked in hand. Get back shot. Anything.

"But here's the thing. I suspect most of these yahoos are in Texas, Arizona, Montana and the like. They will spend their time dreaming about taking you or Bat, or Earp, or even Hardin down. I just doubt they'll have the sense or money to come all the way up here. If one does, you'll handle him like the rest who tried you. I just don't see a bunch of them parading up to Northern California where they are out of their element. These fellas are not train riders. They are more like grub line riders!"

"Thanks, Grandpa. As always, you add sense to everybody else's first thoughts. Dangerous people have been part of my life since ten. As sheriff, why should

I worry? It comes with the trail I ride."

They went on eating the venison loin roasted with potatoes, carrots and onions Sarah prepared in the morning and let cook all day in a black iron pot hanging over the coals on the swing iron.

"Now, we have some worries put aside by Israel, Millie fixed one of her famous pies," Sarah said. She served an apple pie and refreshed everyone's coffee.

"Millie, will you help me with my baking on this little stove? I think I can do alright cooking meals over the fire in the fireplace, but the baking is beyond me," she asked. Millie nodded and smiled. The two husbands smiled too. Two women baking desserts was better than just one.

******

Life went on for sheriff and detective alike in Marin County.

By early December, a colder than normal spell hit. Temperatures were in the upper thirties and rain prevailed.

Pope and Sarah rode in together, kissed and went on to their respective offices.

He hung his heavy canvas ranch coat on the coat rack, followed by his suit jacket and Stetson. He sat his carbine in the rack and poured his third cup of coffee for the day. Sitting at his desk, the gold star glinted prominently on his black vest.

"What's new, Bill," Pope asked his chief deputy.

"Nothing yet, Sheriff. I expect a few wanted posters to come in with the noon mail. Nothing of interest worth your reading in the reports from the three night deputies."

"What do you think of the probability of the town paying for a night marshal and letting us deputize and supervise him? We're a peaceful place, but there still is the more than occasional drunk, mugging and the like. It would keep this office open all day. He could stay here and make maybe four rounds a night," Pope said.

"I think we'd have a chance at it. If not, the county is pretty pleased with you and the office over the smuggler thing. They'd probably approve another deputy or two to cover it as a fallback position," Isakson said.

"I'll catch the mayor at his general merchandise later and see what he says. He'll probably whine about budget. Maybe he will be right. If he seems sincere, I'll take it up with the county commission. You think we'd need two to cover it, Bill?"

"I do. What with illness, family issues and the like. One deputy could do it most of the time, freeing up the second to be another patrol deputy until needed."

"Sounds like a good solution. I may just pass on the mayor for now," Pope thought aloud. His chief deputy agreed. This was his third sheriff since signing on as a deputy twenty years ago. All had been good. This one, Pope, was affable but much younger. He might have some basics to learn. *He showed a lot of potential*, the older man thought.

Pope went to the supervisor and presented his idea. He got approval for one additional deputy as long as the rest of the commission went along. One beat what he had now. The new one would cover nights and he would have to pull one off night patrol to cover when he was not available. Or cover it himself. Or split it with Isakson. Either way, it was doable. The commission would meet and hopefully confirm it in two weeks.

In the meantime, Pope would check with his chief deputy and quietly with other deputies to see who a good candidate might be.

He thought about Martha Lane, then dismissed the idea. With the night deputy position, she would not have to patrol on horseback alone. She would have to manhandle frequent drunks back to the lockup. She would not have any backup. While deputies on patrol did not have backup either, ones did while in town. Their backup was either the chief deputy, the sheriff or both. Just not late at night when predators prowled.

It seemed a distant option to him. With neither Pope nor Sarah at Wells Fargo anymore, he did not have to worry about repercussions from Joe Lane.

He was more worried about whether any nineteen-year-old, male or female, could handle the job alone.

Pope walked by Sarah's new office just as she was coming out the door with her coat on and a leather satchel in hand.

"Off detecting? I was going to buy you lunch," he said.

"Not today. I have to go to Sausalito and check on one of Harry's old clients. See you at dinner," she said as she swung a long leg over Kate's back and settled in the saddle.

"Your shotgun holster is empty."

"I know. But fear not, husband. My shotgun is in the satchel with my notebook. Right with me in case of a gunfight while eating lunch on the harbor," she replied with a smile.

He shook his head and walked off as she rode out of town.

Bill Isakson got back from the post office at one o'clock. The ferry with the mail had been late.

As he and Pope were reviewing new wanted posters together, they heard shots.

Pope grabbed his coat and carbine. Isakson grabbed his coat and a long-barreled shotgun. They both went out the door carefully.

The shots came from the area of one of the town's banks. They moved down sidewalks on opposite sides of the street at the same pace.

Three men with rifles ran out of the bank. They saw the two lawmen and aimed. Bill Isakson fired a load of buckshot. The distance was too great, and it knocked up dust in the street. Pope sought a barrier. He found it in the form of a water trough. Dropping to his belly, he aimed around it as the three sent a barrage of shots towards both lawmen.

Pope aimed his carbine, but a man who had been shopping at the feedstore ran in front of him and he could not fire.

The chief deputy let go another load of buckshot, but to no avail at the distance.

The three jumped on their horses, a black, and two duns, and rode off as fast as possible.

"Bill, check for wounded in the bank. I am going after them! See if you can round up a posse once the bank is taken care of!" Pope yelled.

He sprinted down the street to Caesar and mounted. He always had a couple night's water, coffee, jerky and the like in his saddlebags, so he did not have to stop as he took off in hot pursuit.

Pope started off a quarter mile behind. The robbers' horses were as fast as Caesar, or faster. What they did not have was his endurance.

The chase became five miles, then ten. The robbers were slowing as they pushed their horses hard.

Pope reached back in his saddlebag and put a box of cartridges in his coat pocket. They were .44-40s, so they would fit his Colt revolver and his and Winchester carbine both.

The three hit a point in the road where the left was a steep rock covered slope, and the right had a copse of trees. They dismounted.

One set up at the top of the slope between a large rock. The other two positioned themselves behind trees.

Pope grabbed his canteen and dismounted. He sent Caesar back in the direction from which they had come.

He rolled across the road, avoiding the first rifle shots from the hidden men. He knew exactly where they were from the white puffs from the black powder cartridges. Pope would send the same signal when he fired. He decided to not give away his position yet. Unless on their persons, the robbers did not have extra ammunition. They also forgot the money, hung across the saddle of one horse. They had not taken canteens either. While not a major issue on this cold day, it represented an oversight.

Pope was set up behind a large stump. It had been sawn recently, so was green oak and would stop far more powerful guns than they had.

Pope could just wait for Bill Isakson and the posse. He would give them maybe a half hour. If not here or if the robbers moved, Pope would take offensive action. It was just his way.

One of the robbers fired and the bullet came too close for comfort. Half a second later, Pope fired and saw the bushes rustle where he had shot. So, he fired again. The bushes stopped rustling. He reckoned it signaled a solid hit.

Nothing happened for another twenty minutes. Then, Pope heard hooves pounding the hard packed dirt road behind him.

It was the chief deputy with another deputy and four posse-men.

Pope waved and, using arm movements, had them fan out before getting into carbine range. He had already determined the robbers were shooting smaller caliber carbines like his.

Once spread out, he motioned for them to move in.

Pope opened up on the tree positions and fired all fifteen rounds from his 1873 carbine, then five from his Colt. The covering fire allowed the lawmen and their posse to move in closely.

They released a volley into the woods.

A man cried, "We give up! Stop shooting!"

Pope yelled, "Cease fire!"

Once the shooting had stopped, he yelled again.

"This is Sheriff John Pope. Drop your weapons! Now, stand and throw your hands up! Come out where we can see you!"

They complied and Pope led the posse to them, reloaded Colt in hand.

Once they were disarmed and in custody, he and Isakson walked across the road to the other robber. He had a bullet in his shoulder and one in his forehead. He had died instantly from the second shot.

The deputy with Isakson had been delivering a prisoner to the lockup for charges. He immediately joined the posse. His name was Walter Wood.

"Walter, there are three horses wandering around. Grab a posse-man or two and locate them. One has a bag of money from the bank on the saddle. Find it and take custody of it, please."

The young deputy nodded and, taking two posse-men with him, walked down the road.

They put the dead man over the saddle of his own horse and tied his feet together with a portion of lariat under the horse and a portion around his middle tied to the saddle horn.

Pope led the procession into San Rafael. Townsfolk began to cheer and clap and did so all the way down the main drag to the jail. Isakson sent Walter off to get the undertaker to pick up the body. They searched the man. Identification would have to come from his friend. If he did not have a family to bury him, the sale of his horse and gun would.

Isakson went to the bank. The cashier told him the president was expected back soon. The chief deputy had assisted him to the doctor's with a bullet crease in his right bicep just after the robbery. He gave Isakson the count on the money stolen.

Later, Pope and Isakson returned the bag of money. They counted it in front of witnesses and got a receipt for the amount less a ten-dollar bill they held out for evidence in court.

The two robbers were charged with bank robbery and attempted murder of a peace officer. The district attorney noted there was currently no such law at the time in California, so changed the charge to plain attempted murder.

John Pope, Bill Isakson and Walter Wood did something every police officer holds to be his key objective. They went home to their families at the end of their shift.

The article hit the front page of the San Francisco papers.

Michael Kane had begun to subscribe to several of them after his visit. He read the articles.

I might have to call on John for some assistance real soon, he thought as he folded the paper and sat it down by his chair in Topping Castle.

Real damn soon.

A LOOK AT: ISRAEL POPE, MOUNTAIN MAN (GUN FOR WELLS FARGO BOOK 4)

Mountain man and man hunter, Israel Pope was a calm, forgiving man. But attack him or his family and he became an efficient, stone cold killer.

Pope started out as a river boater, fur trapper, scout, wagon train master, horse rancher and bounty hunter – later in life he became a member of the Kiowa tribe with the name Bear Fighter.

Men and bears fell to his Bowie knife, rifle and tomahawk. A blood brother to the Kiowa's, he was a legend throughout the West.

"G. Wayne Tilman is a remarkable writer about the Old West. You can taste the authenticity he serves up in each tale."

AVAILABLE JUNE 2021

ABOUT THE AUTHOR

G. Wayne Tilman is a full-time author. He retired from the Federal Bureau of Investigation several years ago. Prior to the FBI, he was a Marine, bank security director, deputy sheriff, investigator, and security contractor. He holds baccalaureate and master's degrees from the University of Richmond and has been an adjunct faculty member there, as well as the University of Phoenix, St. Petersburg College and Florida Metropolitan University.

He wrote his first novel over thirty years ago and has now written thirteen novels. Genres include espionage thrillers, mysteries, and Westerns.